TIME TRAVELER
CHRONICLES
Robert Werden

When I wrote this story, the music I was listening to at the time often inspired my narrative. Just like in film, music can set the mood for a scene. I wanted to share the mood those songs set for me with you, the reader. Throughout this book, song titles are mentioned, so feel free to listen to a song at the time when it's referenced in this book. For your convenience, I have created a playlist on you tube for you.
https://www.youtube.com/c/robertwerden/playlists

CONTENTS

Chapter 1: A r r i v a l 1

Chapter 2: Two years later................................... 11

Chapter 3: Recruiting Evelyn Carter..................... 19

Chapter 4: Training Day....................................... 45

Chapter 5: First Mission....................................... 59

Chapter 6: Deep Secrets....................................... 75

Chapter 7: F a k e r 91

Chapter 8: M o o n S h o t 117

Chapter 9: D o w n 125

Chapter 10: D o w n d e e p 143

Chapter 11: D a w n 167

Chapter 12: Little Purple Rocks 181

Chapter 13: A Very Long Scan 201

Chapter 14: A Royal and a Prophet.................... 227

Chapter 15: O r i g i n s 255

Chapter 16: Pack an Extra Lunch........................ 265

Chapter 17: T i m e's U p 281

Chapter 18: M e l t d o w n 293

Chapter 19: Absolute Zero 313

Chapter 20: E x o d u s 335

CHAPTER 1: ARRIVAL

In ten minutes, in Times Square, New York at exactly 8:10 a.m., something extraordinary will happen. The world will change forever when the axiom, "time travel", will make the leap in human lexis from the realm of fiction to fact. The life of Evelyn Carter will be forever altered. Her actions will change the world.

A few blocks away from Times Square, the time is 8:00 a.m. when something beneath the street rumbles and the sound of concrete cracking echoes off the buildings lining the busy intersection. An ear-aching hiss of steam blasts from manhole covers and newly formed fissures in the asphalt.

People walking near West 43rd street and 7th Avenue scream in fear as the shaking and noise continues. The ground shakes, causing them to lose their footing as a hole suddenly appears and swallows up the entire area between the four traffic lights. The well-traveled road collapses in an almost perfect circle, falling twenty feet with a tremendous crash. People run from the surrounding sidewalks, slamming their backs against the brick walls of the adjacent buildings. Those nearby scream in fear, worried the ground they stand on will also give out. Luckily, the sinkhole happens between traffic signal changes and no one gets seriously hurt. A severed underground steam pipe fires billowing clouds of vapor into the air with a thunderous hiss.

An automatic shut off valve quickly cuts the flow of steam, giving way to an eerie silence. The silence is an illusion caused from the temporary deafness of the high-pitched steam blast. As people regain their senses and stumble back to solid footing, the sounds of the city once again normalize. A dust cloud obscures the gaping hole, but soon settles. Crowds of curious New Yorkers gather to look into the newly formed crater.

The blacktop has dropped straight down, and the walls of the hole are perfectly smooth, as if someone used a giant cookie cutter and carefully removed the foundation. NYPD just happens to have a precinct station at that exact intersection, so within seconds cops surround the sinkhole with caution tape. A sinkhole in New York is not new, but at rush hour, it's a recipe for major traffic.

A few blocks away in Times Square, traffic comes to a dead stop. Drivers lay into their car horns like an orchestra tuning up before a concert. From this distance, no one can see what has happened. Add to that, it stopped raining ten minutes earlier so the air hangs thick as the rising morning sun breaks over the buildings, pulling steam from the wet city streets, making it difficult to see.

Evelyn Carter, trapped in gridlock, holds her phone an inch from her ear. On the other end is Greg, the jerk she walked out on twenty minutes ago. She rolls her eyes as she listens to the incredulous lies he's telling. Last night he had the nerve to bring a girl home and actually introduce her to Carter. Listening to Greg justify his indiscretion, Carter sits motionless and now homeless in her dented and faded 2007 white cargo van. The windows are down and her radio plays an old 70's song, 'Shambala', by Three Dog Night. The repetition of the lyrics only adds to her frustration with the traffic and her now ex-boyfriend. Her hand slams against the radio power button. She shifts her phone to her left ear as she listens to the horseshit Greg spews.

She interrupts him mid-sentence. "Listen dickhead, I'm tired of your crap. I don't need you or anyone else to take care of me!"

"Babe, where the fuck are you going to live? You need me!"

"First, you asshole, you don't get to call me *babe* ever again. Second, bullshit, I managed on my own for eight years. I think I can figure it out! I don't need anyone, especially you."

"Well, you can kiss your box of –"

She hangs up before he can finish his sentence. "Fuck you, asshole!" She tosses the phone to the passenger seat.

Her elbow rests on the frame of the window, her head on her hand. Looking out at the people in the square, she breathes heavily in searing anger. Staring at everyone going about their business is more entertainment than being with Greg *'Dickhead'*. At least those people are more animated than Greg and his all day X-box sessions. She watches them walk by while her van goes nowhere. Even *they* walk faster than the cars move. It's normal for traffic early in the morning, but this is ridiculous.

"Come on!" She hisses under her breath.

She doesn't know about the sink hole and thinks, *'maybe If I skipped the bagel and only gotten coffee, it could've shaved a few minutes off and missed this traffic.'* The only problem is this is New York and bagels are almost a religious experience. Also, she needs some comfort food right now, and a big paycheck would be nice.

This old van acts as her mobile office, and she's taken considerable effort to make it look that way. It cost $350 to have the words 'Action News' painted on the sides. A friend found an old satellite dish in the trash and welded it to the roof. The dish doesn't have any function, but it completes the professional appearance she wants to convey. The mainstream news crews from the big networks used to make fun of her van. They don't anymore. In this business, respect isn't earned from the quality of the vehicle; their respect has been earned from the quality of the footage she consistently captures. It's not that she's pretending to be a reporter; she really does report the news for a living. Carter is an independent photojournalist. Her specialty is video journalism, officially referred to as a news stringer.

It became obvious early on that network teams greatly benefit from their professional appearance. Crews with the right look got the great interview or access to the other side of the yellow police tape. So right from the beginning of her career, she knew she would have to look the way they did. She got her news buyer at the network to give her a press pass that she wears around her neck. After a couple of dates, he even hooked her up with a used shoulder-held professional camera. Sometimes the sight of a big camera on her shoulder gets her into a location.

She stores her work gear in the van, but there's not much room inside for her belongings, just enough for a few boxes of clothes and personal items. She has some nontraditional reporter's tools as well, such as a pair of bolt-cutters for when the best video footage is just one padlocked gate out of reach.

In the back of the van, she has a single mattress where a normal news van might have a video editing bay. A van is much cheaper than an apartment. This wouldn't be the first time she lived on the streets. In New York, on the money she earns, having a roommate is a necessity. For Carter, having a real roof over her head always comes with a price higher than the actual rent. Just in the past year, she has moved in and out of four apartments because of drama with her roommates, this last one with Greg, her first boyfriend since she moved to the city. It seems no matter where she lives, whether in her home city of Phoenix or the Big Apple, her choice of men is consistently bad. Each time it starts great, she thinks she knows what she is getting into. Then it's either cheating, drugs or they lose their jobs and sit around all day doing nothing. This time, it was all three, a trifecta.

Every morning it's the same routine. She wakes up at 5 a.m., gets her coffee and bagel, then goes out looking for a paycheck. Carter always puts on the clothes of a professional journalist. She wears some comfortable as hell, well-broken-in hiking boots her Dad got her six years earlier for a trip they never took. Add to that a pair of cargo pants and a button up shirt, which are not flattering to her athletic figure, but definitely make her look like a pro. But what really clinches her journalistic appearance is the black camera gear vest that has the word 'Press' embroidered on the front and back.

Still trapped between cars on all sides, her van crawls at a snail's pace. While sipping on an extra-large cup of coffee and dropping bagel crumbs on her lap, she scans the streets for a story. Some tourists are getting their photos taken in the square. This story has played out the same way every day for a year since she moved here. She watches the tourists take a picture with the fat guy dressed in the Spiderman costume, then refuse to pay him. A walrus-mustached cop steps between the spandex hero and the alligator armed tourist who walks away. The cop holds his hand up to the Spiderman impersonator as a warning. Little does the cheapskate visitor know how close he was from a spider punch to the back of the head. Across the square, other tourists gawk at a half-naked man in a cowboy hat playing an acoustic guitar. These events unfortunately are not the ones that will pay her way into a new apartment. She needs something bigger if she wants a paycheck today.

Even though she is beyond frustrated at the way her day has begun, she is a professional and keeps her focus on finding work. Being an independent stringer, she drives through the city all day looking for the next story. She has a police scanner, so if she hears a call stream through, she will break every traffic law to get to the scene first. If nothing happens, she enjoys watching people and trying to guess what their personal stories might be.

From the window of her van, she watches them unknowingly divulge their secrets. Ken, a guy she dated a few times, works at the TV station as a news buyer. He always tells her that she has an almost supernatural intuition about capturing something at the right moment. For example, she can tell the woman standing on the corner in the red dress who holds a large leather portfolio is waiting to ambush a talent agent. Across the street, she sees a young man anxiously waiting for the latest issue of the New Yorker to arrive. She predicts he's a columnist getting an article published for the first time and wants to buy the issue the second it hits the newsstand. She only has to look at the way they walk or the clothes they wear, and she can piece together an accurate story.

Historical evidence suggests the square isn't the best place for getting a well-paying video. Today though, in exactly five seconds, it will be home to the biggest story in human history.

A strong blast of scorching air slams the side of her van, as if a rocket-powered train rushed past. Something has happened, which she sees from the corner of her right eye. A blue light appears in her right side mirror. Having driven past the square hundreds of times, she has not seen anything like this before. *This isn't a street performer pulling off a new stunt, or even a car accident,* she thinks. Shifting to look out the two rear windows, she sees people in the square lying on the ground. A blue electrical discharge shimmers and sparkles in the center of the square. At first it looks like an exploded electrical service box, except there was no explosion.

She realizes this is the payday she needs.

But only if she can be first to get whatever this is on video will there be a chance of selling it to the networks. Her hands bang on the steering wheel as she stretches her neck in all directions looking for an exit. No such luck.

"Shit. Shit. Shit."

Suddenly she puts the van in park and yanks the keys out. She gets up from her seat, pulls an elastic hair tie from her pocket then scrapes her long black hair into a ponytail. While she climbs between the seats into the back of the van, she grabs her trusty sidekick camera. The back double doors fly open after she kicks them with her booted foot. Jumping out from the van, she lands on the yellow taxi behind it. Her one hundred and twenty-five-pound body crashes on the taxi's hood, which flexes and pops, but she leaves no dent. With the camera recording, she runs towards the disturbance.

Her heart pumps hard as she navigates the street full of cars that stand in her path. As she approaches, tourists and costumed performers lay on the concrete, trying to regain their senses after being knocked down from the blast. She films the people lying on the ground, looking for signs of injury. Injuries, unfortunately are what make the evening news. The shirtless guitar player sits on the curb, staring at his broken iconic six string; it got crushed when he was blasted from behind and landed on it. She records about fifteen people on the cement who all seem fine, just a little shaken.

Carter approaches the blue glowing disturbance, which interferes with the iris on her camera's lens. She lifts the camera, adjusts her focus and exposure, but it's tough for her to capture the intense, shimmering illumination. Through her camera's viewfinder, it's clear this is not an electrical service box. It hovers about three feet off the ground. She steadies her camera and then pulls her face off the viewfinder to see the object with her own eyes.

The object is completely out of place. The glowing energy field pulses and crackles around something unfamiliar suspended within it. Behind the translucent shell, she can see a silver-colored metal cylinder. The ends of the cylinder are dome-shaped with small faceted end caps. The whole thing is only about three feet long and possibly twelve inches thick. It looks smooth but it appears there's some sort of access panels along the surface.

Officer Walrus Mustache runs over and steps between her and the strange object, pushing her back. She will have none of that, and walks right back after he moves, kneeling down to get some close up video. The cop continues from person to person, shoving them back.

Still kneeling, she switches her camera angle as a crowd gathers to get people's faces and reactions. She frames the shots with the metal glowing tube in the background as she records eyewitness testimony describing the blast wave that threw them to the concrete.

One woman who stood only two feet from the object provides the experience in her own words. "It was f-ing crazy! I just came in to the city to buy tickets to a play for me and my girlfriend, when out of nowhere there was this blast of heat and wind. I saw the whole thing. The light was bright blue and then I was flying backwards and landed on that guy over there."

Carter even captures a brave New Yorker attempt to touch the object, only to get an incapacitating shock.

Emergency response vehicles arrive quickly, making it difficult to continue to document the scene.

She knows it's time to stop recording when she sees the big networks show up. Time to upload the footage to the newsroom before the networks can get a live TV feed established. She connects her phone to her camera and uploads the video footage. Ken always pushes her stuff to broadcast. Being the first with the footage pays the most.

"Ken, did you get the file?"

"Yeah, I was just watching it. What happened? What *is* that thing?"

"I don't know, but it's not from this world and that means it's worth big money if you want to use it tonight."

"I have a feeling about this one as well, could be a big payday. I'll let you know."

CHAPTER 2: TWO YEARS LATER

It's a hot dry summer night in the desolate tract sands of Jerusalem, and everyone in the temple palace eats supper with the King. The guards on watch are mostly inside the main corridor near the dining room. They wait for the Kings drunken concubines to emerge after the supper. A party after the party is a nightly gift from the King to his loyal guards.

The year is 948 BC and US Air Force Colonel Bill Adams stands with his back against the outside temple wall next to Frank Reynolds, the teams' documentarian. Frank joined the TTRC (Time Travel Regulatory Commission) a few weeks ago; this is his first time out of the pod. Bill, the pod commander, is a former F-16 fighter pilot. They both try to blend in by wearing period-appropriate linen robes. The guards on their way into the palace rush right past them without even a suspicious glance, like twentieth century sailors on their way to a red light district.

Once they're alone, Bill reaches under his robe for his radio. He presses the button and whispers, "Lieutenant, Frank and I are at the temple. Keep radio silence until my next signal."

"Copy, Colonel." Lieutenant Sue Philips replies from a few hundred yards away, at the landing zone in a desert sand dune.

Bill leans over to Frank and whispers, "Remember, they want footage of all the objects in the King's chamber."

Bill didn't like the idea of a civilian working on field missions. From the moment he met Frank, he disliked him.

11

It's not that he's a bad person or would not do a good job, it's his lack of discipline and constant blustering of his artistic ideas. He only has this job because of his award-winning documentary on the lost tribes of the South American jungles. He has been in the jungle before, but he only observed from camouflaged blinds in the trees.

"Bill, I don't think I'm ready to do this, I thought I was just here to record from inside the pod. Why am I in the field?" Frank presses his head fretfully against the stone wall.

"We don't have time for this, Frank!"

They move gradually along the wall as Frank trembles. Bill looks back at him with an annoyed sneer.

"Frank, you've got to pull it together. You knew we went into the field when you signed up. No one ever said you'd be sitting in the pod all the time."

"I'm a *filmmaker*, not a soldier."

"Just do what I say you'll be fine. If you don't, we could both get killed!"

Bill stares at Frank with mounting frustration. They approach the entryway to the temple. The moon scarcely lights the entrance as they peek into the torch-lit corridor. Bill pulls his face wrap from his desert headdress up, leaving only his eyes exposed. He looks at Frank and suddenly reaches over to snatch Frank's glasses off his face, then shoves them in Frank's pocket.

"There are no opticians in 948 BC."

Frank nods then takes a deep gulp of air. "Sorry, I forgot."

"Hide your camera under your robe and stay beside me. We'll casually walk down the corridor to the Kings chamber."

Frank crosses his arms with the small hand-held camcorder gripped in his palm. He hides the camera in the fold of his frayed robe as they walk briskly down the long corridor. Oil burning torches embellish the walls and offer a dull illumination of their path. Frank sees something in a room at the end of the hall. He pulls his glasses from the pocket Bill had shoved them in and raises them to his face. He squints as he tries to make out the shape of a highly reflective object.

"Colonel, what's that?"

"That isn't our objective today; we can come back for it later." Bill stops at a closed door in the corridor. "This is the room. Let me check for locals."

Bill bends down and pulls a fiber optic scope from his robe. He slides the scope cable under the door and peeks through the eyepiece. "Looks clear, start recording."

Frank unfolds his arms and presses the record button on the camera. He holds it up to his eye just as Bill carefully pushes the door open, which makes a high-pitched creak. Bill tries to be as quiet as possible, but as the squeal from the door echoes in the hall, he intuitively grabs Frank, and pulls him into the room, away from prying eyes.

"There it is." Bill points to the carpet they've come to steal. "I'll grab it; you record the rest of the room."

Bill walks over to a hand-woven green and gold carpet leaning against the wall. It appears glued or sewn around a metallic silver platform that leans against the wall near the king's bed.

Meanwhile, Frank documents other items that one would expect in a Kings chamber—a gold washbowl and jewel encrusted wine jug; all the trophies from battles won. Frank moves rapidly, shuffling his feet sideways around the room, aiming his camera with trembling hands. Sweat drips off his brow, stinging his eyes. He records the many spoils of conflict, gold and gems tossed haphazardly on tables and spilled onto the marble floor.

Bill lifts the carpet away from the wall. It's a lightweight but unwieldy platform. The carpet, noticeably worn in the middle, has seen its share of use, as if someone stood only in the center of it for years. On the edges of the fitted carpet, the tassels are frayed, indicative of heavy wear. Bill moves it to the center of the room, supporting it with one hand as a pivot while he tries to see the bottom. He finds a series of round concave depressions laid out in a pentagonal pattern. The depressions appear machined. Bill lays the carpet flat and stands before it, wondering how to turn it on. He runs his hands over the edges, looking for hidden features, but they're perfectly smooth.

Frank finishes making his way around the room and stops recording back at the door. He shuts the camera off and walks over to Bill, who stands before the carpet with his arms folded.

"So what is this thing?"

"It's King Solomon's flying carpet. The part I can't figure out is where the power switch is."

"Look, I know I'm new here, but how can a carpet from three thousand years in the past fly? Don't tell me *magic.*"

"No. Look, there are things you don't have clearance for yet. Just let me figure out how we're getting this thing out of here without getting killed."

Frank throws his hands in the air. He wonders why he even volunteered for this job. Bill walks around the carpet when the sound of voices in the corridor startles them. Bill runs to the door and peeks out into the hallway. Four palace guards stand a few doors down, talking in ancient Aramaic.

He runs over to the carpet and points to the end nearest Frank's feet. "You grab that end; we need to go now!"

Frank shoves the camera in a pocket and picks up one side, while Bill grabs the other, and they walk towards the door. Bill holds up one hand and makes a fist; the military gesture to stop. He then looks back down the hall at the guards. A few seconds pass, and he drops his hand back down and whispers, "They're looking the other way, let's go."

They move the carpet out the door and head down the corridor, away from the guards, towards the doorway they initially entered.

Bill steers Frank through the corridor, his adrenalin pumping. As they near the exit, Frank turns to look back at the four guards and trips over his own feet. He falls to the ground, dropping his end of the carpet, gasping loudly when his elbows hit the floor. The sound echoes through the stone hallway, alerting the guards to their presence.

One screams, "Gananbua!" *Thief.*

Bill looks back at Frank. "Get up, now!"

Frank scrambles to his feet, grabs his end of the carpet, and they continue running towards the exit. Frank stumbles, trying to match Bill's pace as they head out the doorway and through the sand, back towards Sue, who waits in the pod at the landing zone. Frank, already out of breath, struggles to make it through the soft sand, forcing Bill to pull him along, using the carpet as a tug-line.

They start running up a sand dune when whizzing fills the air. The guards are close behind, firing arrows around Bill and Frank's feet. Suddenly Bill feels the back end of the carpet drop, and he looks back to see Frank has been seriously wounded. An arrow struck in the back of his thigh, missing the bone, and sticks out the front and the back of his leg. Bill drops the carpet and runs back to the now-limping Frank.

Frank staggers, holding out his hand. "Colonel, help me!" The bottom of the eggshell-white robe Frank wears rapidly turns red. The arrow must have hit his femoral artery.

Bill throws his arm around his shoulder. "You've got to run, Frank!"

They come within reach of the carpet just as Frank loses consciousness. He falls, landing on the carpet with an audible *thump*. The arrow protruding from Frank's leg snaps, and Bill looks back to see the guards have made it over the sand dune. He has no weapons to fight, so he turns his body in a combat stance in front of Frank. Bill hears footsteps from the other side of the sand dune as the guards get closer. His adrenalin is giving him extreme tunnel vision. His ears ring as his blood flow increases.

Just then, a shrill hum starts to radiate from the carpet. A yellow glow appears from the underside of the platform. The carpet starts to float a few inches above the sand. Bills eyes widen as he realizes Frank's limp body had found the power switch he had looked for. Bill straddles Frank atop the carpet as it begins to hover into the air. The guards arrive below the carpet, raising their bows, launching a volley of arrows. The ballistic arrows strike the carpet's underside, but do no damage.

Bill leans forward and the carpet moves in that direction, the way a surfer would ride a wave. As they approach the landing zone, Bill uses his radio to call Sue.

"Sue, we're inbound, time on top thirty seconds. Phase in visual, prep for matter collection and departure."

"Copy, Colonel."

"Frank is injured and bleeding. Break out the kit!"

Sue, sitting in her chair in the pod, glides her fingers across the touch-screen console, moving a digital slider to the left. Bill steers the carpet with his feet, looks down, and sees a brief flash of blue plasma light illuminate the desert sand. He leans backwards to bring the carpet to a stop. Below, a bell-shaped object suddenly appears on the surface, the pod time ship phasing in from invisibility. Bill slides his feet closer together and the carpet begins its descent, landing five feet from the ship. Bill jumps off, dragging Frank across the sand.

Sue swivels her chair around and throws open the door for Bill, who drags Frank inside and slams the door.

"Target the carpet outside the door and transport it into the buffer."

Sue taps a few buttons on her screen. Outside, the Guards shoot arrows at the pod. A blue light beam fires from a turret extending from the pods exterior, scanning along the surface of the carpet lying on the sand. Suddenly the carpet disappears.

"We got it," Sue calls.

Bill wraps Frank's leg with a bandage and jumps up to his command chair. "Phasing out in three... two... one..."

Bill stabs a button on the screen labeled 'Return', and the pod vanishes in a flash of light; a momentary plasma pulse sends a shock wave out in all directions, which knocks the guards back a couple feet. They sit up in the sand, dazed as the concussion wave which threw them to the ground wears off.

CHAPTER 3: RECRUITING EVELYN CARTER

After Frank's injury, he unsurprisingly quit the TTRC. The heart of a time ship is the documentarian, and finding a replacement was imperative. Bill and Sue tried to fill in, but their skills were no better than Frank's. The TTRC determined that the skill set requisite for the videographer job had to be more than someone who knew how to manage a camera. After evaluating many types of videographers, the verdict was simple—a stringer was the correct choice.

The TTRC identified hundreds of candidates for this job opening. On the top of the list was Evelyn Carter. Bill pushed her to the front after seeing her in interviews on TV from when she filmed the first time machine which was the genesis for the TTRC. Evelyn had been a stringer for ten years since she left home at the age of seventeen. Her well-documented record of getting to scenes of breaking news faster than her competition as well as amazing story telling through imagery made her an easy selection. Her work documenting the arrival of the first time machine didn't hurt, either. It has been two and a half years after she had first filmed the New York time machine. Over that time, she moved from city to city until deciding to go back home to Arizona, near her parents.

It was six months after Frank quit the agency when the TTRC approached Evelyn on the scene of a small apartment fire in Phoenix Arizona.

***

TTRC agents Bill Adams and Sue Philips pull in to the apartment parking lot. Even though they're both officers in the Air Force, they're not in uniform. Bill wears a pair of cargo pants and a polo shirt; Sue a pair of jeans and a button-up blouse. They get out of their government-issued four door white sedan and watch Evelyn Carter work.

Carter kneels down with her video camera, getting a low shot for B roll of the now extinguished apartment fire. The charred building smokes heavily into the midday sky. Bill walks up behind Evelyn and crouches, putting one hand on his knee, removing his sunglasses with the other. He looks at the LCD display on her camera.

"You have a good eye for this stuff."

"Thanks."

Carter stands unexpectedly with camera in hand and runs toward the side of the apartment. Bill stands just as Sue walks up beside him, and they watch Carter make a dash across the parking lot. As she runs, the camera seems to glide above her shoulder even though she doesn't have a stabilization harness to prevent shaky video. Clearly, she is a professional and highly skilled videographer.

A firefighter winding up a hose sees Carter running past, looking up and then back at what he is doing. He and his team had spent an exhausting two hours extinguishing the raging fire. Something in his brain then clicks. Normally he would not pay any attention to news crews on the scene. After fighting fires for twelve years, he has seen reporters more times than he can remember. This on the other hand, is Evelyn Carter, he knows her, and knows she has an almost sixth sense about things.

He drops the hose to the ground, looking towards the part of the building Carter films, and finally sees what she sees. Up in a window someone's arm is visible, gripping the middle latch.

The fire fighter screams to his crew. "We have a victim in the window!"

Carter kneels, aiming the camera towards the truck. The firefighter grabs a large axe and a portable ladder. With the ladder on his shoulder and the axe in his other hand, he runs up to the apartment wall just under the window. She records him heave the ladder up against the scorched wall and climb up to the window with the hefty axe in his hand.

He reaches the window and calls to the lifeless-looking old woman inside. "Lady, are you okay? Don't worry, I'm going to break the window." He grips the cement window ledge with one hand to steady himself as he swings the axe over his head. The heavy steel head smashes through the top of the window and a blast of hot air and smoke rushes from the opening. He flips the axe in his hand so the underside of the blade hooks on to the metal frame of the window. He yanks hard on the handle, pulling the frame away from the charred brick building. The lifeless looking woman's arm flops out of the window. "I got you lady!" He slides her out of the window and over his shoulder.

At the bottom of the ladder, the firefighter lays the old woman on the grass. He rips off his helmet and tosses it to the side, where it skids across the ground, coming to a stop only to spin like a top on the sidewalk. He checks her pulse as Carter moves in to get a better shot of the woman's blackened face. The victim, almost bald from the fire, doesn't move. Another firefighter drops to his knees next to her and begins giving her mouth to mouth, while the first firefighter delivers chest compressions.

"Stay with me, lady!"

Carter slowly pans her camera between the two firefighter's faces, then back to the old woman. The woman starts to cough as the CPR does its magic. A third Firefighter sprints over with a stretcher and an oxygen tank, and they carefully slide her on to the stretcher in a group lift.

"One, two, lift!"

The third firefighter places a mask on the woman's face and turns the valve on the oxygen tank until there's a hiss of flowing gas.

"Breathe deep, nice and slow."

She puts her hand on the mask and presses it against her own face. She takes a few difficult deep breaths as she stares fearfully into the sky. The old woman's eyes search for something; she doesn't know where she is or what has just happened. Carter captures everything on camera as the old woman finally looks up at the firefighter and places her palm on his cheek.

He smiles down at her. "You're safe now."

The three heroes carry the woman to a waiting ambulance. Carter lowers her camera, using her jacket sleeve to wipe her forehead from sweat, smearing black soot that had coated her face. She carefully puts her camera on the ground, reaching behind her head to remove her hair tie, and shakes her hair out to clear it from fallen ash.

Bill and Sue approach her as she picks up her camera and walking away from the building towards the edge of the parking lot.

Just as the three meet in the middle, Bill extends his hand. "You're Evelyn Carter, right?"

Carter ignores his hand and continues walking towards her van. "Yeah, I'm Carter. Do you need something?"

"Well, as a matter of fact, we do need something. We want to hire you."

They arrive at the van. Carter opens the door to the front passenger side, which makes a squeaking sound. She looks at Bill, then at Sue. "I don't do weddings, sorry."

"How come you didn't call to the fire fighters and alert them about the woman in the window?" Sue asks.

Carter takes off her gear vest and throws it on the passenger side floor. "That's not my job, I just shoot, the rest is up to them."

"She would have died if the firefighter hadn't seen you running to the window, though."

"Yup, and that would have been a different story." Carter forces a smile and reaches to the dashboard, grabbing a cable protruding out of a small cell phone mounted on the dash. She plugs the cable into the side of her camera and types quickly on the phone's keyboard.

"What does the phone do with your camera?" Bill asks.

"I'm uploading my footage to the news room."

"Evelyn-"

"Carter, I prefer Carter."

"Sorry, Carter, we're not getting married, and we don't need a videographer for a wedding. Sue's already married. We're from the Time Travel Regulatory Commission, and we would like to hire you to work on a Time Ship."

She types on her phone. "Ha, you sure *could* use some help, from what I've seen on TV. Your footage sucks."

Bill places his hand on Carter's shoulder. "That's why we're here talking to you."

Carter finishes typing. "Uploaded and filed," she says under her breath, and turns to Bill. "Wait, are you for real? Let me see your ID's."

Bill and Sue exchange looks and pull wallets out of their pockets. They flip them open; a TTRC gold badge shines in the sunlight on one side, and an ID card on the other.

"Those aren't police badges. They look phony."

Bill replies, "That's because we're not cops, we're time travelers."

23

Carter runs her fingers over the length of her camera, zoning out, thinking about when she recorded the first time machine two years earlier. This is the one story she started and never saw through to the end. She remembers watching the videos that were broadcast after each time travel mission on TV and thinking to herself, *If I was holding the camera this would have been a million times better.* Carter wants this assignment, but she wonders why they're asking.

"Would you like some time to think about it?" Bill asks.

"No, I'll do it!"

Bill smiles. "How would you like to take a quick ride, then?"

"Where to?"

"Nevada."

***

Six hours later, about twenty minutes before arriving at TTRC headquarters, Carter rides in the front passenger seat of Bill and Sue's government car. Sue sits in the back and Bill drives. The radio plays one of Bill's mixed CDs. He loves classic rock and has 5th Dimensions 'Age of Aquarius' playing softly over the speakers.

"You've been pretty quiet for the last few hours, Carter. I figured you'd be asking me questions about the TTRC the entire drive," Bill says.

"Sorry, I'm just thinking."

"So, two and a half years ago you were working in New York, what made you move to Arizona?"

"I'm from Arizona, and my parents are there. I sort of went from city to city looking for work. After New York, I went to Atlanta and tried to work for CNN, then I went to Dallas for a while, but when you're broke, you have no other choice but to go where the work is. So I guess Arizona just sort of pulled me back."

"What about the money you got from your Pulitzer?"

"Do you know how much news cameras and equipment cost? That money was gone in a few weeks." Carter turns the music off. "I get what you do, and I get what you want me to do. What I don't get is *why me?*"

"History isn't scripted, Carter, it's fast, it's surprising, and it requires the eye of a person who has instincts to catch the moment. Sort of like what you did back at the apartment fire with that woman. You knew something was about to happen. You kept yourself out of the action and didn't set up the rescue. You were there to document the event regardless of the outcome."

Carter stares out the window at the passing desert scenery, thinking about what she might see in this job. She knows there are so many events in history never recorded. *What an opportunity,* she thinks.

Bill says, "Sue is the engineer for our pod."

Carter looks at Sue. "Pod?"

Sue leans forward from the back seat. "That's what we call the time ships, just easier to say. I'm a physicist, and have degrees in engineering and physics related to what we do. Bill is the pod captain and you're being recruited to be the documentarian."

"These pods can move through space as well as time, right? So why didn't we use the pod to get to the base instead of taking this long car ride?"

Bill points back at Sue with his thumb. "Sue always wants to skip the long rides and take the pod shopping, but time ships are not a taxi service."

"Right..." Sue wears a condescending look as she fans her face with a note pad which has scribbles of equations on it.

Bill pulls a plastic ID card and lanyard out of his pocket and hands it to Carter. "Here, I almost forgot, this is your temporary TTRC base ID card."

Carter takes the lanyard and places it over her head, looking down at the ID. "You already have all my info on here, even my driver's license photo."

"We've been watching you for a while now; you're on the top of a very short list."

Carter turns up her top lip as she stares at the three-year-old photo. "I hate this picture. So, I get a gold badge later, then?"

"Oh, we're here," Bill says.

Carter sits up in her seat and lowers the visor as the setting sun turns the sky red. Ahead is a large tower, with an armed guard on top. Another guard at the bottom walks out from a small shack and stands in front of a sun-beaten wooden barricade arm. The car comes to a stop as the guard walks up to the driver's side window and bends down to look inside.

"Colonel, Lieutenant, Miss. Carter.... You're cleared for entry." The Air Force guard salutes them and waves the car through.

"That's it? *That's* the security for the base?" Carter asks.

Bill snickers. "No, see that mountain ahead there?"

Carter lowers her head to peek under the sun visor. "Yeah, oh it's inside the mountain?"

"Yes, that's the base up ahead. The guard we passed is there to let us know we're clear to drive through the minefield. Had he not approved us and entered a pass code at the guard shack, the transmitter that disables the mines before we drive over them would not have functioned. It's sort of a dead man's switch," Bill explains.

Carter rolls down her window and leans out to get a look at the ground as they drive. There's no paved road, just tire tracks in the desert sand from other cars that had driven there before. The tire tracks are everywhere. "How come all these tire tracks are not in the same path?"

"Don't worry, we're all safe. The mines become disabled as we drive close because of the transmitter built in to the car. We don't need to stick to one path, and it makes it more confusing for people who are thinking about sneaking up on the base to see so many tire tracks." Bill points to the GPS screen on the dashboard. "See the green light? That means it's safe to drive through the mines. Had the guard not entered the correct code, it would be red."

After about two miles of driving, he brings the car to a stop in a tunnel opening on the side of the mountain. The tunnel is unremarkable in design, just a simple corrugated steel half round tube sticking out of the side of the mountain. Inside, off to the left, is a small mirror-coated window. Presumably, there's a person on the other side of the glass. Bill stops the car and he and Sue hold up their ID's.

"Do I need to show my ID, too?"

"No, they know you're with us."

Bill raises his hands, touching his fingertips to the inside roof of the car. He gives Carter a wink and a nod. Carter turns to look back at Sue, who also has her hands on the roof. Carter, wearing a scared look, raises her hands and pressing them hard against the roof.

Suddenly a low hum vibrates the frame of the car, growing louder and louder, until there's a bright flash of green. Everyone is flash blind for a second until Bill and Sue lower their arms and look over at Carter.

"You can put your arms down now, the scan is over."

Carter rubs her eyes. "What did we just get scanned with?'

Bill tilts his head in a slightly cocky manner. "I have no idea, but after my first scan, they told me to eat less red meat."

He laughs as they resume driving, descending deep into the dark tunnel, and presses a button on the car dashboard, which brings up a night vision display which projects on the windshield.

"Bill, how come you don't use your headlights?"

"It's just a security feature. We drive in dark; if any light is picked up by the tunnel sensors a security lockdown is initiated."

Carter stares at the heads up display in front of Bill. It shows the shape of the winding tunnel ahead. "Bill, when I was younger, my parents took me to a haunted house on the boardwalk in New Jersey. This driving in the dark is bringing back memories of that child hood experience, and it isn't good!"

"Sorry, we have to do this. Do you want to hold my hand?"

It's evident that they're not going *in*, but underneath. The road curves into a spiral as they drive deeper and deeper under the mountain. Suddenly a rotating red light on the ceiling breaks the darkness, illuminating a massive steel door that has begun to open. The door is twenty feet tall and twenty feet wide, sliding up into the tunnel ceiling. As soon as the car passes through, Carter turns and watches the heavy steel door close. It should have made a loud bang from closing so quickly, but instead, there's a high-pitched hiss of a pneumatic piston, which has slowed the impact at the last few inches before it hit the ground.

It's pitch black once more. Carter's pupils dilate as she yet again tries to adjust her vision. Suddenly a second steel door slides open, and a bright light blasts out. Carter squints, holding her hand up. At some point before the door opened, Bill had put on his sunglasses, ready for the light at the end of the tunnel.

Carter struggles to regain her daytime vision as she looks at the massive underground parking area that they're halfway through. "Shit!"

Sue leans forward from the back seat. "That's what I said the first time, too."

The car pulls up to a parking spot next to a row of buildings. Bill shuts off the engine. "Are you ready to see more?"

Carter unhooks her seat belt, gazing in wonder out the window. They're in a tremendous cave which is thousands of feet from floor to ceiling. She looks out and sees buildings as tall as New York skyscrapers. The view goes on further than she can make out detail. There are bright blinding lights mounted to the cave ceiling. They're so bright they simulate daylight.

Carter turns to Bill. "It's like the entire mountain is just a shell! How is this even possible?"

Bill looks up at the cavernous complex. He points at the walls of the mountain. "They built this place for an entirely different purpose. Originally this was going to be a continuity of government facility. In the 1960's they planned on moving VIPs here in case of a nuclear war. It was much smaller back then. Then a discovery in excavating allowed us to literally hollow out the mountain and the ground underneath it. We're actually standing about three thousand feet below the base of the mountain. Above us, the mountain walls are almost a quarter mile thick. We have forty miles in both directions hollowed out under ground."

"What kind of excavating tool can do this?"

"In due time, be patient, all will be revealed," he says in a spooky voice.

They walk from the parking lot to the sidewalk along the street at the edge of the city. For an underground military base, it looks similar to any American city. There are tall buildings, short buildings, retail and industrial. There are people everywhere in the bustling underground city. Some are in military uniform, others wearing civilian clothes or lab coats. Cars and military vehicles drive throughout the streets.

"This is like an underground town; there's a barber shop, a restaurant, oh my god!" Carter stops dead and slaps her hand on Bill's chest. "Is that a Wal-Mart?"

"Yup, they play a big role in all this."

"So all this is for the TTRC?"

Sue responds, "No, this is a multi-department hub for various uses. The TTRC is just one small section. We all get to share the facility with other Government and Civilian projects that need high security."

"How many people are down here?"

"Well there are a few thousand base personnel, but there's room in this hub to house about half a million people should there be a disaster."

They make their way to the TTRC headquarters. As she fixates at the immense city above her, she veers off onto the artificial grass of the road verge, not paying attention, which forces Bill to walk behind her with his hands at the ready to catch her if she trips. She feels like a child in a toy store for the first time.

She sees a blurred object pass rapidly through a translucent tube above her head. The ten-foot diameter tube runs just above the buildings east to west, and extends as far as the eye can see.

"What's that tube up there?"

Bill looks up. "Oh that's a base to base transit system. We built that back in the 70's. It's almost worldwide now. It's really cool how it works. The tubes have the air vacuumed out so there's no friction. The car inside is propelled by the same magnetic drive system on trains and roller coasters. Without the friction of air to slow you down, we can travel at incredible speeds. We can go from this hub to a hub on the other side of the planet in less than twenty minutes if we needed to."

She shakes her head in awe. She knew the military had secrets, but this is almost a form of future shock. The city appears bigger than any city on Earth.

"How do you keep all this stuff a secret for so long?"

Bill laughs. "Well, we slowly leak the secrets to the public as needed. We just gave the tube transport technology to that guy who makes the fancy electric cars. He and many other companies help us distribute secret tech to the public. In return, we get money from our investments in their corporations to fund more research and construction. It's a pretty good arrangement."

They arrive at the TTRC building, which is a six-story structure about four blocks from the main parking lot. Bill swipes his open wallet against the magnetic pad on the door, and it slides open. Carter feels underwhelmed walking in the building. The plain tan walls and sparse décor is not what she expected, having anticipated a high-tech facility with lots of activity. The TTRC receptionist welcomes them with a wave as they walk past her desk. Carter smiles, but her eyes show she is almost embarrassed.

They head toward the double bank of elevators directly ahead. After they enter, Carter notices the cheesy music playing softly in the background. She looks at the button pad as Bill presses sub level three. As the elevator reaches its floor and the doors open, the three walk out to a long hallway. Bill points out the rooms as they pass.

"That's the crew lounge; on the other side of the hall is the cafeteria. The food is good, but I suggest going to one of the base restaurants if you've the time. If you just want a burger or something to eat fast, then the cafeteria is convenient. Here's the geology lab, and this is the collections department."

Carter stops in front of the collections department window and looks inside. There are many people wearing clean room suits examining various objects. She sees a group of technicians' using what looks like an x-ray machine on a golden box.

"Is that the Ark of the Covenant?"

Bill looks in the window. "That's what they're trying to figure out now. We just collected it last week. Here we are. Hangar Bay One."

They turn into a simple set of double doors. Ahead in a room the size of an airplane hangar are six of the time ship pods. They sit on mechanical clamp stands. To the side are a small control room, ready room, and gear room with lockers.

"I recognize this from TV! This is where the time ships—I mean pods—come and go."

She finally feels grounded with some familiar surroundings. The hangar bay is the only room on base that's live broadcast over TV and on the internet.

A man in military uniform walks out of the control room. Bill turns towards him. "Carter, allow me to introduce Major General Roy Wilson, He is the TTRC base commander."

Wilson raises his arm towards Carter. "Ms. Carter, I've been eagerly awaiting your approval, welcome aboard."

Carter shakes his hand. "My approval?"

Wilson looks at Bill. "I thought Colonel Adams would have mentioned, we've been doing your background check and security clearance for a number of months now."

Bill shakes his head. "No sir, we hadn't discussed that yet."

Wilson turns his head back to Carter, gripping her hand. "Well I'm confident you're the right one for the job and you will do well here. Good luck with your training Ms. Carter."

Her eyes shift to Bill. "Training?" She looks back at Wilson. "Thank you, General."

"Please, you're a civilian, call me Roy, only Colonel Adams has to call me General," He says, walking away.

Sue waves goodbye. "I'm going to engineering, I'll catch up with you later, Carter."

"So let's go check out our pod shall we?" Bill gestures towards the first pod in the row.

Next to the line of six pods is a cement pedestal about three feet tall and two feet in diameter. A metal cylinder lies on its side, hovering inside a blue glowing energy field.

Carter veers away from the pod to see the pedestal. "This is the original time machine I filmed! Right? "

"Yes, this is that very same one. It's what started the entire program."

Carter slowly circles the pedestal. "I watched the news for a while, but when it got into all the arguing over what it was, and how it worked, I stopped paying attention. It got too technical and the arguing got political."

"Well, I'll catch you up on what happened so far. You recall there was really no way to hide its arrival. After your news footage went public every news agency immediately picked up the story, by lunch time there were panels of so called experts who speculated on what it might be."

"Yeah, I remember that part. Everyone thought it was a bomb. Then that scientist broke the story that he thought it was a time machine. The thing I didn't understand was how did he know what it was if it had the force field around it?"

"Well, he was working on experiments relating to generating frequencies that match similar ones being listened to through radio telescopes. He had this theory, that the background noise radio astronomers had been listening to for years, were actually changing every second since the big bang. He published a paper years earlier, claiming the frequency was the universes clock. When he was brought in to consult on the cylinder, he used his universe frequency measuring equipment. When he saw the same readings from the energy field, he then went on TV and announced this is a time machine. He also claimed it was a time machine that we built sometime in the future and sent back in time to us. Of course, that part has yet to happen since he doesn't work for the TTRC right now."

"Right, I remember that part played over and over on TV. He said if you can change the frequency, you can travel through time."

"That's only half the process; you needed to also temporarily leave the universe."

"That's where I got lost." She holds her hand over the blue energy field.

"After months of running every experiment to try and penetrate the energy bubble surrounding it, suddenly a couple panels mechanically opened on the cylinder. Do you see that one right there?" Bill points to a LCD display screen.

"Yeah, I remember that. It's the five-year count down."

"Right! That panel covering the LCD screen slid open and a timer counting down from five years was running. Now it's at two and a half years. In addition, the other round panel next to it also opened. That empty spot there contained the backup field generator. That was the sphere that dropped down through the force field and landed on the floor. Since we still couldn't penetrate the shield on the cylinder, we determined there was another generator inside and this one that dropped out was a secondary. We think that whoever sent the cylinder through time wanted us to get the generator, so we could easily reverse engineer it."

"So that's what makes the blue force field?"

"Yes, and it also makes the phase field. The phase field was the missing link to making time travel possible. Inside the time machine, the phase field takes anything inside it, out of phase slightly with the universe. Then the frequency generator sends out a signal to a specific time you want to go to."

"How does sending a signal make you travel in time?"

"Think of it this way, Carter. The universe has a clock, and no matter where you are in the universe, that clock is set to the same time. Instead of seeing a digital read out or an hour and minute hand, we see a constantly advancing radio frequency. We can read that frequency and calculate what the frequency was one hour ago, or even one hour from now.

It's extremely easy for us to generate any frequency we want throughout all of time. The part that makes the magic happen is when that frequency we generate impacts with the phased out energy field. Since the time machine is out of phase, it's instantly synchronized with any frequency we throw at it. Therefore, if I generate the frequency that was from three weeks ago, the phased field will synchronize with that frequency and instantly transport us there."

"That makes more sense than that documentary on the science channel. I wish they would have just said what you said for us regular people. One thing you didn't explain though is how come we can see this cylinder, but when you go on time travel missions you're invisible?"

"We actually stumbled onto that during unmanned trials last year. One of the software programmers, who developed the user interface program, messed up the phase in and phase out programming software. This mistake caused the prototype to vanish. Originally, they thought they lost the prototype, but when it returned after the pre-programmed trip time expired, the video tape from the on board camera showed it never left. It sat right on the table and recorded the hangar bay for the entire time it was supposedly gone. They then realized they could modify the phase field to give us a cloaking device."

"So this cylinder doesn't have that capability?"

"Well we're not sure, because the phase field is still up and we can't turn it off. Maybe when the countdown timer finishes in two and a half years it will shut off."

She laughs. "Or explode."

"There's that, too."

They make their way to the first pod, which is a bell shaped craft similar to the old capsules astronauts flew in the Apollo moon missions. It has a domed top and a wide bottom, bigger than the old capsules at about fifteen feet in diameter at the base and fourteen feet tall. The outside is painted a flat white with riveted metal seams. There are no visible windows, but halfway up the body are silver metallic panels which wrap around the pod's surface. The door on the front is a little bit shorter than the five-foot-seven Carter stands. On the side of the pod is a name plate that reads "POD ONE." Under the plate is a stencil that has "Pugs", "Boa" and a blank space which looks recently painted over.

"Pugs, Boa, what does that mean?"

"Well, all aviators have call signs, but my call sign when I flew Air Force jets was not really appropriate for public viewing, and the General didn't think that was the best call sign for the mission we're on. The public doesn't know our real names for security reasons. So since I have two Pugs at home, he nicknamed me pugs. I think though he was also using my last name Adams in there as well. You know that old TV show? Sue has a huge boa constrictor at home, so the General nicknamed her Boa."

She turns away from Bill, walking around the pod. "I'm not telling you what pets I have."

He bows his head. "Don't worry, I won't tell the General you have a cat."

She whips around. "Let me guess, background check?"

He nods, standing in front of the pod door, gesturing for her to go in. She climbs up the set of rolling stairs placed next to the pod. As she walks into the doorway and looks in, she sees three swivel chairs mounted to the floor. There's a wraparound window, which is the mirror coated wraparound panel she noticed on the exterior. The window sits at shoulder height when sitting in the chairs, which makes it difficult to see out. It wraps around half of the pod. A chrome rail above the window, which also wraps all the way around, has a camera mount that rolls on dolly wheels.

Carter looks at the camera mount as she runs her hand along the rail, checking its smoothness. "Good tracks, bad camera mount, though."

Bill examines the mount. "You're the expert, Carter." He points at the middle chair. "That one is yours. When you need to swing the camera around over our heads, just yell 'duck'." As Bill pushes the mount along the curved rail, it slides smoothly and comes to a stop at the end of the window frame.

"Can we replace this camera mount with a quick release? I might need to go handheld."

He puts his hand on the camera mount. "Sure, whatever you need."

She explores the inside of the pod, looking at the control panels mounted in front of each chair. Near the main door is another small door, which she opens. "Good I was wondering if there was a bathroom."

Bill sits in the left seat. "Yup, and it has a mini shower for those long stinky missions."

She closes the door and turns towards the right hand seat. "This is Sue's seat?"

He nods. "Are you ready for a test ride?"

She puts her hand on the camera rail. "Where's my camera?"

"No camera for this one, we'll just go around the block once."

She sits in her seat. "I'm ready."

Bill shuts the pod door and jumps back to his chair, doing a full rotation as if he is a kid playing on a swivel chair. He reaches over to the microphone button. "Pod One, ready for test run."

The speaker inside the pod squeals, then a voice comes over. "Pod One go for launch, be back in time for dinner."

Bill leans forward and flips a master power switch, causing all the control panel lights and screens to illuminate. A screen in front of him displays a long series of numbers next to the word "frequency", and under that another says, "Space coordinates".

He turns to Carter. "Any requests?"

"Anywhere I want?" On his nod, she says, "How about ancient Egypt? I've always wanted to see that."

"You want to see the building of the pyramids?"

"Yes!"

Bill types on the touch screen. A button appears with the words "Phase now?"

Bill's finger hovers over the button. "Ready?"

Carter puts her hands on the armrests and squeezes them tight. She doesn't know what to expect, and she squeezes so hard that her knuckles start losing their color. "Ready!"

Bill pushes the button, and the pod starts to vibrate. An electrical discharge hum starts, and gets louder until a flash of blue light flickers. Then total silence.

Bill swivels his chair around. "Take a look."

Carter stands and leans into the window, gripping the camera rail above her. As her eyes adjust to the sun light, she can see they're flying. Just off to the side is a large square grouping of stones on the ground which forms a platform in the sand. The pod, about four hundred feet off the ground, hovers completely still. She looks down and finds thousands of people beneath them, pulling large slabs of stone up a giant ramp made of sand. The ramp is nearly a quarter mile long at a very slight incline. There are only about three levels of the great pyramid at Giza completed.

"The people on the ground don't see or hear us," Bill says softly.

Carter smiles but quickly looks back out the window. Now mesmerized, she finds it difficult to accept what she's seeing. This cannot possibly be real. It's like watching a documentary in really good 3D.

"You want to see something freaky cool?"

"Sure, what?"

"Watch this!"

Bill hops back in his seat and grabs a set of flight control sticks you would normally find in an airplane. As he pushes the sticks, the pod starts to move. Carter grips the camera rail in anticipation, only to realize there's still no feeling of movement inside the pod, but it begins dropping altitude until it's only inches above the sand.

"Ready?" Bill moves the pod across the surface of the desert sand. Suddenly he brings the pod to a stop. "Well?"

"Well what?"

"Turn around."

Carter lets go of the rail and turns. Right in front of her is a man sitting on the pod floor, sharpening a metal tool with a flat stone. Carter takes a step backward and lets out a gasp. "How did he get in here?"

"He's not actually in here, we're out of phase so he can't see, hear or touch us. I just parked the pod on top of him. From his perspective, he's sitting in the hot sun doing whatever it is he's doing."

Hesitantly, Carter walks over to the man and puts her finger out to touch his shoulder. Just like a ghost, her finger passes through his body.

She pulls her hand back. "That *is* freaky."

"You don't need to whisper, he can't hear you." Bill brings the pod back up in the sky and backs off from the pyramid site. "Now watch this, we have a fast forward dial."

Carter looks at him with wide eyes, then back out the window. Bill puts his hand on a big metal dial and turns the knob to the right a little bit at a time. The view outside the window begins to speed up, first looking like people are moving very quickly, then as Bill turns the knob further, they become blurs. He turns the knob even more, and the people disappear from view, and the stones they had been pulling

40

appear to be moving on their own. About halfway done with the building of the pyramid, the action suddenly reverses, and the stones start to disappear. Carter whips her head around to find Bill with a huge grin on his face.

"Just kidding." He turns the dial forward again.

Carter watches as the construction completes, and more and more structures appear around the pyramids. The complex of buildings looks immaculate, the top of the pyramid shining with a golden capstone. The familiar sides seem glass-smooth from a layer of white limestone and plaster covering the jagged granite blocks.

Then the pyramid begins looking older and older, losing its smooth coating. Many of the surrounding structures around the pyramid appear to sink into the sand, along with the bottom of the pyramids. Sand seems to come in and out like waves on the beach, covering the entire structure. Just as the action seems to stop, an entire modern city appears and the pyramids rise from the sand. The fast-forward ceases. Out the window, the surroundings move at normal speed. People wear modern clothes, taking photos.

Carter's head jerks back as the time lapse completes. "What year is it out there?"

"It's today, the day we left the hangar bay."

Carter stares at the people who cannot see the pod. A tear starts to form in her eyes. What she has just witnessed is unlike anything she's ever seen in her life.

"Are you OK?"

"Yeah, it was just a bit overwhelming to watch so much history pass so quickly." She wipes her eyes with the back of her hand. "There was a story being told through that window, even though decades where passing every second. I could see the story play out even at that speed. I watched as millions of people were being born, living their lives, working, loving, raising families and dying, faster than the blink of an eye. I'm used to stories playing out in real time. So much slower is how I've processed events in my head all my life and career. It's like my brain just got reprogrammed to see the world in a completely different way, in a way that people have never seen before." Carter turns towards Bill and a small tear runs down her cheek. "Sorry if I got into the moment, I'm just a little unprepared for the experience."

Bill smiles. "That's why we recruited you, it's that instinct you have to the story." Bill reaches over to his screen and presses his finger on the button marked "Return." The pod vanishes and returns to the hangar bay.

CHAPTER 4: TRAINING DAY

At the hangar bay, Pod One arrives back from the test flight. Bill steps out first, offering his hand to Carter. She steps down to the staircase and sits down on the bottom step.

"Wow, I feel like I have a bit of jet lag." She massages the back of her neck.

"That passes in a few minutes. Sometimes I still feel it, if we just do a quick trip." Bill pats her shoulder and starts towards the control room.

Carter follows. "How much time has passed here?"

Bill fills out the travel log on the computer console inside the control room. "The same amount of time that we were gone passes here. They programmed the pods to do that so we don't lose or gain time during missions. We could come back a second after we left if we wanted to, but the higher ups wanted to have an accurate record of how long each pod spends in mission time." He finishes entering his mission report in the computer, then turns to the coffee pot. "Want a cup?"

"Sure; light and sweet please."

Bill smirks. "I know."

"So, what's next?"

"Well, now you have a bunch of decisions to make. The first one is, do you want the job? I'm thinking from your reaction during the test flight, that would be a yes?"

Carter nods cautiously.

"All right. The next choice is where you want to live. You're six hours from home, so a commute may not be the best choice. The base is two hours from the nearest town."

They enter the crew lounge and relax in some recliners.

"Well, where do the others who work here live?"

"Right here in Hub Town. My place is a few blocks from here, in Tower 42. Sue is also in the tower. It's a small 1,100 square-foot apartment, but the rent is free and you can walk to work."

Carter sips her coffee, contemplating such a big life change.

He continues, "I already took the liberty and have a place reserved for you, if you want to go take a look. If you like it, we can arrange to move your things. Oh we won't forget your cat either."

"Let's go see it."

They walk over to Apartment Tower 42, in the east side of town.

"Why is this called Hub Town?"

Bill opens the front door of the apartment building for Carter. "There are multiple hubs, how many, even I don't know. I've only seen two others. I guess because each one connects via the tube transit." Bill pushes a button to call the car. "Officially, we're just Space 30 on the location list. Each base underground is called a 'space,' and above ground we call them 'areas.'"

"Like Area 51."

"Yup."

The doors open, and Carter and Bill enter the elevator.

"So, what was the original purpose of the spaces underground?"

Bill hesitates. "Well, I'll tell you a bit about it, but there are some things I don't have permission to tell you yet.

Someone proposed a way to protect a large amount of the population in the event of a disaster. You know; nuclear war, natural disasters, etcetera. So underground seemed like a good place to prepare. We have access to underground water through aquifers and we can tap into the Earth's geothermal energy for heat and our power needs. Technology in the 1960's was very limited, but later on, I'm not sure exactly when, a particle beam was discovered that could remove rock using almost the same tech as we use in the pods to phase in and out of space time."

"So you phase out the rock and then put it... where?" She asks as the elevator doors open once more.

"Well, we just delete it. We used to remove material to form a space and then aim the beam somewhere else to deposit it, but someone decided just to flush the buffer so the matter just disappears permanently. I guess it's safe to do that, but I'm not sure. Sue would be the one to ask about that."

Bill stops in front of an apartment door. "Here it is; Apartment 10 E."

Carter slips past him. "There's already furniture in here?"

He follows her into the room. "Yes, but we can remove it if you want to decorate yourself."

Carter looks around. "No. I like it. You should see the shit hole I'm in now—oh wait, you probably already have." She finds Bill is smiling. "You aren't watching me shower or anything creepy like that, are you?"

Bill raises both hands. "No, no. Your shower habits don't play into your security clearance."

They laugh.

Bill walks back toward the door. "Well, I'll leave you to get acquainted with your new surroundings. There are some clothes in the closet along with all your basic toiletries. You can make a trip to the base store for anything you might need. Use the computer on the desk over there in the office to email me a list of things from your home you want transported here for you. There's a file on the desktop, which has an accurate inventory of all your personal belongings. Just click on the box next to each one you want transported. My email address is already on the contact list, so you can just attach the document and click send. I've had them stock your refrigerator with food; its stuff you probably like."

"Thanks, I think I'm getting used to this Big Brother thing; it's not even fazing me anymore."

Bill stops. "Oh, there's a mobile phone on the desk and it has everyone you need to know on speed dial already. So feel free to do what you want and tomorrow I will give you a call before I come by to get you. There are some shops and restaurants open twenty-four hours a day on base. Food on base is free, of course. Just don't pig out, we need you fit for duty." He pauses once more. "Have a good night, Carter. We have a big day tomorrow." He leaves, closing the door behind him.

Carter's new apartment is a two bedroom; the second one converted into a home office. The rest of the floor plan is a basic wide-open space with no walls separating the living room, dining room and kitchen. The apartment is lavish and modern for government housing. Better than the one bedroom she came from which backs up to a smelly restaurant.

In the refrigerator, she finds some very familiar items that she normally buys. Their placement is the way she would normally organize. "Okay, this just gets creepier by the minute."

She thinks, *it feels like an invasion of privacy, but then again they do think of everything.* After sitting on the sofa for a bit and drinking a beer, she realizes she doesn't even know what her salary will be. Carter grabs the cell phone from the office and messages Bill.

Bill: Maybe it's too late to ask, but what does this job pay?

SEND.

A few seconds later Bill replies: *How much do you want?*

Seriously?

It's GS15, so just over 100k.

That's more than I was going to ask for. See you in the morning.

Carter grabs her ID lanyard and takes the elevator back down to the street to get a better lay of the land. When she gets to the street, the first thing she sees is a small box on a metal pole next to the apartment labeled 'Town Maps'. When she opens the map, she realizes how large the town actually is. Forty miles in both directions, all underground, so far from one end to the other that it's impossible to see to the end.

"Okay, so Tower 42 is on the outside edge of the town, and from here, if I go left I can get to this seafood place."

The seafood restaurant, called 'Neptune's Pantry' is fairly busy. She enjoys a lengthy meal and tries not to stare at the other base personnel who eat their meals. Everyone seems happy as they sit and laugh just like in any other restaurant she has ever visited. After eating, the server asks for her ID card.

"Did you enjoy your meal?"

"Yes, it was amazing. I love king crab. It was so good."

"Good, I'm glad."

Carter looks at the host, noticing she is a woman in her sixties. She wonders for a moment how people are hired to do restaurant jobs in a base with such high security.

"Can I ask you a question? How long have you worked here?"

"Oh, going on five years now." She forces a smile. "I came down in the '80s as a DARPA researcher. When I retired, they let me stay in my housing and gave me this job." The host hands her back her ID. "Well, have a good evening."

Carter heads back to her apartment and swipes her ID card to open the door. She settles in for the night, lying in bed trying to process everything she had seen, but for some reason the host in the restaurant keeps popping into her thoughts. *Is she really retired, or has she been prevented from leaving?*

***

The next morning Carter gets ready to leave when the phone rings. "It's Bill. I'm waiting outside in the car whenever you're ready."

Carter tucks the phone between her cheek and shoulder as she laces up a pair of boots. "Okay. I'll be down in two minutes."

Down on the street, Bill waits in the car. Carter comes through the double doors and gets in the passenger seat. "So where are we going?"

"It's training day. We're going about five miles from here, where you'll learn some of the rules and take some basic medical evaluations. Then we're going to go over some security items as well as a little basic survival and self-defense."

"Why would I need self-defense and survival training? I thought we just observed and blended in."

Bill takes a breath. "There was an incident recently, the documentarian was injured by a local time occupant and was unable to defend himself. He survived, but quit the program because he felt he wasn't prepared properly for the situation.

So now we give you the basic skills you'll need in case of an emergency."

"Was that person the one whose name was painted over on our pod?"

"Yes. I blame myself for not preparing him adequately. So I want to make sure you're prepared."

Bill and Carter arrive at the training facility, and Carter spends an hour in class learning the do's and don'ts of time travel, such as never interfere unless under direct orders from the TTRC, and never reveal you're a TTRC agent to the general public, to avoid the possibility of someone forcing her to alter time.

The public knows agents exist, but the identity of the agent must be secret. The first time traveler known to the public had been removed from duty because of the unwanted attention and threats of blackmail by those who wanted the time line altered for personal reasons.

She also learned the two-man rule, which applies to all personnel who have access to time travel equipment. *"During any operation which may afford access, a minimum of two authorized personnel must be present."* This rule had been adopted from the military nuclear weapons program to prevent unauthorized access to time travel equipment.

After the long day of poking, prodding, and learning basic necessary skills for operation and survival, Bill and Carter drive back to Tower 42.

Bill pulls the car in front of the entrance. "So, how're you holding up so far?"

She slumps back. "I'm good, but I'm pretty tired. It's funny. I could go for twenty straight hours chasing fire trucks and police cruisers, but for some reason I'm exhausted."

Bill snaps his fingers as if he had forgotten something important. "It's the sun!"

Carter gives him a puzzled look.

"Your body needs sun light on a daily basis to maintain the right vitamin balance or something like that. You have a map of the city yet?"

"Yes. I got one last night."

"Good. On the map there are sun towers spread throughout the city. Take your bathing suit and some sunblock up there and get some sun, you'll feel much better. Also, when you go operational you will get natural sun light through the pod windows and when we go on collection missions. You can also go to the pharmacy and pick up vitamin supplements. Just ask for 'Sun Pills' and they'll give you what you need. We all suffer from lack of sun, so I sometimes forget to tell new people. Sorry about that."

Carter sighs. "So how do the sun towers work?"

"Go up and see for yourself."

Carter gets out of the car and Bill drives away. She goes back up to her apartment and checks her drawers for a bathing suit and lotion. Sure enough, they're right where she would have put them herself. She changes into the bikini, and then puts on a t-shirt and a pair of jeans.

It's only 3:00 p.m., so she heads down to the nearest sun tower, which is only five blocks away. The walk is even more exhausting than she imagined it would be, and the no-sun theory starts to make more and more sense. She arrives at the entrance to the sun tower, a ten-foot-wide metal cylinder from the ground in the cave right up to the roof. She presses the button next to the door.

"It's an elevator," she says aloud.

After the long ride up, the doors open to reveal a domed structure under the desert sun. There's a large swimming pool, lounge chairs, and refreshment stand. At this point,

Carter is learning to expect surprises like this. *'Now all the national debt makes perfect sense,'* She thinks.

She strips down to her bathing suit and takes out her lotion. After finding an empty seat, she spends a couple hours in the sun, swimming in the pool in between, until her cell phone dings with a new text message.

Glancing at the LCD screen, she sees the message is from Bill.

Dinner?

Sure.

Pick you up in 45 min at your apt.

Okay.

***

At 6:00 p.m. there's a knock at Carter's door, and she calls, "Come in."

"My ID doesn't open your door!" Bill says from the other side.

She opens the door. "Sorry about that, I figured you had the God pass or something."

Bill laughs. "Nope, I'm not God, not even close. I've met him, he's taller than me."

Carter turns to Bill, wide-eyed, but says nothing. Bill lets the tension rise for a minute, and then lets her in on the joke.

"Kidding!"

"I knew you were kidding." She laughs.

"Of course I was; he's shorter."

Carter grabs her phone and ID and walks towards Bill at the doorway. "So, is this a business dinner?" She says, a slight flirtation in her voice.

"I'm afraid so. I want to get to know you."

Carter frowns. "I think you know more about me already than I do."

"Well then, maybe it's more about you getting to know me. Get an idea of how I do my job and where you fit into the big picture."

"Gotcha, works for me."

They leave on foot, walking to a small Chinese food restaurant a couple blocks away.

"So, how are you adjusting so far?"

"Well, I think I'm getting over mind-blowing things faster as each hour passes."

"Brings back memories from when I got my security clearance and first found out about this stuff. The fantasy to reality conversion in your head takes some getting used to. It's rare that I feel the awe of learning something mind blowing any more. I envy you."

"You envy me? You mean the feeling of disbelief in almost everything you see or learn? Or feeling like you're on a hidden camera show and it's all a joke, or even a dream?"

"Yeah, it's like when you get something new, and you're so excited to learn everything about it. Sort of like when you get a new cell phone, and you spend hours playing with it, but then in a couple of days, it just sits in your pocket all the time."

"That's an interesting analogy. I guess that's sort of the same feeling."

"Here's the restaurant," Bill says.

They enter and order from the menu, chatting for a bit until their drinks arrive.

"We're going to be working together, going on missions, spending hours or even days in the pod together," he says, holding a glass of beer in his hands.

Carter listens, sipping from her own beer.

"We'll get to know each other, and you'll also get to know Sue. You and I will be working together, sometimes it'll be easy, sometimes we'll be chasing a car or flying tandem with an airplane, or even under the ocean watching an event take place. We'll need to react to situations that might be mostly unknown or not as we remember reading about them in the history books or pre-mission reports."

"Sure, sounds like a normal day for me."

"In this case though, you'll have a partner, so I want to make sure you're prepared to share information so we both can do an adequate job as a team. Sue is part of the team as well, but her duties on the pod focus more on the technical side. My job is to fly the pod in a way that allows you to film the events so the most information can be collected without having to go back and do it again."

"Yeah, they mentioned something about that in the rules class this morning. Something about the same crew passing through their own time stream and a paradox."

"Exactly. We don't really know what would happen, so we're very careful to use the onboard telemetry from past missions to avoid passing over flight paths where another pod may be. We're invisible to the people on the ground, but we're also invisible to other pods that might be in the same time and space. So it's important that when we're on a mission, we gather the footage of the event the first time. Especially when being up close to the subject is required." Bill pauses to clear space for the food the server has brought to the table. He slips a pair of chopsticks out of a cloth holder. "I just want to make sure we function as a team. Simple communication and quick response times for what you need to shoot, is what you will need from me while I'm piloting. Full coverage and detailed footage is what I will need from you so we get the job done in one take."

Carter nods, munching on an egg roll. "Well, in real life I only got one take, so I think I can get the job done. I guess me not working alone anymore is something I need to focus on."

Bill slurps up a bit of lo mein, and with a mouth full of noodles says, "Sounds like a good start to me, and Carter, as fantastic as all this may seem, this is real life."

"Sorry, I meant my past life. Wait, that sounds wrong."

"No, I get it, this is a big transition."

They spend about an hour discussing the details of past missions, interesting discoveries and funny things he had seen while time traveling.

"History books are amazingly inaccurate." Bill says over coffee, the meal now finished and cleared from the table. "In the year I've been going on missions, we have had to rewrite the history books dozens of times. Amazingly, as famously stated by a renowned scientist, *'The worst type of evidence in science is eye witness testimony, yet it will get you convicted in a court of law.'* I'm paraphrasing of course. So we're holding histories writer's feet to the fire."

"It's a good thing video exists, because I'd hate to have to explain what I saw when I was a stringer. I don't think I would have gotten paid."

The two get up from the table and head back to the apartment building.

Carter says, "I think I have a good idea, at least better than yesterday, on what we're doing and why we're doing it. I can see the importance now more than before. I guess it all boils down to learning from the mistakes of history, and to do that, we need to know exactly what happened. Not just what people said happened."

They ride the elevator up. "Get a good night's rest, tomorrow is mission day."

"Goodnight, Bill."

CHAPTER 5: FIRST MISSION

The next morning Bill arrives at Carter's door with two paper cups of coffee and his elbow to press the doorbell. The door opens and Carter stands there in a towel with her hair dripping wet.

"I thought you were going to call first?"

Bill pauses. "Sorry. I thought I said 7:00 a.m., I brought you a coffee, though."

Bill hands her one of the cups, and Carter reaches to take it, when the side of her towel slips. She quickly grabs it back, but not before Bill gets an eye-full of her incredible figure and one of her breasts.

"You sure are physically fit," he says, trying to diffuse the awkward moment.

Carter gives Bill a look as if to say *'naughty boy,'* and turns back into the bedroom, closing the door behind her.

He walks in and goes toward the kitchen. "I'll just put your coffee on the counter."

Carter stands behind her bedroom door with her back pressed against it and takes a deep breath. Then, walking to the closet, she lets her towel drop to the floor. She grabs the olive drab one-piece jumpsuit she found hanging in her closet. Stuck to the jumpsuit is a yellow sticky note which reads: *'Mission Uniform.'* Setting it aside for the moment, she puts on her bra, a pair of underwear and a white t-shirt, then steps into the jump suit and zips it up. She uses her towel to dry her hair as best she can, looking at herself in the mirror mounted beside the dresser. She grabs an elastic hair tie, and puts her hair into a ponytail.

Meanwhile, Bill paces in front of the window, waiting for her until the door opens.

"There's my Stringer."

"Yeah, I'm in Go-Mode now."

"'Go-Mode?'"

"When I put my hair in a ponytail, that's *'Go-Mode.'* I'm all business when I'm in Go-Mode, and until the hair comes down, I just keep on going. It's sort of a tradition I created for myself when I first started working as a stringer."

Carter walks through the kitchen, scooping up the coffee cup as she passes the counter it had been placed on. "Let's get to it, Colonel!"

"After you, Miss."

***

They arrive at the TTRC hangar bay and step into the ready room next to the control room, where Sue already sits on a chair in the front row.

"Good morning, Lieutenant." Bill nods.

"Colonel, Carter, good morning. You look like you've been here for years in that uniform. I almost didn't recognize you! It's good to see this side of you."

"Good morning, Sue. Yeah, it's a side I never contemplated being seen in. Bill saw another side of me today, too," she says with a telling smirk.

Sue looks at Carter, confused. Bill walks between the women, holding a mission folder that he'd grabbed from a tray on the way in.

He clears his throat. "Shall we get started, ladies?"

Carter takes a seat next to Sue as Bill walks to a podium at the front of the room, flipping through the folder in his hands.

"OK, Mission 63. Looks like we have a request from Geology today. This is...one second." He scans the details of the brief. "Oh, right. This is a repeat mission but from a different angle. We're doing an up-to point mission on the Antarctic today.

Carter leans forward. "What's an 'up-to point' mission?"

"An 'up-to' is where we go back in the timeline to the beginning of the formation of something and record the progression up to a specific event. In this case, we're going to record the Earth, specifically the continent of Antarctica from the beginning of Earth's formation to the time when it froze over."

Carter pushes back in her seat, gazing off to the side of the room. Bill grabs the folder and wraps it into a tube, making his way towards her. "Do you have any questions, Carter?"

"No. I just never really thought about the South Pole not being frozen before."

"Oh, yeah, you'll see why on the mission. The positions of the continents as they appear now are much different from where they started. We did a few time lapses on the planet in previous missions, but they were all from positions around the equator. Geology wants us to track the Antarctic as it shifts position so they can see the changes in the shape of the land mass as well as get a more accurate idea of what's under the ice."

"Well, I guess this is going to be an easy mission, then?"

"Carter, your job is just call out movements to me. Say 'up,' 'down,' 'left,' or 'right' as you're recording, and I'll follow your cues. Say 'hold' when you're in position."

"How many years are we going back?"

Bill unrolls the folder and flips to the first page. "5.6."

"Five million years?"

"No, 5.6 billion years."

"That's insane!"

"Don't you love it?"

Sue walks towards the hangar entrance. "I'm going to run the checklist, Colonel. We'll be ready in five minutes."

"Roger, LT, I'm going to get Carter her gear now."

Bill leads Carter to the gear room connected directly to the ready room and points toward a table displaying various camera equipment. "This is your main camera here. I don't think you'll need any of the audio gear for this operation, but there are a bunch of batteries and memory cards in that case to the left."

Carter does a quick scan of the gear laid out before her. "Oh good, P2 media. Kind of old school, but reliable. At least it's hot swappable."

"Hot-what?"

"Hot swappable media is a memory card that can be removed while the camera is still recording, so if I run out of memory, the camera automatically switches over to one of the other three memory cards. I can pull the full one out and replace it with an empty one. This way, I never have to stop recording."

"You sure do know your stuff."

Carter picks up a big digital camera and an aluminum case filled with digital memory cards and camera batteries. She and Bill carry the gear out to the hangar bay and climb aboard Pod One.

"Last one in shuts the door, Carter," Sue says with a hint of laughter.

"Right." Carter drops her gear on the pod floor and reaches out to swing the pod door shut. She looks at the door when she closes it, and under the door handle, someone had written the letter 'G' on the inside with marker.

"What does the 'G' stand for?"

"It was a stupid joke Frank made before he left," Sue replies. "We need to paint over that."

As the crew takes their seats, Carter hooks the video camera to the rail mount above her chair and locks the dolly wheels in place. Bill and Sue run through a pre-flight checklist, and Bill requests permission to launch from the control room.

"Pod One ready for launch. Request permission to embark."

The speaker in the pod crackles. "Permission granted, Pod One. You are go for mission Zero-Six-Three."

"Roger that, Control. Pod One departing." Bill punches in the time and space coordinates listed in his mission-briefing folder to the pod's navigation computer screen. "Three, two, one, phasing." He presses the phase button and the pod hums with the familiar electrical discharge sound. There's a flash of light, and then complete silence.

"Whoa, there's no gravity," Carter whispers, looking out the window. She stands and feels the magnetic pull on her boots to the pod floor. Reaching up, she grasps the handle on the camera that she mounted on the slide rail. She turns it on and places her eye against the viewfinder, adjusting the focus ring around the lens, zooming in on a small spec between the sun and the pod. "Is that the Earth?"

Bill looks out the window. "Yup, there she is, only a few hundred thousand years of age."

"But we're so far away; I can't get any fine detail in the view finder."

"We're not far away; the Earth is only about twenty thousand miles away from the pod window."

Carter pulls her head from the camera and looks over at a smiling Bill. "What's the joke?"

"No joke. This is the beginning of the Earth, it's 5.6 billion years in the past, and currently the Earth is only four miles in diameter. It has a lot of growing to do."

"Wait. The Earth was just a rock floating in space? Like an asteroid?"

Sue answers, "Precisely. Well, to be more specific, this is the largest rock in a dust belt that's orbiting the sun at this distance. The micro gravity this one rock generates is enough to attract more and more particles of dust over a period of about a billion years until it's big enough to actually be classified as a minor planet. Right now inside this rock is a crystalline formation. That crystal structure needs a few ingredients to begin growing."

"What do you mean grow? Like a life form?"

"No, Not exactly a life form. Remember when you were a kid; they used to sell those crystal growing play sets at the toy store? You mix the colored powder into salty water and wait. By the next morning, the entire container is filled with little fragile crystals. It's like that."

Once again overwhelmed by what she heard, Carter shakes her head.

Bill turns around to his flight controls and presses forward on the control sticks lightly. "Here, let me give you a visual."

He flies the pod forward to the primordial Earth; slowly the rock starts to fill the view looking out the window. He stops the pod just as the surface of the Earth is only inches from the window.

"Get ready; we're going in."

Sue sits in her chair with a wide grin. Obviously she's done this before, and knows what Carter is about to experience.

Carter looks back at Bill. "Now what?"

"Now this." Bill taps on the flight sticks and the pod starts to move forward passing through the outside of the Earth. As the pod passes the surface it suddenly gets brighter in the pod.

Carter peers out the window, and sees a huge hollow core filled with luminescent white crystals lining the inner shell of Earth.

Sue explains, "These are radioactive crystals, so they generate their own heat, and the micro gravity pulls in hydrogen and all sorts of noble gasses that are floating around in space. Those gases penetrate the shell of the micro planet and react with the radioactive isotopes to feed and grow these crystals."

Carter films everything, looking through the eyepiece. "It looks like we're in a giant geode. Tell me more about it."

Sue continues. "Eventually the increasing gravity causes more and more material that's floating nearby in space to collect and form the miles thick crust we know from our own time period. However, at the heart of the Earth even in our present day, these same radioactive crystals are still growing between the lower parts of the mantle and the upper crust. Drawing in the raw materials they need to feed off through ever-increasing gravity. The growth is exponential too. The Earth in our time is growing hundreds of times faster than it did four billion years earlier."

Bill pulls on the flight sticks and backs the pod back out of the shell of the Earth. The pod continues to back up until the Earth is once again a little brown spec in Carters camera lens.

Carter stops recording, pondering the ideas she has just been exposed to. "How come I have never heard about this before? I thought all missions were disclosed to the general public."

Bill responds, "Well this mission was originally going to be published, but after the first mission we discovered something else that caused this to be classified as top secret for security reasons. You're cleared for this information, but we'll go over that later when this mission has concluded."

"Got it, so what's the game plan for this mission?"

"So here is how we're going to do this, I'm setting the fast forward to about twenty-five million years per second, which comes out to forty seconds per billion years. So the entire event will take about three minutes to play out from start to finish. Antarctica is on the equator right now, so we'll watch the Earth grow larger for about sixty seconds, and then you will see the Earth start changing color as more and more hydrogen and oxygen forms into clouds and then water. All the land will disappear for a minute or so, but then all of the sudden there will be a rapid increase in water as the cloud density gets to its maximum.

Water is what really fuels the crystal growth, so the Earth will really pick up speed and you will see the water will start changing from dark to lighter blue as the crust grows wider. As the Earth grows, the expansion forces the seas to become shallower. That's when you need to be ready to direct my flight controls."

"So, will the pod be orbiting the planet as we film?"

"Yes, the early Earth rotated very slowly in the beginning, and the navigation computer is already programmed to stay locked on the changes of the Earth's rotation so we don't just see a spinning blur.

You'll see the continents suddenly lift out of the oceans. The continents are what's left over after the crust splits and new crust is pushed into the gaps. The mantle of the Earth at this point is so hot from the radioactive crystals growing inside that the crust is molten in sections. So this churning molten rock is pushing the higher cooler solid rock upwards.

I'm going to lock our orbit around Antarctica, but when it appears at the equator, it will start slipping down to the southern pole. When you see it moving in your view finder just give me commands of down up left or right. Sound easy enough?"

Carter imagines the scene, playing it out in her head, then opens her eyes. "Got it. I'm ready, let's go for it."

Bill claps his hands and swivels his chair back to the control panel. Sue monitors the engineering screen on her work center, and Carter positions herself on the camera.

"Time progression in five seconds." He counts down and puts his hand on the fast forward dial. "Three, two, one. Progression locked at twenty-five mil per second."

Carter presses record on the camera and squeezes her eye against the viewfinder. Just as Bill described, the Earth starts to get bigger in the lens of the camera. At first, it seems to grow smoothly but, as the surface of the crust becomes larger, it also gets closer to the pod. She looks through the lens and sees the crust of the Earth is rolling and churning repeatedly like a boiling pot of sauce. From time to time, the surface becomes smooth like glass, and then suddenly thousands of tiny pock-marks appear from meteor impacts that occur so quickly the actual meteors are invisible.

Suddenly, the planet fills the majority of the window as the surface vanishes in a thick white cloud of vapor. The clouds don't last long, disappearing in an instant and giving way to a dirty icy surface. The Earth spends a few million years as a solid ball of ice, which passes quickly on camera. Then the thick ice surface starts to crack and the crust of the Earth starts to penetrate to the sun light as if it was a seedling germinating from below the soil. Hundred and thousand-mile-wide sections of land thrust out of the ice, being born again after millions of years under the frost.

As the landmasses take over, the ice slides up and down away from the equator, leaving visible scars from the grinding of miles thick glaciers. The massive weight of the ice paints patterns and carves valleys on the rocky surface of the continents. The ice melts and clouds circle the planet in a blurry pattern of the newly formed jet stream. With the ice almost completely melted around the equator, the oceans flood sections of the landmasses creating lakes. The warmer, more saturated planet starts to grow more rapidly as the water seeps into giant crevasses in the Earth's newly formed fault lines. Like a potted plant, the soil sponges in the water. The multimillion-year famine for nourishment is finally over as demonstrated as the Earth swells from the rapid core crystal growth.

The Continents continue to rise out of the water and the Antarctic continent finally becomes visible. The deep brown continent becomes larger and larger as the Earth's size continues to increase. The oceans get shallow more and more as the Earth diameter stretches them out to only a few dozen miles deep.

Bill's body faces his control surface, but his eyes lock onto Carter as she constantly adjusts the focus on the camera and aiming the lens at the continent. "How we doing, Carter?"

"Still stable, I'm watching for it."

Antarctica's colors change, from a brown rocky tint to a deep red around the coastline. Suddenly a brilliant hue of green blasts along the Antarctic coastlines and blankets the entire continent.

"Oh my god, the colors! This is incredible. It looks like the commercial for the paper towel where they place the towel on the counter top and the colored liquid instantly spreads through the sheet."

"You're doing great, Carter, keep on it."

Carter watches through the camera as the mountains break through the level surface of the land, pushing the growth of green out to the sides.

The Antarctic continent shows signs of plant life through the clouds which grow thicker. Suddenly there's movement of the continent. A series of explosions appear in the ocean to the north. A red ring of fire and smoke circling a huge section of the ocean forms, getting wider and wider—volcanic activity on a massive scale. As it progresses, all the continents on Earth spread further and further apart as Earth continues to expand.

Carter calls out, "It's shifting south."

"Roger, changing orbit south."

Carter watches the ring of fire fill the atmosphere with ash and smoke. "Down and to the left."

Bill pulls back on the sticks as the pod starts moving lower below the Earth's equator.

"Faster, go down, faster."

Bill looks over his right shoulder, trying to lift himself out of his chair without letting go of the flight controls. He pulls back on the controls even more. "We good? We good Carter?"

"Yes I got it, keep at that speed, it's stabilizing in its shifting speed. OK—hold position."

Within seconds the pod hangs directly below the south pole of the Earth and the Antarctic continent is now settled into its current resting place, where it exists in modern time. Carter records the continent start to lose its lush green color and the ice once again reclaims the land.

"Looks like we're approaching your up-to point."

"When the land is all white, you can stop recording."

Carter waits a few more seconds, her body and arms relaxing though her eye is still pressed against the viewfinder. A few seconds later, she pulls away from the rubber eyecup, making a sucking noise as the moisture from her perspiration breaks the suction. She stands in front of the camera and lowers her hands, pivoting her neck to look back at Bill, who sits smiling with a look of approval. She takes a deep breath and exhales, reaching up behind her head and removing her hair tie. As she shakes out her hair, she falls into her chair and starts to smile. She looks over at Sue, who waits for a word to come out of Carters mouth.

"That was bad-ass crazy!"

Everyone laughs, and Bill gives Carter a thumbs-up as he reaches over to press the Return button on his screen.

"Wait, can we just sit for a minute?"

Bill pulls his hand away. "Sure, I'll bring us back up to the equator so you can take a look." He gently moves the pod out a bit from the Earth and settles it in a stationary point above Mexico.

"Before when we first got here there was no gravity in the pod but now I can feel it under my feet. I still need the magnets on the shoes, but I definitely feel it in my head."

"Sue can explain that to you."

Sue swivels her chair around. "We feel the gravity even out here nearly five thousand miles away because we're stationary. If we were moving in an orbit around the Earth as fast as the International Space Station flies, then our speed would cancel out the Earth's gravity and we would all be floating. Right now, we're a little bit more than twenty-five percent of Earth's gravity.

Bill stands and slaps Carter on the arm. "Congratulations Carter, you're officially an astronaut."

Carter laughs. "I guess I am." She turns and looks out the window of the pod, gazing at the Earth below, which still looks very different from what she's used to. "What year is this now?"

"We're currently 126 million BC," Sue replies.

"So dinosaurs are down their right now?"

"Yes, would you like to see some?" Bill offers.

Carter pauses, overcome with excitement, her face lighting up. "Definitely! Should I film them?"

"No, you just enjoy the view; I'll fly us over some heavily populated areas."

Bill lowers the pod into the atmosphere and heads towards the land mass that will eventually be Texas. As the pod gets lower, the dense forests become clearer. A large volcano spews lava near the center of Texas, and an even larger one sits in the Midwest between future Nevada and Utah.

The pod holds altitude about three hundred feet off the ground in northern Texas. Bill skims over the land at about one hundred miles per hour as he tilts the pod towards Carter's window so she can get a better view.

"There's one!" She calls out.

They pass over the slow moving Paluxysaurus, which is a four legged long neck herbivore. Bill continues to fly and then suddenly changes course toward something he sees off to the left.

"Carter, look ahead of my window."

She looks over his shoulder. Ahead in the distance is a flying Quetzalcoatlus, a large bird like dinosaur. "Holy crap, that thing is huge!"

Bill nods. "Yeah, looks like a thirty-foot wing span." He pulls the pod next to the majestic flying creature and matches speed with it.

Carter steps back over to the camera and starts recording. "This is for my personal collection."

"No problem, have at it."

They follow the Quetzalcoatlus a little longer and then look at some herds of other animals along the ground. Eventually Bill stops for the day and hits the return button on the console.

Back at TTRC headquarters, Bill and Carter are in the ready room after stowing away the camera gear and retrieving the recorded video for the geology department.

"Carter, I'll drop this video off at geology if you want to head on home."

"I thought maybe you might want to show me around the city a little more, maybe get some food."

Bill grabs the memory card and puts it in his jump suit pocket. "Sure, tag along with me and we can head out after I drop this off."

She follows him out of the hangar bay and down the hall to the research lab where a couple eager geologists wait for the arrival of the video card.

"Doctor Evans, Doctor Flynn, here's today's Antarctic footage you requested."

Evans takes the memory card. "Thanks Colonel. Who's this with you?"

"Doctors, this is Miss Carter, she's the one who made that video for you today."

"Miss Carter, if the video looks as good as you do, I'm sure we'll be more than pleased with it."

"Calm down, Evans." Bill gives Carter a smirk.

"My hero."

"Sorry about that Carter, these guys don't get out much." Bill snaps his fingers. "Speaking of getting out, Carter and I are off duty now, so we'll see you later."

Carter looks at Bill as they start walking away and whispers, "Much later."

Evans waves as they walk out the door, then he looks at the memory card in his hand and turns towards the video player on the workbench behind him.

CHAPTER 6: DEEP SECRETS

Bill and Carter head back to their respective apartments to shower and change for an evening out. Bill arrives at Carters apartment at 6 p.m. Approaching her door, he extends his finger to press the doorbell but stops, turns, and walks back down the hallway. As much as he enjoyed the view from his last unannounced arrival, he feels it's better to take the polite approach this time. He reaches into his pants pocket and pulls out his phone to warn Carter of his impending arrival in a text message.

Carter, I'm heading to your apartment in a few minutes, is now a good time to swing by?

Carter is in the shower when she hears her phone chime. She throws the curtain aside and reaches into her jumpsuit pocket that's on the bathroom floor.

I'll be ready in 5 minutes.

Okay.

Bill leans back against the wall in the hallway, a few doors down from her apartment. He looks at his watch, which reads 6:03.

"Five minutes to kill. Now what?" he thinks.

Meanwhile, Carter rinses the shampoo from her hair and jumps out of the shower. She makes it all the way to her bedroom before she realizes she had left the shower running. Like a billiard ball bouncing off the side rail, she runs back to shut the water off. On the way out of the bathroom, she grabs a towel and vigorously rubs her head with it then wraps it like a turban. She runs to the front door wearing only a towel on her head to peek out into the hallway.

Bill hears the door open and he sees Carter lean out into the hall, looking in the opposite direction. He slams his back against the wall and hides behind a large fake plant as she looks left, then right, and quickly shuts the door.

Bill, still firmly pressed against the wall, checks his watch again. 6:05. At the same time Carter stands naked in front of her bedroom mirror, blow-drying her hair. She runs to her closet, where the movers had stacked boxes of her clothes while she'd been on the last mission. She rips into the boxes, looking for something suitable, and feels something move against her ankle. Looking down, she's startled to find that the movers had also brought Mayonnaise, her white Persian cat.

"Get in your bed!" She commands the cat, who continues to express his love for her ankle.

She puts on a pair of skinny jeans and a button-up shirt, turning to the mirror for a quick look before running to the kitchen and checking to see that the cat has food and water.

In the hallway, Bill holds his phone, playing a game. He looks at his watch; 6:07. He puts his phone in his pocket and walks up to her door, leans in and listens for any sounds. Not hearing anything, he presses the doorbell.

Carter, putting on her shoes, hops on one foot all the way to the apartment door before swinging it open.

"Come on in, I'm almost ready," she says, slightly out of breath.

Bill walks in and stands next to the couch.

"Have a seat, I'll just be a bit."

Bill sits and looks out the window as Carter goes back into the bedroom. She grabs a bottle of perfume and sprays it in the air, then walks through the berry-scented mist. She snatches up a lipstick and opens it, but then, staring at herself in the mirror, she squints disapprovingly. *Too much, too soon.* She realizes she's obviously treating this as a date, and thinks *maybe I should slow down a bit and not read anything into going out with a coworker.*

Bill sits on the couch with his palms on both knees. It's a good place for your palms if you intend to keep them perspiration-free, even in an air-conditioned apartment.

Carter walks back out of the bedroom. "Ready. Where are we off to?"

"You look nice." He pauses for a reaction, but before Carter can speak, he says, "Sorry, I didn't mean you don't normally look nice."

She smirks. "Don't you know anything? You should never apologize after paying a girl a compliment."

Bill feels awkward and embarrassed. "You're right; I won't let it happen again."

They laugh and head out the door. On the elevator ride, they stare at the decreasing floors on the digital display above the button pad. Carter uses her peripherals to examine the pair of khakis he wears. He's older than she is, but not by much, with short dark hair, trimmed to military regulation. Though attracted to him, she's uncertain if she should show it, as her record of failed relationships races through her brain.

The doors open and Bill walks out, looking at Carter, who still stands in the elevator. "Coming?"

She snaps out of her trance. "Sorry, was thinking if I put food out for the cat."

They walk to the parking garage where a sea of white, black and tan four-door sedans fill the parking spots.

"Do you want to drive, or should I?" he asks.

"I don't have a car here, so you better do the driving."

"Your car is over in 10 E parking spot, but if you want me to drive, that's fine."

"Wait, I have a car?"

"We all do, the ID card starts it."

"In that case, I'll drive. I need to learn the town, anyway."

"Works for me. It's over there, to the right."

They get in her black government-issued vehicle, a medium sized four-door sedan with slightly tinted windows. The door locks and ignition have a sensor which allows access, and the car started when she held her magnetic ID card against it.

She drives up to the street and comes to a stop. "Left or right?"

"Go left; there's a place where some of us hang out about fifteen minutes from here. Good ribs, tap beer and there's usually good live music. They also have pool tables if you like to play pool."

"I love pool, and ribs, and beer."

Bill laughs, sensing Carter is trying to fit in. As they drive, he points out different places in the city. The streets are modeled after any other city in America, with the exception of buildings which are obviously government related every few blocks. Defense Research Building 5, or Joint Operations Central Command Annex B. Between these buildings are all the amenities you would expect in an urban community—fast food, dry cleaners, clubs and other entertainment. The layout seems to have repeating occurrences, as if the planners wanted to make sure workers didn't have to travel far to find the comforts of a hometown, while making sure the workers in each facility only congregated with each other.

As they drive, they talk about the Antarctic mission.

"Bill...you mentioned that the mission discovered something that was classified, am I cleared to know about that?"

"Yes, you're cleared, but I have to warn you that this information as with all classified information can never be spoken of with people outside the program. Also, knowing this information is something you may not be prepared for, as it might alter your view of pretty much everything you've come to know about humanity."

"What's the big secret?"

"We discovered that sometime before the last worldwide extinction, there was a civilization of people who existed on Earth. They were advanced in culture and technology far beyond what we're today. The sun, a few hundred thousand years ago, went through a series of coronal mass ejections."

"What does that mean?"

"Coronal mass ejections are basically giant explosions on the surface of the sun. These explosions were sending deadly radioactive material, randomly into space. Now this still happens today, but back then it was more frequent.

So, the people of this ancient society began to contemplate their own extinction. They started searching for a safe place should one of these CME's hit the Earth. Technology they had created, allowed for tunneling deep into the Earth looking for caves or other safe locations for their society to seek shelter. This is the same tech that we used to create the spaces for our underground bases.

Anyway, after years of looking deep within the Earth these ancient people discovered that there was an empty void in the deepest of deep spots in the planet. They found that there's an entry at both poles of the planet to get into the center of the Earth. The discovery of this sanctuary didn't come too late, soon after its discovery, solar activity started to increase. The people of this ancient civilization moved to the inner parts of the planet and there they lived and survived for centuries. They didn't just *survive*, they thrived. They realized that the technology they possessed allowed them to completely abandon the surface and live happily in the deepest place of the planet.

Now I've never seen this place, but I have met a few of the people from there. They have an agreement with the current surface dwelling human culture that allows for the continued parallel evolution between our two civilizations. Those who remained all those millennia ago on the surface shed the technology they had, but not by choice. They lived to survive only, and eventually relearned the technology to what we have today. The ones down below continued their advancement, and decided that a separation between cultures was required."

"Wait a second. You're saying there are people way more advanced than us living in the center of the planet?"

"Exactly. They've been advancing for just about six hundred thousand years. Four hundred thousand of it has been inside the Earth."

"You're not joking, are you? What do they look like? Are they like us?"

"Well there are multiple races, some of them look similar to us, but there are some vast differences in appearances among the races, from what I have been told."

"How big is the hollow space in the planet?"

"The Earth, from what I know, is completely hollow. There's only about eighty to one hundred and twenty miles of crust, mantle then the crystal section, and an inner layer of mantle and another crust, which makes up the center of the Earth's surface. In its center floats a power source that simulates the sunlight with day and night and the energy of the sun needed for life.

They're very protective of this society, so we have an agreement to keep their existence a secret. That secret is something that seems like it may become harder and harder to keep though."

"So, there are magic elves living in the Earth?"

"Funny, I wish it was something we could joke about. There's tension; I'll just leave it at that."

"So what does this have to do with our last mission?"

"The fact that the Earth grew is not the secret we're trying to protect, it's the agreement to not disclose the existence of what's in the center of the Earth. The agreement we have is not something we would violate. We wouldn't stand a chance militarily if we decided to try. Admiral Bird found that out in the 1940's."

"Oh, here's the club." Bill points to a neon sign on the front of the club which reads 'Hangout 18'.

Carter turns into the parking lot, which is filled with mostly government issued cars. Music from inside can be heard as soon as they step out of the car. Through the windows, they see people playing pool and eating dinner.

Bill turns to Carter when they get to the club's entrance. "The discussion we just had isn't part of our public mission objectives; I just wanted to get you up to speed on why we need to keep this off the record as far as the full disclosure mandate of the TTRC dictates. This is not a secret about time travel; it's a secret that directly relates to the well-being of the human race today."

"No, I understand." She wonders though, *what threat these center Earth people pose.*

They walk into the club and some classic rock is playing, Journey's 'Don't Stop Believing' over the karaoke stage speakers. The club is small, only a dozen tables and ten booths. Three pool tables sit near the front, a stage in the back with some karaoke screens hanging from the ceiling and a piano on the stage.

"For a government base, there sure are all the comforts of home," she says.

"You obviously haven't been on a base before. Most government installations do their best to keep you from wanting to leave."

Carter looks down at the floor as they walk towards a booth, thinking about the woman she briefly spoke with at the seafood restaurant. "So are we *allowed* to leave, or...?"

Bill laughs. "Carter, you're not a prisoner, you can leave anytime you want. We just do better work if we stay close by."

They sit across from each other, and a server comes to the table, placing menus in front of them. Her nametag reads Sarah, and she seems to be in her late forties, with long blonde hair tied back in a ponytail.

"Draft beer, Bill?" Sarah asks with a southern accent.

"Thanks, Sarah."

"And for you, Miss?"

"It's Carter, I'll also have a draft."

"Would you two like some hot wings, or are you going to order dinner?"

Carter flips open the menu and scans it. "I'm pretty hungry; I'll take a full rack of ribs."

Sarah looks at Bill, who smiles approvingly. "Same for me, full rack with a bowl of that spicy chili."

"Sounds good, I'll take a chili as well," Carter adds.

Sarah jots in her order pad, then looks up and smiles. "Be right back with your beers."

"Thanks, Sarah," Bill says.

Carter sips the beer Sarah delivers, sucking foam off the top. "Does Sue ever come outside of the command center?"

"Well, Sue's married to a guy who works in Hangar Bay Two, and she pretty much heads back to her apartment after work because they rarely see each other."

"Ah, I see."

He drinks about half his beer in one swig. "Sue's great, she does a fantastic job as pod engineer and she has a great personality once she warms up. I just think Steve, her husband, is a little jealous."

"Why?"

"Sue and Steve used to work on a pod together. They started dating, then got married. But the rules prohibit that, so Sue moved to our pod."

"It must have been tough for her to have to stop working with her husband."

Bill takes a sip. "Yeah, if this was any other military assignment she might have quit, but she enjoys the missions."

"So what's Hangar Bay Two, more time ships?"

"They're the same pods, but their mission is exploration of space, not time travel."

Carter leans back in the booth, holding the mug handle with one hand. "I never heard about that on the news. So Steve goes out to the other planets in the solar system?"

"No, he's on habitable world charting in the Andromeda galaxy. Under the Congressional full disclosure mandate, we only have to reveal time travel related information. Space exploration, even though it uses the same technology is considered top secret. The pods go out star-to-star and check to see if they have planets. If there are planets, they check each one for habitability. If the planets have life on them already, they send that information to the General who assigns that to the crew in Hangar Bay Three."

"So Hangar Bay Three investigates if there are people?"

Bill finishes off his beer and wipes the excess from his mouth, nodding. "Precisely, and if there's intelligent life then there's a specific crew who observes them for future missions and possible contact. "

Carter takes a sip just as the ribs and chili arrive. Sarah places the plates and bowls on the table. "Let me know if I can get y'all anything else. Bill, are you singing tonight?"

"Not tonight, this is more of a business dinner."

Carter unfolds her napkin and stares at her plate, trying not to make eye contact. She knows it's a business dinner, but hearing him say so is a little disappointing. She hasn't had a friend in a while, but she knows she needs to keep focused and learn about her new world.

She picks up her fork and knife cuts the ribs apart. "You do karaoke?"

Bill puts a spoon full of chili in his mouth. "Yeah, from time to time, if there's enough beer."

They dig into the chili and ribs, chatting about the last mission. After they finish, Carter looks over at the pool tables. "Do you play pool?"

"Sure, but not professionally."

They get up from the table and play a couple games of Eight Ball.

"So, when you were a kid what did you want to be when you grew up? Was it a stringer?"

"Actually, I *did* want to make movies. I had a video camera when I was fifteen. I got it as a birthday present. My Dad got it for me because I wanted to make funny videos. However, I ended up getting distracted."

"Distracted by what?"

"Just stuff."

"Sorry, I wasn't trying to pry."

"No, it's cool. It was because of the fights my Mom and Dad were having. When I left home at seventeen, that's the only thing I took, other than my bag of clothes."

"The fighting drove you out?"

"Yeah, my Dad was fine, but he didn't make much money, and Mom just kept on his case all the time about the bills. The thing is, she didn't work, so she was just as much to blame. I couldn't handle the fighting, so I walked out in the middle of the night."

"Is that how you became a stringer? Because you had the video camera?"

Carter racks the balls on the pool table and walks around to the end to make the first break. She slams the cue hard against the balls as they bounce together.

"Yeah, I was walking down the street in Phoenix, when I heard a gunshot one night. I pulled out my camera and aimed it toward the sound, and a man came crawling out of a liquor store with blood trailing behind him. I recorded the whole thing. The storeowner walked out behind him and shot the man in the back of the head. After it was over, I kept recording and listened to everything people were saying. The shop owner came up to me. He was Korean and spoke very broken English, but he described how the man had just tried to rob him and that he was just defending himself.

I didn't say anything, I just let him talk. He still had the gun in his hand and I was actually scared he was going to shoot me because of what I saw him do."

"So what did you do?"

"Well the police arrived and I kept recording. They set up tape to secure the scene, a man walked up behind me with a big professional camera on his shoulder. He saw that I was filming, and he asked me "what did you get?" I told him I got the whole thing, and we watched my footage. He pulled five hundred dollars out of his pocket and asked me to buy my tape. I asked him why, and he told me he was going to put it on the news. He was a stringer, and had contacts with the local TV station.

I told him I'd take the money, but I also needed a job. We worked together for a few months, but he was more interested in my tits than my footage. After that, I went independent."

"And you've been doing that ever since?"

"Yeah."

Carter basks in a mental state of the kind of relaxation she hasn't had since she was a teen. She has a good job that doesn't eat up all twenty-four hours of her day, a nice place to live with all expenses paid, and the time to enjoy herself out side of work.

They head out to the car and drive back to Tower 42. Bill hands Carter a pill.

She looks at it in her palm. "What's this?"

"It's for after you drink. It gets rid of the effects of alcohol."

Carter takes the pill and swallows it without even thinking. She trusts Bill, and even though a few weeks ago she would have assumed the pill was a knockout drug, she dismisses those instincts. Within thirty seconds, she feels the slight buzz from the beers she drank disappear.

"This is turning out to be the weirdest week of my life."

"Ha, you have yet to see weird, I heard we're approved for a collection tomorrow."

"You mean going *outside* the pod?"

"Yes, but I don't know what we're collecting yet."

"Do you know what year?"

"Nope, we don't usually know until right before the mission for security reasons."

She's intrigued by the thought of walking around in another time. Most of the ride home she's quiet, thinking of what tomorrow will bring. Bill watches as her eyes seem to stare at the road ahead without truly seeing.

"Don't worry about it, Carter, we have this thing down pretty good. Everything will be planned out by the higher ups to ensure a good mission."

After Carter gets back to her apartment, she puts her mobile phone next to her personal phone that has been on the desk charger for two days. She's almost forgotten about her past life and the people she left behind. She hadn't even called her parents to let them know where she'd gone. She opens the home screen on her personal phone and finds five missed calls from her Dad, twenty messages from Elliot, the editor at the news station, and two messages from Phil, the guy she'd been hooking up with for a few weeks.

She calls her dad first.

"Hi Dad!"

"Evie!! Where have you been?"

"Sorry, I got a new job and I've been in training."

"Oh that's great, champ, where are you working, FOX, CNN?"

"No, I'm actually working for the government doing video work. It's great, I'm having a blast!"

"I went to your apartment when you didn't return my calls, and they said some movers took your stuff out in the middle of the night and paid off the rest of your two-year lease in full. I figured you got abducted by men in black."

"Well, you're not far off. I'm working in a place that requires me to keep my job a secret."

"Is it the time travel stuff?"

"Um, no."

"What else is happening? Are you seeing anyone? Maybe a rich general or something?

"Um... Not yet Daddy, I just started a couple days ago. I'm just trying to get myself settled."

"Are you on a military base? Do you have a place to stay?"

"Yes, I'm in an apartment on base, with all expenses paid, so you don't need to worry about me anymore."

"Baby, I never worried about you, I'm proud of what you've accomplished. I just want to know you're happy."

"So far, so good, Dad, I'm pretty happy right now."

"Well, whatever you're doing I know you'll be the best one there. I love you Eve, always remember that. Just give me a call from time to time to let me know you're still alive."

"I love you too, Daddy. I'll call every week, I promise."

Carter disconnects and places her phone down. She sits silently at her desk for a few seconds before getting up and heading for the living room to watch television. As she flips through the channels, she finds the CNN network and watches the news.

She sees a report of a train derailment only a mile from her old apartment in the city she just moved from. Still used to springing into action, she has an instinctual urge to get on the scene of the wreck. Her breathing gets heavy as she watches the video and slowly starts to relax her stance, sitting back down. She develops a slight grin, as she realizes that's not her job anymore.

She walks into the office and opens the messages from Elliot and Phil on her personal cell. Phil is looking to hang out at 2 a.m. yesterday, and Elliot is asking why she missed the train accident.

Sorry Elliot, I'm out of town on a paid assignment. Not sure when I will, or if I will be back. I'll text you if things change.

She switches over to Phil's messages. *I'm with someone else now. Time to move on, sorry.*

She places the phone on the charger and gets in bed, staring at the ceiling. Her eyes lock on a small defect in the paint above her. She starts to smile, then closes her eyes and falls asleep.

CHAPTER 7: FAKER

Excited about her first extravehicular mission, Carter woke early enough to stop for a cup of coffee and a bagel from the diner just across the street from the TTRC building. Her jumpsuit is freshly ironed, and she even had time to sew on an embroidered nametag she had ordered at the base uniform shop. She walks into the hangar bay ready room a full thirty minutes early.

Her phone buzzes; it's a message from Bill. *On my way down to pick you up.*

I'm already at the ready room.

Oh, Okay.

Bill is also excited to get on with today's mission. Collections are rare, and knowing this, he'd been even more excited to see Carter's reaction.

The TTRC congressional committee must vote on a collection. Sometimes these ops take months for approval. Experts on the objects in question debate the merits and risks to the timeline of making the collection. *This* mission, however, progressed quickly through the channels.

Bill arrives at the ready room to find Carter sitting in the front row alone with her bag of camera equipment tucked between her feet.

"Morning Carter, glad to see you're punctual."

"Good morning. Yeah, I kind of got up early and didn't want to bother you. I stopped off at the diner and got some breakfast."

"Oh good, breakfast is the most important meal of the day. I'm sort of bummed about missing our new morning routine, though."

Carter blushes. "I bet you are."

Bill stops and thinks for a second, realizing she's referring to the towel malfunction. "Is Sue in yet?"

"Uh... I haven't seen her in the hangar bay yet."

Just then, the sound erupts of a pod phasing in. The familiar electrical discharge and a plasma blast echoes through from the hangar bay.

"Oh, Pod Three is returning from their mission."

Bill and Carter walk toward the bay and find Pod Three hovering above the docking clamps. The four clamps begin to close and latch onto thick steel bars on the pod's landing feet. The pod powers down and the door flips open. Major Karen Lewis and photographer Ian Jacobs step out.

"Good morning Major, how was your op?" Bill asks.

"Successful sir, cargo is intact and ready to be transferred to holding."

Carter peeks inside Pod Three's door, hoping to see the cargo. Lieutenant Phil Brennan, the pod's engineer, exits holding a small touch screen tablet. Behind her, Carter hears squeaking, and turns to see two Air Force personnel wheeling a large metal cylinder which looks like the New York time machine from a few years earlier, except much larger. At about eight feet long and two feet in diameter, it has a small glass window on the top.

Phil uses the tablet to open a panel on the pod exterior. A small electric motor whines as the pod's matter transfer turret extends from the open panel and stops about one foot from the side, then fires a thin green laser at the floor. The beam strikes the concrete just in front of the rolling cart, and Phil uses his tablet interface to aim the green beam at a small glass indention on the end of the large cylinder. He presses a button on the tablet labeled 'Transfer'. A hum builds, and then a burst of white light blasts from the turret. The cylinder window illuminates for a second. Everything is silent again as the turret powers off.

Carter watches the procedure with the urge to ask what the item is, but decides against it. The Airmen wheel away the container as Carter and Bill walk back to the ready room. Just then, a loud banging echoes from the container. Carter stops to look. One of the airmen turns a valve on the side of the cart, which activates a rush of gas into the container. Almost immediately, the banging stops.

"Bill, is someone in there?"

"Don't worry about it."

"Do you know who it is?"

"Let's talk about this later, okay?"

Bill puts his hand on Carters shoulder, guiding her to turn back towards the ready room. She realizes he would not have brought her into the hangar if he didn't want her to see the transfer of a person. She takes a breath and tries to focus.

Bill goes up to the mission tray near the podium and picks up the briefing folder for Pod One. Carter sits in the front row and realizes Sue still isn't there. She looks back to the ready room door, then at her watch, when the rapid sound of footsteps echoes from the hangar bay.

Sue, out of breath, bursts through the door. "Sorry I'm late; I was down in Bay Two helping Colonel Philip's engineer work out a software bug."

"No problem, is it fixed?"

"Not yet, looks like there's an intermittent problem during cloaking but nothing dangerous."

"Keep me apprised of the progress, LT."

"Yes, sir."

Bill opens the folder before him and begins reading for a few seconds. "OK troops, our mission today is a collection operation from Biotech department. We're heading to 1875 California. We're to meet up with local Native Americans who grow an extinct plant used in their medicine. This is a meet and greet mission, so we need to go in disguise as local settlers who are trekking across America."

"So how am I going to hide this 21st century camera gear?" Carter asks.

"We're leaving the big camera in the pod and you'll wear body cams sewn into your costume. We have that ready in the gear room. This plant originated in India, and it grew on tall mountains, but Native Americans supposedly also grew it out in the mountains of California. It's been referred to by such names as Panacea or Sanjeevini. The plant still exists today, however, there was a mutation in it sometime in the past, and it lost all its healing qualities.

Legend has it, the Hopi grew this plant. Stories say it gave them the ability to fight off any illness, increased their life span, and could speed up the body's natural healing to the point where a warrior who had been struck down dead with an arrow in his heart came back to life after only rubbing the oils on the wound. "

Carter glances at Sue, then back at Bill, wearing the look of someone who feels they're being played for a fool. "All right, is this my hazing or something?"

"I know it sounds fantastic. Trust me, this is a real mission. This collection came from the higher ups as a priority. We sometimes get missions that make little sense, or seem like the risk isn't worth the reward, but what you have to realize is all of these missions fall into a bigger picture."

"Sorry, I was just expecting us to be going after the Holy Grail or King Arthur's sword. A plant never occurred to me."

"Well, according to the guys in biotech, they think this plant—as it grows today—has signs of being genetically modified by design to suppress the healing abilities. So someone in recent history did something to it on purpose."

"So that means they had a motive for changing the plant. Is someone planning on attacking us with a bio-weapon or something?"

"I knew you were smart, Carter. That's exactly what they fear. We don't know why someone modified it, but we can't take a chance that someone might already have such a weapon, and if they do, and this is the only cure, we need to be prepared."

"So why do we need to make contact?"

"Well, we're not sure if the plant just works on its own or if other ingredients are added. So we're going to go in and see if we can convince the Natives to demonstrate the medicine." Bill closes the folder and tucks it under his arm.

Sue stands up. "Am I going into the field as well?"

"Maybe, it depends on what comes up. Right now you're in the pod, monitoring."

"Understood, sir."

Carter asks Sue, "Do you do field work at all?"

"Sometimes I get out, but the best place for me is in the pod in case of an emergency. If something goes wrong, I can pick you guys up or send out the distress beacon."

"What's the beacon?"

"A small square metal box that travels back to our point of origin and relates where we are if we get stuck."

"Have you ever had to use it before?"

"Only a few times. Early on in the program, we had breakdowns. Beacons were used to send a message back to the present, relay back the details of what the problem was and where they were stuck."

"So, the beacon is a mini time machine."

"Yes, and we can record a message or upload details from the pod computer to it. Just enough information to tell the control room what went wrong. Then it homes back to base, and another pod can dispatch for a rescue."

They walk to the gear room where the day's mission supplies wait for them—costumes of period clothing and a couple leather satchels. General Wilson walks in behind them with a leather gun holster and a single action revolver.

Carter looks at the pistol the General hands to Bill. "What's the gun for?"

"Ever since Frank got injured, we always go in armed. We've never had to kill anyone, but we don't take the chance of being killed, either."

"You're not worried about altering history if someone dies?"

Bill snickers, then flips open the load gate on the side of his old western six-shooter, and dumps a bullet into his hand. He holds it up to show Carter. "See this? The tip of the cartridge has no bullet in it. Instead, the brass shell has this blue colored wax plug with a small needle sticking out. The ammunition in this gun shoots a tranquilizer dart. If I *have* to shoot someone, they'll just take a nap."

"Smart!"

"Yup, and the little pin head delivers an instant knockout to anyone it hits. The only thing left behind is the wax that breaks apart and the pin, which dissolves. The only evidence will be a small welt, like when you get hit with a paint ball and a small pin hole."

Carter laughs as she picks her costume up. "This is what we're wearing, huh?" She walks into the changing booth and scrutinizes the button-up blouse, long wool dress, and bonnet with a small camera embedded in it. She also has a pair of well-distressed leather boots, a corset, and puffy bloomers. "How am I supposed to fit in this corset? Did anyone measure my chest at all?"

Sue is in the booth next to her. "They're sort of one size fits all with underwear."

"Well if I put this thing on, I'll have a chin rest with the way this pushes everything up so much." She tosses the corset aside. "Bill, I can handle this puffy underwear that go down to my knees and this dress but I'm not wearing this corset, I won't be able to move in it." She peeks out from behind the curtain. "Did you hear me?"

Bill walks out of his changing booth in cowboy boots, tattered cattleman pants, and a white button-up shirt. He has an old frontiersman hat in his hands and the gun belt over his shoulder. "Well that's up to you, but the bra won't be invented for twenty-nine years, so that's something to think about."

Carter rolls her eyes and pulls her head back in behind the curtain. She stands there for a few seconds, throws her hands in the air. "Fuck it," she mumbles under her breath, removing her bra and putting on the blouse. She finishes with the rest of the costume and stands in front of the mirror, realizing her nipples are visible through the sheer fabric. She tries puffing the blouse out, but it doesn't help. She grabs her bonnet camera, whips the curtain back and storms into the gear room. Bill and Wilson look at her, and then promptly down at the floor.

Sue reaches into her locker and pulls out a tan wool scarf, which she tosses across the room to Carter. "Heads up, Carter."

She catches the scarf with one hand then flips it around her neck, laying the ends over her chest. "Thanks."

"No problem, you should have been with us in Haiti last year when we were getting something off the HMS Bounty."

"Topless, right?"

"Yeppers."

Sue and Carter laugh as they walk out together to the Hangar Bay, but Bill and General Wilson stay behind.

"Bill, I want you to test out the plant if you can. This time period is right at the edge of the treaty and they will be relocating soon. This should be just at the time when the reports of traders claiming they got this medicine were at the highest level. Things were really good between the tribe and the government at this point, so you shouldn't have any problems."

"Got it, I'll try to get a few specimens with roots intact also."

Bill walks out to the pod and finds Carter and Sue already aboard.

Carter turns to him. "Last one in shuts the door, Bill."

Sue snorts, trying not to laugh.

Bill swings the door shut. "Right."

They go through the checklist and when Bill gets permission to launch, he engages the time phase sequence. In a flash, they arrive at their destination.

"OK, 1875 California. We should be able to find a local tribe pretty easily."

Carter checks the hidden camera in her costume bonnet, and then puts it in her lap. "So are we going to hide the pod somewhere and walk?"

"No, we need to find a covered wagon. The natives need to think we're locals."

Bill pilots the pod in cloaked mode up in the air to get a better view of the area, flying north, and notices a small mining town down below.

"Down there, we should be able to procure a couple horses and a wagon in that town. Carter check inside those satchels, we should have some money in one of them."

Carter grabs one of the distressed leather bags and flips the top flap open. Inside she finds some old gold coins. "Found them. There are about forty gold coins in here that say twenty dollars each."

"Yeah, each one is an ounce of gold. We should be able to get what we need for about one hundred dollars."

Bill lands the pod behind a stable. There's no sound or movement of the dirt below the pod as it touches down. He taps on the control panel and an electrical hum buzzes from the pod door.

"Right, the door is in phase, but we're still cloaked, so we can come and go through the door."

"Am I doing any recording for this part?"

"No, we're just buying a wagon and finding out where the local medicine man is."

Carter swings the pod door open. The air-conditioned interior suddenly changes as warm California air rushes inside. They have landed in the shade of the stable building. It's just after 2 p.m. local time, so the sun is high in the midday sky. From outside the pod, the only thing visible is the door opening. Bill and Carter step out through the door and close it behind them. He scoops up a handful of dry dusty dirt and rubs it into his pants and shirt.

"I suppose I need to get dirty, too?"

"No, I just like immersing myself in the role."

Carter bends down and copies Bill, rubbing dirt on her clothes. They smile at each other as they muss themselves up. She reaches up to Bills face and wipes her dirt stained hands across his cheeks. "Now you look the part."

They walk out from behind the stable to the unpaved streets of the recently built mining town. The buildings are new and still smell of the milled wood they were made from. Townspeople walk along, going about their business, and horse-drawn wagons roll past the saloon across the street.

They walk up to the stable doors where they see a man building a wagon wheel. Bill approaches him.

"Good afternoon, sir. We're looking to purchase a covered wagon and some horses, are you the man to see about that?"

The merchant, standing at a traditional wood workers bench, looks over. "Yes mister, I have what you need. Just you and the little lady?"

"Yes sir, that's correct. We were brought out from the east by friends, and now we need to make it the rest of the way on our own."

The merchant walks to the side of his shop where two wagons have been parked. "This one right here will cost you one hundred and thirty dollars, and I have two horses I can sell you for fifty dollars each."

"That's more than I thought it would be. Two hundred and thirty dollars, then?"

"Yes sir, supplies in a mining town tend to fetch a premium."

"Of course they do."

Bill hands the money to the merchant. "I also need a bit of information as well, if you have it." Bill drops each coin into the merchants cupped hands. "We're looking for a Hopi medicine man that is trading in a leaf that rumor has it cures everything. Do you know where we can find this man?"

"Sure I know him, are ya sick?"

"No, we're bringing the medicine to my wife's sick mother out west."

"Sure, he is right down the road, about fifteen miles. He sometimes comes by and trades for things in town."

"Do you know his name?"

"He just likes being called Medicine Man."

"Medicine Man, of course. Sir, thank you very much."

"I hope your mamma feels better, young lady."

Bill hooks up the horses to the wagon and offers his hand to Carter to help her step up. He jumps in and sits next to her in the spring supported bench seat. They drive down the street the merchant had pointed them towards, and Bill pulls out the wireless earpiece from his pocket and places it in his right ear.

"Lieutenant, bring the pod back up above us and follow us over that hill."

"Copy, Colonel." She powers up the pod and ascends to one hundred feet above the stable, spotting Bill and Carter about halfway down the road. She moves the pod above them, keeping speed with the wagon. "Right above you, sir."

Bill looks up to the empty sky above the wagon and salutes the invisible pod. They make their way over the hill about half an hour later, where Bill stops the horses and gets out, walking around the back of the wagon.

"This should do nicely. Sue, park the pod right here in the wagon."

"I'm descending now, sir."

Carter hops down and walks towards Bill. "The wagon is too small to hold the pod, how are we going to hide it?"

"We're only going to use the wagon to get in and out of the pod door. The only part phased in will be the door, just like back at the stable. This way, we can use the wagons tarp to shield us from view when we're opening the door. Sue is going to lock the pods position to a point in the back of the wagon, so as I drive, the pod will move with it."

"So the only thing people on the outside will see is the pod door floating in the middle of the wagon?"

Bill laughs. "Only if the door to the pod is open. If the door is closed the wagon will look empty, and if someone gets in the wagon they will be out of phase with it, just like when we were over the man in Egypt."

"It'll look bigger on the inside!"

Bill closes the back flap to the wagon. "I suppose it will."

Sue docks the pod. "Locked on sir, ready to go."

Carter asks Bill, "Won't Sue be bouncing all over the place because she's in the pod that's connected to the wagon?"

"It's not a physical connection. She's connected virtually, kind of like a balloon floating on a string."

They get back on the wagon and resume their trip down the road. By nightfall, they see some campfires burning up ahead.

"I think that's the tribe. It's late though, we shouldn't sneak up on them while they're sleeping. Let's set up here for the night and head over to meet them at dawn."

Carter leans back in the seat. "Wait, we have a time machine, why don't we just fast forward to the morning?"

"Come on Carter, how often do you get to go camping while getting paid?"

She laughs. "Good point. Do we have supplies for the night?"

"Everything we need is in the pod."

They go to the back of the wagon, where Sue opens the pod door for them. Once inside, Bill slides open some panels on the interior walls where packaged food and water are stored.

Bill tosses Sue an MRE. "Chicken, right, Sue?"

Sue nods. "Thank you."

"Carter, what would you like? We got beef, chicken, pulled pork, pasta, chili?"

Sue spins her chair around. "No chili!"

Carter looks at the shelf full of military MRE packs. "I'll take the beef, I guess."

They all go outside the pod and set up a campfire next to the wagon. After eating, Bill retrieves a pair of binoculars. "I'm going to go up that hill and take a look around the area."

"Do you want me to go with you?" Carter asks.

"No, I just need to check if there's something beyond the hills we know about it beforehand." He straps on his gun belt and checks the gun to make sure it has tranquilizer loads. He also reaches into his coat pocket and feels around for the box of extra real ammunition he brought.

Carter and Sue sit by the fire drinking tropical punch in tin cups as Bill heads off. Over the past few days, Sue has been left out of the after work social events and Carter thinks that she might be feeling neglected.

"So you're married right?"

"Yes, to Steve. He also works in the TTRC."

"Yeah, Bill said he's in Hangar Bay Two."

"He's on a mission right now in another galaxy, looking for planets."

"That's so cool, have you ever gone with him?"

"Sure, that's actually how we first met, I was on his team, but the situation changed between us. When the General found out we were dating he told me I needed to transfer to another pod. They needed an engineer on Bill's team, so they transferred me to Pod One. Now we hardly see each other. Thankfully we get weekends off, unless we're on a mission that runs long."

"I never asked Bill if he was married."

"As far as I know he's never been married. Seems to me he prefers to be flying around and going on missions rather than dating. I've never even seen him go out to dinner with anyone, even when Steve and I invite him along, he always comes by himself. I remember though, there was this girl from DARPA named Cathi he dated once, but she disappeared one day. I don't know if they broke up."

"Oh that's weird, we just had dinner together two nights in a row."

"Really? That's interesting," Sue says with a sassy tone in her voice.

"I think they were more like business dinners, because we mostly discussed TTRC stuff. But we did play pool last night."

"Well I can tell Bill's comfortable around you. He hardly talks to me, or anyone for that matter. Just take it slow, remember this is a job. Trust me, you don't want them to think you're not focused, or have anything that could compromise the mission."

About ten minutes later, Bill negotiates his way down the hill and back to the wagon. "OK ladies, lets unfold the cots in the pod and get some sleep."

***

The next morning, Bill and Carter drive down to the tribe village. As the wagon rolls in, they're met with friendly waves from the local Hopi natives. These villagers are very familiar with trading from the frontiersmen over the years. Young children chase after the wagon as it rolls to a large adobe structure in the middle of the village. Bill stops the wagon and jumps down to the dusty, well-traveled ground.

A young Hopi woman greets him. "Welcome."

"Good morning, I'm looking to trade; we're in search of medicine known to the Hopi from this plant." Bill holds up a pencil sketch of the Panacea plant he'd traced from a photo back at the base.

"Yes, we have many of this. Come with me."

She escorts Bill and Carter into the adobe structure. Bill subtly points to Carters bonnet as they walk through doorway. She reaches under her bonnet and starts recording the interior, slowly turning her head from side to side. The traditional cabin is set up like a general store. Inside are woven baskets lining the walls, filled with all sorts of roots and herbs. In the center, a fire crackles as an old man sits and stirs a potion in an iron pot.

They approach the old man as the woman speaks to him. "They wish to trade for this medicine."

The man looks up at Bill and speaks in perfect English. "Whatcha got to trade?"

Bill kneels and opens his satchel. "Please look inside and take what you want for an even trade."

The medicine man rummages through his satchel and pulls out the remaining gold as well as some period silk and other items. He doesn't seem interested in anything.

He points to Bills gun. "Let me see that pistol."

Bill pauses for a second, then stands up and unhooks his gun belt. He hands it to the medicine man, who immediately starts spinning the cylinder while holding it up to his ear.

105

"I heard about these new ones, but what's a Ruger?"

Bill puts his hand up to his forehead and stands silent for a second, trying to think of a reason he would have a replica of a Colt peacemaker made by a company that would not be founded until 1949. "Oh, that's my name. I'm William Ruger." Bill looks back at Carter, who smiles. "I bought it as a sample and it had no name on it, so I had the blacksmith chisel my name." Bill takes the gun from the Medicine man, then turns around to face Carter, and quickly empties the six tranquilizer darts from the gun into his hand and dumps them into his pocket. From his other pocket, he pulls out a hand full of real bullets, turns back to the medicine man, and hands him back the gun. "Here are some bullets I made."

He shoves the bullets in his pocket and tucks the gun in his sash. "Deal." He reaches inside a wicker basket which overflows with moist leaves and grabs a few handfuls, filling up a leather pouch, and tosses it to Bill.

Bill catches the bag. "Will you give me one live plant so that after my long journey to my wife's sick mother, she can put it in the ground and have more for when she gets sick again?"

The medicine man laughs and grabs the bag. He opens it and pulls out some of the leaves, pointing to the jagged edges of the leaves that have small round tips. "See that? Those are seeds. Plant them high on the mountain with much rain."

"Thank you. Can you show me how to use the medicine?"

"Sure, give me your hand."

The medicine man takes Bills wrist and turns Bills hand palm up. He reaches under his sash, pulls out a large knife, and quickly draws the blade across Bills palm. Bill tries to pull his hand away, but the medicine man is too strong.

The cut begins to bleed, and the medicine man presses a leaf against it. He forces Bills fingers into a fist and waves his hand over it.

"You say the old Hopi prayer... Abracadabra." He snaps his fingers and opens Bill's hand, then spits in it. He takes a cloth and wipes away the blood, revealing the wound which has already closed and a red scar that formed in a matter of seconds.

Carter leaning over Bill's hand, aiming her camera at the wound. "Does it still hurt?"

"I don't know, I mean, I think it hurts but for some reason I think my brain is being tricked into it." Bill flexes his hand a few times. "No there's no more pain." He extends his freshly healed hand to the medicine man and offers to shake. "Thank you, medicine man."

The medicine man refuses the offer. "I'm not touching that hand, I just spit in it."

Everyone in the room laughs. Bill and Carter thank him and walk back toward the wagon. After they get on the wagon, Carter says, "What kind of horse shit is this? I mean, did he even cut you?"

"Trust me, I was cut. I wasn't expecting it, either. This is some amazing stuff."

Carter looks down at her ankle, which she had cut a couple days earlier. She reaches into the bag and pulls out a leaf.

"What are you doing?"

"The other day I scraped my leg on a bush near the apartment building. I just want to see if this stuff really works." She rubs the oily leaf on her scabbed cut, which reopens the wound. Instantly she sees the oil sizzle on her cut, and the wound starts to heal. "Shit, that was fast."

"Yeah, I can't even believe my own eyes after watching it."

"I was blown away. I got the whole thing on video."

"Good, I don't even think the magic word or the spit had anything to do with the process."

"Funny. So are we ready to go back to base?"

"Yes, we'll go over that hill and then abandon the wagon."

As the wagon reaches the top of the hill, they notice three men on horseback riding towards them. When the men get in front of the wagon, one stops his horse and turns it sideways to block the road. He pulls his rifle from the saddle holster and aims it at Bill and Carter. Carter presses the record button in her bonnet instinctively as the other two riders circle the sides of the wagon.

The man in front calls out, "Good morning folks, how are y'all doing?"

Bill eyes the men on either side. "What can we do for you, stranger?"

"Well since you ask, you can hand over any valuables you happen to have on you."

"Look mister, we have a little money if that will make you go away."

"Well that's a good start, but how about you sweeten the pot and throw in that pretty little lady you got sitting next to you?"

"I'm afraid I can't offer her to you mister, she's my wife." Bill reaches into his satchel and pulls out the gold coins to show the robber. "I have lots of gold you can have." He pulls out a few of the tranquilizer bullets as well, pinching one between his fingers. Carter looks down to find Bill passing her one as well, and accepts the dart.

"Mister, here take this gold." Bill steps down off the wagon with the stack of gold coins in his right hand. On his way down, he pretends to slip and slaps his left hand on the rider's leg, injecting him with the tranquilizer.

Carter copies him with the rider on her side as Bill hands the main robber the gold. When the robber reaches to take it, Bill drops the coins and slaps the other dart into the robber's palm.

The robber looks confused, staring at his palm, and tries to signal his fellows to take action, but both are already lying face down on the back of their horse's necks. The bandit lets go of the leather reins and falls sideways off the horse, landing with a loud *thump*. Bill retrieves the gold coins and walks back to the wagon.

"Bill, what will happen to them?"

"In about an hour they'll wake up. They'll be sick for a few hours and probably puke, then they'll be fine."

He and Carter walk around to the back of the wagon and go inside the pod to find Sue laughing. "You do know I had all three of them targeted with the stunner, right?"

Bill pats Sue on the shoulder. "What fun would that have been?"

Carter plops down in her chair and pulls the bonnet off her head, shutting off the camera in the process. "Well. that was interesting."

"You OK there, Carter?" Bill asks.

"Yeah, I think I'm pretty good. I've been through some adrenalin-pumping situations in my life, but that was one for my record book. I'm actually ready to do it again if you want to go find more robbers."

Everyone laughs and Bill squeezes his hand on Carter's shoulder. "I'm glad we got you on our team. You sure proved your skills today."

They take their stations and head to base. Carter rides an endorphin high when they arrive back in the gear room to change into their base uniforms, and is surprised to look at her watch and see it's only 4 p.m.

She leaves the changing room and approaches Bill as he ties his boots. "It's still pretty early in the day, what are you planning on doing?"

"Well I'm going to listen in on the interview of the person we saw come in on Pod Three yesterday. Do you want to come?"

"Who is he?"

"Well, that's what we're trying to find out. He's been in holding all night because we're waiting for the interviewer to arrive from Ohio."

"What are they interviewing him for, anyway?"

"We think he might be a con artist. He was found with center Earth technology pretending to be the god Kukulkan and ordering an entire culture to work for him mining gold in Mexico."

"Wow, that's creepy. Does this happen often?"

"Yeah, more often than most people realize. There are numerous occasions in history where entire civilizations have been duped."

"The real Kukulkan was the God of the Toltecs and some of the Mayan ruins are constructed in his name, but this guy was found in the year 900 BC, which is a long time after the original."

"What a dipshit, let's go nail this guy."

She follows Bill down a few floors to the interview room. When they arrive, they're led by a few Airmen to an observation room. They sit in the movie theater-style seats behind the one-way glass, looking into a room with a table in the middle.

General Wilson and some others walk in the observation room. Wilson sits next to Bill. "Colonel, how was the medicine collection op?"

"Successful, sir. I'll have my report as well as Carter's video on your desk tomorrow morning."

"Very good, glad to hear it. Carter, did you have any problems going in the field?"

"No, General, we had everything under control, I even managed to make a camp fire with a flint."

After a couple minutes, the interview room door opens and the detainee is brought in, dressed in a white jumpsuit and wearing handcuffs and leg chains. His skin is coated with a gold powder which seems to cover his entire body. The Airmen secure his cuffs to a metal post in the center of the heavy steel table and his leg chains to posts embedded in the concrete floor.

"General, we're ready when you are, sir," one of the guards says, facing the divider window.

Wilson pulls a wired head set microphone out from a compartment in the arm of his chair and puts it on. "Bring in Dave."

Dave Conners, the interviewer from Ohio, enters and stands in front of the table facing the detainee. A few silent moments go by until he addresses the captive. "I understand you speak our language?"

"I speak many languages. I am God."

"Sir, if I am to understand you correctly, then you possess powers of God as well?"

"I do."

"So the chains that hold you down should be no challenge to escape, then."

"If it pleases me, I will break these bindings and kill you with them. Why did you take me from my palace? What is this place?"

"I'll make a deal with you. I will answer your questions if you answer mine."

"Why should I answer to you?"

"Well, unless you use your divine powers to break these chains and walk out of here, you'll be held until you give me answers."

"What is your question, mortal?"

"Are you from Agartha?"

The detainees face goes blank as sweat forms on his forehead. "You know of Agartha?"

"Of course we do. We have a treaty with them. We talk and trade with them and have done so for nearly sixty years."

"Where am I? On the surface, or below?"

"You're underground, but not in Agartha. You're in a facility run by surface people."

"That is impossible, surface people do not have the technology I have seen here."

"Well, that's because you're no longer in your own time. We have brought you forward into your future."

"You possess the ability to time travel? Does Agartha have this technology as well?"

"No, this is one technology they haven't achieved, and we haven't shared it with them."

"I assume then, that you are not sending me back to my time for fear that I will inform the council of this."

"You assume correctly." Dave turns to the window. "General, we're done here."

"Wait, I can share technology with you."

"What technology do you have?"

"I know how to tunnel through stone and iron."

"We already have that technology. Can you tell me how to make an artificial sun?"

"I do not know how that is done."

"Then we're done here. You'll be turned over to Agarthan security. They will determine your fate."

"No! They will lock me away, please, I can help you."

"Guards, take this faker back to holding." Dave exits as the detainee is escorted out. Wilson, Bill and Carter head to the hallway and watch the guards take the prisoner to the elevator, and Dave joins Wilson. "This is the fifth one we've captured and learned nothing from."

"I know, it's not looking good."

Dave walks off, leaving the three in the hallway. Carter asks Wilson, "General, what's going on?"

"I know Bill told you about the civilization that lives deep in the Earth. Well, some less-than-reputable people from this place, which they call Agartha, over the past few hundred thousand years have left Agartha and come to the surface. In Agartha, it's a crime to come to the surface. It's an even bigger crime to impersonate a god, prophet, pharaoh, or interfere with the natural development of our civilization. However, some people from Agartha do it anyway from time to time, and because they have advanced technology, they're perceived as the gods they impersonate."

"So we collect them when we find them? How does that affect the time line?"

"We consult with scholars and other historians before we make the collection. If history changes, we don't even notice the change because it has already happened from our perspective. The only people who know the timeline changes is the crew in the pod who did the collection."

"Sounds kind of dangerous to me."

Bill interrupts, "It's very dangerous, but we have to do what's right if the risks are not too great."

Wilson continues, "We have sacrificed stopping quite a few of these fakers because the impact would be too great if we removed them. I don't want to even think about how many people died because we couldn't take action to stop it." Wilson walks off in complete disgust.

"I hope I didn't get him mad," Carter tells Bill.

"No, this is part of the job. We get more go's than no go's in this type of thing. Don't worry about it too much. As long as you do your job as well as you've been doing it, the General will be happy."

"So this guy who was pretending to be a god, what effect did it have by pulling him out?"

"Well, as soon as he arrived here we checked the history and it appears the Mayan civilization dispersed shortly after his collection. Since we don't actually see a change, we asked the crew of the pod what they knew before they went on the mission, and they said it was fairly similar, with the exception that there were more structures and pyramids from their timeline perspective."

"So only people who are in the mission see the changes to the time line?"

"Yes, they spend time trying to see what effects their actions will have before they allowed him to see where he was. As soon as the transfer to the cylinder took place, we put him to sleep. If the effects of taking him are unacceptable, then they put him back and he doesn't even know what happened, other than a few seconds in the storage tube."

"Wait, so he didn't even know he had been taken?"

"Of course. Remember yesterday when they brought in the chamber on wheels and put him in it? Well, the procedure works with the same technology we talked about for making this cave. The same particle beam equipment is used to remove him, and he doesn't know he was removed. Then they release him from the beam into the awaiting chamber where he is knocked out and kept in a medically induced coma."

"So he stays asleep long enough for us to check for a negative side effect."

"Right, then we woke him up. Once we decided to wake him up, he was at that point never going back."

"Sounds like you thought this stuff through. The only other question I have is what happens if there's a disastrous effect from our actions, and when a pod returns, time has changed so much that we don't even exist?"

"Well, that single pod can go back and undo the action. In that case they can either put the collection back, or go back a little further and make sure whatever actions they took don't happen."

They walk off and head towards the elevators. Carter asks, "I've been thinking about the revolver you gave to the medicine man... It wasn't from 1875, was it?"

"No."

"Interesting, and you're not worried about *that* disrupting the timeline?"

"No, it was an insignificant anomaly. Things like that rarely have an effect."

"So I could've worn a bra, then?"

Bill smiles, as he presses the elevator button.

CHAPTER 8: MOON SHOT

Carter and Bill exit the elevator on the hangar bay floor level. As they walk to the video archive room to drop off the mission video, Sue comes out of Hangar Bay Two with her husband.

"It's July 20th," Sue says, passing by Carter and Bill.

Bill stops. "Oh yeah, I almost forgot. Who's going?"

"We're overbooked this year, looks like we have twenty-eight VIPs."

"So we need an extra pod?"

"I think so, Steve and I are going to see Wilson and find out if they need an extra."

Carter looks confused. "What's so special about July 20th?"

Bill turns to her. "It's the day we landed on the moon for the first time back in 1969. Every year the government hosts VIPs from all over the world to come on board the pods to watch Neil and Buzz land."

"That's so cool, are we going?"

"That's what Sue and Steve are finding out now. Do you want to go?"

"Hell yeah."

Carter and Bill head into the video archive and turn over the memory card from the day's mission. Bill's cell phone rings. "Lieutenant, what's the word?" He pauses. "We'll meet you in the Hangar Bay." Carter gets a big smile from Bill. "Ready to go to the moon?"

"Absolutely, this is so exciting."

"Well, try and curb your excitement, because we're bringing four VIPs in the pod with us, so we need to be professional and only speak to them if they ask us direct questions."

"Got it, Colonel. I won't say a word." She salutes him.

"Knock it off, smart ass."

A few minutes later Bill, Sue and Carter sit in the pod waiting for the VIPs, when they hear General Wilson's voice call out, "Pod One."

The three get up and stand in a row in front of the pod's door.

"Gentleman, Madam Prime Minister, this is the crew of Pod One. Their names are classified due to security reasons, but you can call them by their ranks, should you need to speak to them. The Colonel is the commander of the pod, the Lieutenant is the engineering officer, and the young lady at the end is the documentarian—she's a civilian."

The crew shakes hands with all four VIPs as each climb into the pod.

Bill enters behind them. "Allow me to fold down the jump seats behind you. If you would like to stand, please feel free, there will be no physical movement during our flight that you will notice."

Carter closes the door and takes her seat. The VIPs decide to stand so they can get a better view out the windows.

Bill turns to Sue. "Verify all pods ready for phase."

"Yes sir, all pods report ready."

"Very good. Attention all pods, this is Pod One actual. Prepare for sync on my mark."

Carter notices the different command Bill used. It isn't his usual wording. "What is sync?"

"It's when more than one pod is traveling to the same time and place. We turn over control to a lead pod so we don't all land on each other. The software sends us at the same time, but separates us in distance by ten feet in a straight line."

"Makes sense, sorry for the interruption."

The Governor of Ohio leans over to Carter. "Don't worry, I was wondering the same thing."

Bill continues, "All pods synchronizing to Pod One computer in three, two, one mark."

Sue reports, "Software sync complete, ready for group phase out sir."

"Copy that Lieutenant, phasing now."

In both bays all pods in the mission phase out simultaneously. As the VIPs watch through the window, a blue flash gives way to complete darkness. Bill and his crew get up from their chairs to allow the VIPs to get a better look.

They stare out the windows. From their vantage point inside Pod One, all they see is the slightly mountainous lunar surface they hover over. The pod is only a few feet off the ground, along the rim of a crater.

Bill walks up to the control panel. "Excuse me for a moment, Governor." He takes the microphone off the mount and pulls it around the VIPs. "All pods report in."

One by one, the other six pods report that *'all conditions are normal.'*

The Governor comments, "Where are the other pods, Colonel?"

"They're invisible sir, just like we are to them, and will be when the Eagle Lunar Lander arrives with our two astronauts in about four minutes."

"Ah, yes I forgot about that part. Amazing how much more color there is than I've seen in photos. Look at the reds and browns."

Sue replies to the Governor, "Yes sir, those are the various metals that oxidized millions of years ago, when the moon had somewhat of an atmosphere."

They watch out the pod windows, watching for the approaching Lunar Lander. The only female VIP—the Canadian Prime minister—points. "Look, there they are!"

They all lean into the windows. Bill pushes gently on the small of Carters back, gesturing for her to join them. She moves to the side where Sue normally sits, and the Prime Minister notices Carter inching closer. "Please step in. Is this your first time observing?"

"Yes, Prime Minister."

"Mine too, I've been on the list for two years. You're lucky to be a crew member."

As they look on, the lunar lander gets closer and closer until suddenly the bottom of the lander's rockets fire and dust blasts out from all sides. The lander comes in much faster than expected, and everyone becomes visibly tense as the rockets fire against the dusty surface. After what felt like an eternity, the lander comes to a stop and the landing rockets shut off. Everyone applauds and cheers after the rockets stop.

Bill steps up to the VIPs. "OK folks, there's a little over six hours before Armstrong steps on the surface of the moon, so if you would allow us, we'll need to take our stations so we can skip forward to that point."

The crew takes their stations, and Bill moves the pods forward to a couple minutes before the LEM door is opened by Armstrong, planting his feet on the lunar surface for the first time.

The VIP from England—a wealthy banker—comments, "Too bad we can't hear the radio transmission."

Sue slaps herself on the head, then runs over to her console and presses a few buttons. "Sorry about that, I forgot to turn the speaker on."

Suddenly an extremely clear transmission of Neil Armstrong's voice comes over the speakers to loud applause. They watch as he climbs down the ladder and utters the famous "small step for man" speech.

Bill grabs the microphone. "We can leave now, but if you would like to stay and watch for a while, I have no problem staying put."

A couple seconds later, each pod reports they would like to stay and watch the Astronauts plant the American flag and set up equipment.

The Senator of Kentucky looks off to the side and stares for a few seconds. "I thought you said we couldn't see the other pods, Colonel?"

"That's correct, Senator."

"Well I see all six of the other pods lined up right next to us."

A look of horror comes over Bill's face as he jumps up faster than he has ever moved in his life. He runs between VIPs, knocking them aside. Sue is right behind him, running to her workstation at lightning speed.

"Shit LT, what the hell happened?"

"Sir, I don't know, it's that software glitch I saw in the other pod earlier this week."

"I've got to get us out of here now, we're visible to the astronauts, and it looks like they're looking at us. Jam their communication signal."

Bill grabs the microphone. "All pods prepare for emergency phase." He makes a fist and slams it against the return button. Instantly, they arrive back at the hangar bay. He turns to the frightened VIPs. "I apologize for the scare, we needed to take emergency action to prevent a time line disruption."

The VIPs regain their composure and step out of the pod to the hangar bay, where General Wilson waits with a smile. "Welcome back, how was your trip?"

The VIPs look back at Bill, who steps out of the pod as the Governor turns back to the General. "It was fantastic, General. Your crew did a bang-up job."

"I'm glad you had a good time." The General gestures the group toward the hangar bay doors.

Carter and Sue stand behind Bill as they watch the group leave. Bill turns around to Sue. "Get over to archives and find out what damage we did, report back as soon as you know something."

Sue takes off, and Carter looks at Bill with fear in her eyes. "How bad is this?"

"I don't know, but this might be a paradox." Bill paces back and forth in the hangar bay. While Carter just watches him. A few minutes pass when Bills mobile phone rings.

It's Sue. "Sir there's no official report of anything, but I found a report from a ham radio operator. He says he was monitoring the astronaut's medical channel and he wrote down a conversation he heard between Aldrin and Armstrong. They were reportedly talking about a bunch of UFOs hovering over a crater watching them while they were working on the surface of the moon. I did some more checking and the report was discredited and forgotten about."

Bill's knees wobble as he starts to relax his muscles. He sits down on the hangar bay floor, rubs his hand on the top of his head, and exhales loudly. "That's just plain dumb luck. We're so fucking lucky. Priority one now is to trace down that software glitch, even if it means building a whole new program from scratch."

"Yes sir, I'm already heading to engineering now."

Bill lays his phone on the floor and looks up at Carter. "It's okay, we're safe. It was written off in history as a bogus UFO sighting."

Carter lets out the breath she had been holding for what seemed like hours. She removes her ponytail, shakes it out, then sits next to Bill, tilting her head on his shoulder.

CHAPTER 9: DOWN

As Sue spends the weekend running down the software bug that keeps disabling the cloak on the pods, Carter relaxes in her apartment on Saturday morning. She sits on her couch flipping through the TV channels and eating cereal that's mostly sugar in a bowl that's too large.

She finishes eating her breakfast and stares at some random movie that's on the TV. Her cat is lying on the couch next to her.

"What do you think I should do today, Mayo?"

The cat looks at her and purrs. With Bill only a few levels away, she wonders if she should call him and ask if he wants to do something. However, she is also thinking about what Sue was saying, how she used to be on a pod with Steve. Maybe it would be best if she and Bill didn't appear to have too close of an after work relationship. She decides to get in her car and drive around.

***

She winds up on the main street, passing the familiar places she had already seen. Ahead is a combination coffee shop and bookstore.

"*Looks like a good place to relax,*" she thinks.

After browsing the aisles, she purchases a copy of H.G. Well's *The Time Machine*. "Might as well read up on this stuff."

She enters the café, which is average sized with a dozen small tables and lounge chairs along the window. After picking out a chair, she relaxes and reads while sipping cappuccinos. Out the window, she watches as various military and civilians stream in and out for coffee and baked goods. She likes to listen to music while relaxing and reading, so she puts her headphones in and plays music from her phone.

After an hour or so, a tall man wearing a dark blue robe walks into the café with a uniformed army general. The tall man has very pale skin and a bald head. Carter might have mistaken him for an albino, with the exception of his eyes, which are a vibrant blue like her own. She can't help herself but stare as he and the General order coffee and pastries.

The tall man notices Carter, smiling while he waves. Carter smiles back, feeling slightly embarrassed for being caught staring. She often finds herself staring long past social norms because she's constantly working out the story behind everything she sees.

The tall man walks over to the window next to her while he waits for his order. He looks down at the cover of Carters book. "How is the book you are reading?"

She's listening to 'Broadicea' by Enya on her headphones, and can't hear what the man asked. "What? Oh...the book? It's OK, I don't normally get a lot of time to sit and just read, so I don't have a lot to compare it with."

"You can always make time to enlighten yourself if you put your mind to it." He bows awkwardly.

"Yeah, I guess you're right."

He walks closer to the window of the café and looks up at the artificial day light bulbs mounted to the roof of the cavern. "Not exactly realistic, is it?"

Carter looks up. "You mean the fake sunlight? No, but I'm planning on going to the sun tower today to get the real stuff."

"Ah, the sun towers are delightful; I wish I could spend more time on them, as well."

"So why don't you? As you said, you can make time."

He smiles and looks over at the General, who just received his order. "Unfortunately, my access to some things here are limited."

She glances down to the laminated ID badge hanging around his neck. It reads in big black letters 'Diplomatic Access Level One' with no name or photo.

The tall man glances at Carter's ID. "It was pleasant to meet you, Miss Carter. Perhaps we will see each other again. "He reaches into his robe pocket, pulling out a small business card, which he gives to her.

She takes it without looking at it as he offers hand to shake. "You too, and what was your name?"

"I am Ambassador Dennia from Agartha."

Carter feels a cold chill run through her body upon hearing where he is from. "It's nice to meet you Ambassador."

The General walks over with the cardboard beverage tray. "Ambassador, we're late."

The Ambassador, still holding Carters hand, glances at the General then back to Carter. "Good luck at the T...T...R...C..." He releases Carter's hand, turns around, and walks out of the café.

Carter picks up her half filled cup of cappuccino with a shaky hand and drinks the rest to get rid of her sudden onset of dry mouth. As she watches through the window, she sees the General and Ambassador drive away in a four-door sedan similar to the one she drives. She looks down at the business card.

Diplomat
Ambassador Aros Dennia
Access Level One
465-9981

Carter had just met a person from Agartha the day before, but he had been pulled from the Agartha, which existed nearly three thousand years ago. He was obviously not a good person, as posing as a Mayan god proved. Even though she recognizes the Ambassador was quite different and very pleasant, she still feels uneasy.

Carter orders another cappuccino and attempts to read a little longer, but keeps glancing at the business card lying next to her coffee cup. She grabs her book and the Ambassadors card then drives back to her apartment. When she gets inside, she goes into the office to retrieve her base phone and sends Bill a text.

Bill, sorry to bother you on Saturday, but I was just out having coffee and I met an Ambassador from Agartha. I wanted to let you know, just in case it was important.

About a minute later, Bill replies. *Did you get his or her name?*

Yeah, Aros Dennia.

Hmm. Did he tell you his name?

He gave me a business card with his phone number on it.

That's interesting. Give me a few minutes. I need to inform General Wilson.

Bill, there's something else, he looked at my ID badge and he seemed to know what TTRC was.

Yes, they all know TTRC. They're not fans of our division.

Yikes! Should I be worried?

Hang tight for a bit. You don't need to worry; He's not a threat right now.

Okay.

Carter sits down on her living room couch for a few minutes in silence, watching her phone. An hour passes before Carter's phone finally chimes with a message from Bill.

Carter, I'm over at headquarters with Wilson. We need you to come in as soon as you're ready. You can come as you're dressed, no need to suit up.

OK. I'll be there in ten minutes.

***

When she gets to the hangar bay, she hears lots of different voices coming from the ready room. She hurries to get there faster, and upon entering, notices almost every one of the twenty chairs filled with men and women in officer's air force uniforms, including General Wilson and Bill.

Carter feels a sensation of claustrophobia wash over her—not because the room is small, but because there are so many people looking at *her*.

Wilson extends his arm to invite her to stand next to him, facing the group of officers. "Team, this is Miss Carter, she's the new documentarian for Pod One."

A low rumble of "hello" erupts from the crowd.

Carter crosses her arms, uncomfortable having so many people staring.

Bill sees her nerves and whispers, "Relax; they're on your side. They're here to support you." He walks to the side of the room and drags a chair over for Carter. Then he goes to the podium and opens a very thick folder. "Ladies and Gentlemen, as you already know, Carter received a card from Ambassador Dennia this morning. I'd like to take this time to update her on what we've been talking about so she's caught up on why we're all here on a Saturday instead of playing golf. "Carter's cleared for this level of security, so we're going to speak frankly about the situation. Carter, as you're aware, we're in a diplomatic relationship with Agartha and have been for roughly sixty years. Part of that agreement includes boundaries where we don't cross into their territory, and they don't cross into ours. Our Ambassador has just as limited access to Agartha as we give to Dennia. Now other than Ambassadors, on an unofficial basis, there are exceptions. If a high ranking official from either side wants to invite a guest, they usually can. So here is somewhat of an opportunity for all of us to get information about Agartha that has not been updated since 1947. The Ambassador you met is one who is known to invite a guest to see Agartha, or at least the capitol city. It's part of their custom to offer a way to contact them, i.e, the business card as an invitation to meet again."

Carter leans forward in her chair. "Why would he even invite me? I mean, he doesn't know me, we just met this morning."

Bill tries to put on a straight face, but most of the men in the room are not as successful. "Carter, not to put too fine a point on it, but the people of Agartha mostly share common physical traits, and the men of Agartha hold women with *certain* physical characteristics in high regard."

She sighs and stands. "Can you give me a minute, please?" She walks out of the ready room and into the gear room, feeling like she did during her old life, dealing with people who liked to use her.

Bill holds up his hand to the group, following her into the gear room. He shuts the door behind him.

Carter stands facing him as he walks inside. Her arms crossed against her chest, she gives him a look unlike any he's seen her wear before. "So, what? You want me to sleep with this guy?"

"No, not at all, that's the last thing I want to happen. I should have talked to you before . I'm not asking you to do anything other than meet him and possibly get a tour of

Agartha. I'm sorry; I shouldn't have sprung that on you in front of everyone before making it clear what we would be asking of you. I promise I'll never do that again."

She stares silently at his face, which clearly expresses that he is truly sorry. "Tell me what this is really about, then."

"Last time anyone went to Agartha in any meaningful way was in 1947. The data we have is that old. We know that this particular Ambassador has invited three other women to the capitol city, and they were all women from the base. Unfortunately, the women who went weren't trained or observant enough to give us any details that could be useful."

"So why did he choose *me*? There were other women in the café this morning."

"Well...what we've observed is most Agarthan women are tall, pale skinned, blond haired, blue eyes, and...the women have small chests."

"So my shortness, dark hair, and big tits are why he approached me?"

"I don't know for sure, but the other three women he invited had those characteristics."

"Wait, if you want to see this place, why don't you just use the pod and take a look?"

"We tried that. We don't know why, but the entire place is protected by something that rejects our ability to phase in. The only way in is through the methods they have, and they hold the keys to that lock. The polar entrances are sealed, and there's only the tube transit system now."

Carter still feels offended but realizes how important this information could be, considering how many people are sitting in the ready room on a Saturday morning. She sighs her assent and walks back in the ready room to retake her seat.

Bill heads back to the podium, and Wilson joins Carter, whispering, "Sorry, we went about this the wrong way. It won't happen again."

Bill continues. "Ladies and gentlemen, I'm sure we're all in agreement that in our rush to hash out a plan for an intelligence gathering operation, we failed to take the time to inform our number one asset in the mission beforehand. I think it falls on me as her direct supervisor to apologize for the way I went about it, and for causing her any embarrassment."

"Thank you Colonel, I'm good to go. Let's continue the briefing."

"So where we're at now is, the Ambassador has given his card to Carter, and we would like to ask her to accept his offer to meet. If he invites her down, we want her to ask if she could get a personal tour of any part of Agartha that our own diplomats haven't been able to go. At this point, any intel will be invaluable."

Carter raises her hand.

"Carter, you don't need to raise your hand, this is your mission," Bill says in a low voice.

"I have a few questions. How am I supposed to get him to bring me down? What am I looking for once I get there, and what happens if I get caught?"

"We'll develop a step-by-step response, and we'll go over the possibilities that might happen during your conversation with the Ambassador. Once you're with him on base, you should ask about his home, where he grew up, and other things like that, so his own desire to show you those things becomes his idea to take you there. Now, as far as surveillance equipment, the only thing we can do is give you a camera. If you're caught with it, you'll have plausible deniability. So a cell phone with a camera will be the likely choice. Now, all base personnel who enter the tunnel to Agartha must be logged so we know who's there. This will make it impossible for him to detain you. You'll have the same diplomatic immunity as he has here. Even if they see the camera, they'll just eject you back to the base."

"Fine, as long as I don't have to sit in an Agarthan jail or join his Harem."

A jovial rumbling fills the audience, which makes Carter feel comfortable and in charge of this mission.

General Wilson joins Bill. "Now, there are a few things we want to know, and we'll give you a complete list so if you see or hear any of them you'll remember, but some obvious things are what type of shield prevents us from bringing pods in, and what type of travel technology do they have? Is it limited to Earth and air travel, or can they travel in space, and if so, how *far* into space can they travel. I'll give you the list."

Over the next thirty minutes, she speaks with about half the people in the ready room. They're very interested in her personally and her ability to pull off the operation. Some express their concern that she is not a trained agent, and they show their reservation on her being discovered and destroying further chances for visitations. But the majority are confident that she has the right personality to complete the mission. At the end of the meeting, she agrees and is given the go ahead to enter Agartha.

Carter and Bill decide to wait until Monday to have her make the call to the Ambassador on the car ride home.

"I want to apologize again. I'm really sorry you were treated this way."

"It's fine. I reacted the way I did because in my old life people treated me like an object. I know you would never ask me to do something like that."

"I wouldn't, not ever."

Carter eyes lock onto his with a renewed admiration. Not many men have treated her with respect, and now she feels bad that she reacted the way she did. She's tempted to show affection towards him, but resists for a multitude of reasons.

"So, why do the Agarthan men have this affinity with women who look like me?"

"We're not really sure, but the dominate race of Agartha are mostly tall, slender, blonde hair, blue eyes. The women are skinny with very few curves. I guess it's just because it's something different, but we've never asked the actual question."

"Did you speak to the three other women who accepted his invitation?"

"Yes, we wish we knew they were going beforehand, but none of them were in the TTRC and we haven't made public that our pods cannot penetrate their shield yet. So we decided not to broadcast that we were interested in the shield out of fear of them realizing we can't get in on our own. I mean, obviously they know we have the pods and they know what they're capable of, but from our best guess, they currently don't know what they're *not* capable of or the treaty might be different."

"Is the treaty something they adhere to?"

"As far as we know, the last time they've been out in our world was before 1947."

"And I'm assuming from the nature of my mission, we don't adhere to the treaty?"

"Technically, we *have* adhered to it. Only those invited have gone down. If you get invited, the treaty will still be intact."

"Are those other women still alive? Did they have sex with him?"

"Yes, and I don't know. However, if you'd like, I can get you their phone numbers."

"No. I don't need to know because I'm not fucking him."

"Well, that's a relief."

***

Sunday morning, Carter wakes up nervous about her upcoming encounter. She decides to put it out of her mind and reminds herself it's just a mission. Maybe today will be the day she actually relaxes with her book at home and in her pajamas.

About 3:00 p.m., after she's shelved her novel and started watching some old movie on TV, her doorbell chimes unexpectedly. She answers the door to find Sue.

"Hey, are you busy?"

"No, of course not, come on in."

Sue comes in and stands next to the couch.

"Sit, do you want some coffee?"

"Sure, light and sweet, please."

Carter pours out two cups and brings Sue one. "You look like something's bothering you. What's up?"

"Well, I debated coming down here, but I felt I should talk to you."

"About what?"

"I need to tell you something, but I'm hesitant."

"Well, whatever it is, I can be trusted, my background check made sure of that."

Sue sips her coffee. "It's about Bill."

Carter wraps her hands around her warm cup. "Uh huh?"

"Look, I know Bill. He and I have been working together for a year now, and I know what's going through his brain pretty much before he does."

"OK...what's going through his brain?"

"You."

"Oh."

Sue looks at Carter with concerned eyes.

Carter clears her throat. "Well, I like Bill too, but I also like this job."

"I know, and that's what I wanted to talk to you about. Bill talked to me yesterday in confidence and told me he was finding it difficult to maintain a completely professional relationship because he can't stop thinking about you. He was thinking that if he transferred you to another pod and maybe swapped you out with Gary on Pod Two he could relax and be able to talk to you, but not as your supervisor."

Carter is shocked, suddenly worried that Bill will do just that. She really likes being on missions with Bill and Sue. "What do you think I should do?"

"Honestly, I don't know. This is the best crew we have had, and I don't want to lose you."

"So you're saying I should confront him and tell him I'm not interested?"

"I'm not telling you to do anything. I just thought you should know there's friction, and that friction needs to be fixed. Sorry, that's my engineer talking."

"No, I get it." Carter sips her coffee, staring at a random spot on the carpet.

"Well, I did what I came to do; I hope you can figure out what needs to be done. I really enjoy working with you, and so does Bill."

***

At about 10 p.m., she watches TV without really seeing. There's some show about lizards on, and has been on for close to an hour. She didn't even have dinner because she's been buried in thought all day. After growing tired of non-action, she leaves her apartment to find whatever restaurant is closest.

She stands by the elevator bank, looking at the two choices before her. If she presses the arrow pointing down, she goes out and forgets what Sue said in her apartment that afternoon; if she presses the arrow pointing up, she confronts Bill.

She stands in front of the two buttons, staring at their frosted orange glow. Then she notices one of them is faulty, the light bulb blinking haphazardly. Instinctively she presses that one, the doors open, and she gets in. A few seconds later the doors swish open again, and she gets out. Her stride starts out slow, then her speed increases faster and faster until she reaches the door. She pauses for a few seconds, then presses the doorbell.

Bill opens the door. "Carter, what are you doing here?"

Carter's face is serious. "You're a smart guy, right?"

"Most of the time, sure."

"I talked to Sue."

"You did, huh?"

"Yes, and I want to make sure our team stays together."

"I do too. I understand." Bill lowers his head, looking down at the floor.

"I don't think you do." Carter advances forward, pressing her body against his as she wraps her arms around his neck. Her heart beats so strong she can feel it in her ears. Bill places his hands on her hips.

She looks him in the eye. "If you're smart enough, you can keep the team together." She lifts herself up to her tiptoes and kisses him deeply on the lips. After a few seconds, she stops to gauge his reaction.

Bill looks at her electric blue eyes, which dart back and forth as she looks at his. "I'll make it work, Carter."

She reaches up behind her head and ties up her ponytail.

"I guess it's go time?" He asks.

She replies with a smile and no hesitation. "Yes it is."

They both disappear behind the door as Carter shuts it with the heel of her shoe.

***

The next morning, they wake up together in his apartment. They stare at each other for a couple minutes before Carter breaks the ice. "Remember, you promised you would make the team stay together."

"I will, Carter. Can I call you by your first name yet?"

"No, I like when you say Carter."

"You're the boss, then, Carter."

"Here? You bet I am."

Bill kisses her and rolls out of bed. He looks back at her lying in his bed. "You're stunning."

She smiles as her cheeks flush. She puts her hands on her breasts for coverage while Bill stands at the foot of the bed.

"Breakfast?"

"Yes sir, please."

Bill gets dressed and cooks up eggs and sausage links while she takes a fast shower and puts on her clothes. As she and Bill eat, he looks at her, thinking through his promise to make sure the team stays together.

"The door is the boundary," he says in a commanding tone.

"The door?"

"You said I have to keep the team together, and my orders are, outside the door to my apartment or yours is the boundary to us, and what we did last night. I don't want to see a wink, or hear a flirt or *honey* or *dear* or anything unless we're behind one of those two doors."

Carter laughs as she takes a sip of coffee. "Aye, aye, sir."

"That's the Navy. I'm Air Force. Get it right."

Carter puts her cup on the table too roughly, which makes the flatware *ching*, leaping out of her seat and onto Bill's lap. Her legs wrap around his waist as she kisses him.

Bill looks at his watch. "I guess we're going to be a few minutes late."

She leans back and looks at him with a scowl. "A few minutes? No, no, no, I don't think so, soldier."

***

Later at TTRC headquarters, they walk into the ready room where Sue sits and waits, looking at her watch. "You guys were supposed to be here an hour ago."

"Sorry, Carter had to drive me because I left my car here on Saturday, and she had some sort of stomach virus this morning."

Carter places her hand on her stomach and squints.

"You still feeling sick?" Sue asks, concerned.

"No, I think I sweat it off this morning."

"Oh good, that's always a good sign. I always know I'm getting right when the sweats start."

"Yeah, I'm feeling pretty right."

"Cool, well I'm going to set up the link between your cell phone recorder to these micro cameras."

Carter pulls her cell out and hands it to Sue. Sue uses the Bluetooth transmitter sewn into the lining of a short red leather jacket to connect to the cell phone.

139

"The button on the collar is camera one, and the button on the left sleeve cuff is camera two. Both will record at the same time. As soon as you're ready to record, hit the volume up button on the phone four times fast. You'll see a small green LED under the fold of your sleeve blink a couple times. That means it's recording. It's not high definition, so try and keep your motions slow due to the low frame rate. The list you memorized is also on your phone in the notes section, in case you need to reference it."

Carter takes the jacket and slips it on. "Good fit. I like it, it's cute."

"You can keep it when the mission is over. We made it for you, anyway."

"Thanks Sue!"

Bill puts his hand on Carters arm. "Now go to the café and sit for a half hour or so before you make the call. We don't know if they can trace cell locations, so we have to make it look like you were off duty. Sue's still working on the software glitch, so everyone else is off today as well. You should be able to get away with it."

"Got it."

"If there's a problem, call me on your phone. I'm not sure what the range is past the tunnel entrance, but if you're not back by 23:00 we'll make an inquiry at the tunnel guard station and say we need you on base for work related reasons. They'll be required to come and get you under treaty rules."

"So be back before midnight, got it."

"23:00 is 11 p.m."

"I know but Cinderella had till midnight." Carter gives Bill the thumbs up as she turns and walks out of the ready room. He sits down and watches Sue take the seat next to him. They both sigh almost at the same time.

Sue turns her head towards Bill. "Our little girl is going out on her first date."

"Don't start."

"Relax boss, she'll do fine."

"I know, I'm just a natural worrier."

"Come on. I'll buy you a coffee and croissant."

"They're free."

"Okay, you pay then."

CHAPTER 10: DOWN DEEP

Over at the café where she had met Aros Dennia two days earlier, Carter sits with another cappuccino and a new book. This time she's reading *Chariots of the Gods*. She decides to read a few chapters before calling the Ambassador, but after sitting there for a few minutes, she looks up to see the Ambassador standing before her.

She hastily shuts the novel. "Ambassador, sorry, I didn't see you come in."

"Miss Carter, how nice to see you again. I thought you might have lost my card."

She reaches into her pocket and pulls the card out. "No, I actually have it right here."

"Oh, that is wonderful. How is it that you have found time to read again, and on one of your work days?"

"Work's shut down for some maintenance, so we all got the day off."

"How fortunate for you, and for me as well."

"How do you mean?"

"Well, I am planning a visit to the sun tower so I can look up at the sky. It is a rare treat to be up there when the sun is obscured by clouds. My skin does not fare well in bright sunny days. Would you like to escort me and possibly share some lunch?"

"That'd be nice, Ambassador."

"Please, Miss Carter, you should call me Aros, we are now old friends."

Carter feels comfortable around Aros now, her hesitation about calling him having been conveniently resolved by this coincidental meeting. "I'd like that."

***

Aros and Carter drive in separate vehicles to one of the sun towers. They arrive and take the long elevator ride up together. Aros exits first, clearly excited to look through the dome into the sky. He obviously doesn't get much opportunity to see it. He tilts his head back as rays of sun barely penetrate the clouds. It's one of the rare days in the Nevada desert when it's overcast.

"We do miss seeing the sky and the stars. It is one of the drawbacks of living so far below."

Carter and Aros walk towards the tower restaurant, which is situated poolside.

"Aros, I don't know much of your city, but I've been told you have an artificial sun, so why is the *real* sun so much different?"

"When we left the surface we were just like you, and decided to make a sun that provided all the same benefits as the real one, minus the harmful ultra violate rays." He pulls a chair out for Carter at the outdoor restaurant table. "So, in our haste, we failed to realize that after a few hundred thousand years, our people would be unable to return to the surface. If we are exposed to these harmful rays, we could die after only a few days of exposure. If I need to spend time in the sun, we have medications and creams we can apply for a temporary solution. In the past, we used gold dust as a method of blocking out the rays."

"So why not slowly reintroduce UV back into your light source?"

"I wish it were that easy. The majority of our population has no desire to return to the surface. We have made the choice to retreat from the sun, and now we must live with that decision. Plus, we have built a society over hundreds of thousands of years, and our population is far too large to blend with those on the surface."

"It sounds like a wonderful place. I'd love to see it one day."

"Ah, Miss Carter, that day could be today if you have the time."

Carter checks her phone. "Well, I'm due for a meeting at 11 p.m., can we be back before then?"

"I'm sure I can arrange that."

They spend another half hour in the sun tower when the clouds start to clear above. As they make their way out of the tower, she follows him to a small building near the northeast part of the city.

She calls Bill on her phone. "Hey Bill, it's me."

"Hello, what can I do for you?"

She realizes Bill is responding so formally in case the Ambassador might be able to tap her phone. "I just wanted to let you know I made a friend and I'm taking a ride to see his place, but I'll be back before the meeting tonight at 11 p.m."

"Thank you, see you tonight."

A little while later both their cars arrive at the entrance to Agartha's diplomatic tunnel. Carter follows Aros as he leads her to the guard station.

"Miss Carter, please scan your ID card with the guard."

A US Army officer and two armed soldiers stand by the set of double doors. Simple wood doors with no locks are the separation between worlds.

Carter tries to maintain a smile the entire time. She intends to keep the Ambassador in the mindset that all is well and everything he shows her makes her happy, which should keep the tour going as long as possible.

Aros places his hand on Carter's back and leads her through the doors. She feels the urge to pull away from his uninvited touch, but maintains character. As they pass through the doors, there's a familiar sight when she sees one of the rapid transit tube cars that are used throughout the city. The tube is oriented vertically to drop them down into the ground.

"Please take a seat," Aros politely offers.

She sits in the transparent plastic car suspended on a gimbal, which rocks slightly as she sits.

"As we get to the midpoint between Agartha and the surface the mechanism will rotate us to the proper orientation so we are not upside down when the gravity changes."

"Oh, I see."

A larger cylinder lowers around the car, the sound of rushing wind sucked out by a vacuum system. When the tube reaches a pure vacuum, all sounds outside the car disappear. They descend into the ground and enter a transparent tube that lines the hollowed rock channel which had been excavated for the transit system. Very quickly the car picks up speed, and within seconds is going so fast the details of the rock wall it passes through become a complete blur.

"Why don't we feel the movement?"

"It is built into the transport to automatically cancel our inertia. When we get to the midpoint you won't even feel the rotation as we transition the gravitational difference."

"Isn't the midpoint at the center of the planet? I mean, the planet is hollow, and your artificial sun is at the center."

"No, our gravity is based on the pull of the mass of the Earth just like you feel on the surface, except our surface is on the inner shell, while yours is on the outside. Imagine you were to take the moon and slice it in half. Then you scooped out the center like you would to ice cream. If you were to walk on the moon after that, the gravity on the outside and the gravity on the inside of the shell would feel the same. The place in which you're walking does not matter, what matters is the overall mass of the moon itself. Our artificial sun is technology; it does not have any mass in itself other than the solar shade, which is just a thin shell." Aros leans forward, looking at the instrument panel which shows their depth. "Get ready, Miss Carter, we are about to pass through the midpoint and the crystal source."

Carter remembers from her first mission seeing the crystals in the primordial Earth, though there was just a hollow space in the center of the planet. Now there's an equal amount of crust on both the outer and inner shell which sandwich the crystal portion of the planet. A few seconds later, the blur of passing rock are replaced with a dimly lit cavern thousands of miles deep. The same crystals she saw on her mission have grown to incredible size. Now they give off their own light source and are thick as cities, thousands of miles in length. The atmosphere clouds with heat distortion, and Carter watches as they start rotating in the car to orient themselves the opposite way. As she observes the distortions, she realizes the crystal chamber is not filled with gases, but water. They're passing through water which is extremely pressurized and super heated.

"So, Miss Carter, what do you do at the TTRC?"

"I'm just a technician in the IT department."

"I see, that must be a gratifying job for you."

"It is, I love working with computers."

Aros seems interested in the TTRC, but not so much in what they do. He appears to be just making polite conversation as they make their way through to Agartha.

Carter watches as the car once again enters into the rocky crust of the Earth, but now that gravity has reversed, they perceive their direction of travel as ascending. As the car gets closer to the surface of Agartha, the blur of passing rock slows. Suddenly they come to a complete stop, and the car moves through a series of mechanical trolleys to a chamber similar to the one they entered in the base city. She attempts to calculate how fast the car must have been going to make such a long-distance trip in only ten minutes, but instead of formulating an answer, she simply thinks, '*That was fucking fast.*' As soon as the doors open, Carter activates the video recorder on her phone. She checks to make sure the green LED flashes, and then follows Aros towards the exit.

They both leave the transit car and walk into a small room that has smooth white walls and floors. The dim room is no bigger than her apartment, with images on the walls displayed on what look like frameless embedded monitors. The images are of various buildings and other structures, both constructed and natural. She stands in front of the monitor for a few seconds, trying to capture the pictures in her recording, but realizes this room is probably well documented by her own people.

She turns back to Aros. "Is this Agartha?"

"Yes, it is called Shambhala. We are in the capitol of Agartha."

Aros leads Carter out and they walk side by side, casually strolling down a long hallway. There are no windows, but open doorways along the corridor. The hall itself towers above them, thirty feet to the arched ceiling. She and Aros pass many Agarthans along the way, until finally she spots some Agarthan women. They wear dark robes that reach their calves; a few wear shorter robes which end at mid-thigh. After learning male Agarthan taste in females, Carter is more interested in what the women of Agartha are like. She passes one who seems to be young like her, and very tall, about six-foot-three. Her robe is a dark red, tighter than most of the others. Carter can see the woman has almost a straight figure, with slender thighs and no curves normally associated with a typical female. The woman has breasts similar to that of a preteen girl.

She aims her sleeve and collar camera at everything she thinks will be of interest, noticing that the men she passes are extremely polite, not gawking or staring, but she catches some of their eyes as they pass and realizes they're doing their best to look at her without being caught. She wonders *'is this because Aros is with her, or if this is just their custom?'*

The women she passes are a completely different story. Almost all of them not only look directly at Carter without smiling, but they seem to be fixated on her body and make it extremely obvious, to the point some stop in their tracks and watch as she passes.

"Aros, I know so little about your people, do you have multiple races in Agartha, like we have on the surface?"

"Of course, but none of our other races are anything like what you know."

"Can I see them while I'm here?"

"Well, you might see some if we were to go out into the capitol city, but, like your people, we have many lands separated by oceans, and there are tribes of people who tend to stay in specific areas."

"Are you at peace with them?"

"We do not have separate nations as you do. Our culture is a peaceful one. That is not to say we do not have conflicting ideas or crime. For the most part we are in a harmony because we have learned to accept each other's differences, and we do not try and change each other."

Carter finds the thought of this a little hard to accept, considering the relationship between Agartha and the surface is so limited. However, she keeps that opinion to herself. "It sounds like a paradise; one that took a long time to create."

"Yes, Miss Carter, it did take a very long time. We left the surface to survive the sun during a time of dangerous solar activity, and it wasn't the smoothest transition. We had many generations of hardship before we were able to begin creating a new civilization."

Suddenly as they turn a corner, the light from the dim artificial sun fills the hall ahead of them. They exit the building and are greeted by a very light green grass lawn and unusual trees and flowers that grow very thin and tall. It seems like the plant life stretches to get more sunlight.

She looks up at the city, which is very clean, the architecture very modern. Most of the buildings are made of metal formed into rounded edges. There are very few sharp corners anywhere in the city. It seems the shape that's most prevalent in design is that of a flattened sphere. She looks up in wonder. Carter realizes she needs to record the layout of the city, so she fakes being blinded by sunlight so she can use her sleeve camera while pretending to shade her eyes.

Luckily, it's cool, so her leather jacket doesn't seem out of place. She and Aros walk about two hundred yards to a parking lot filled with small vehicles. They look similar to automaker concepts from the 1950s. Aros approaches a silver car that looks like an egg which has been partially flattened. As he gets closer, both sides of the car slide open like pocket doors. He offers his hand to Carter and holds her gently as she sits in the passenger seat on the right side. Aros walks to the other side and sits down next to her. The interior of the vehicle has no instrument panel or steering wheel, but plenty of leg and headroom. As the doors slide shut, Aros issues a voice command to the vehicle in a language she had never heard before.

"I didn't know you spoke a different language in Agartha."

"We have an Agarthan language, but since we've been back on the surface at times, we have learned all of your languages as well. I myself speak six languages from your civilization. But many people here do not speak anything but Agarti."

The car begins to hover and then speeds off above the city. It appears the vehicle is either electric or powered by a source other than gasoline. It also has the same inertial dampening system that the transit car had. As they travel, Carter does her best to aim her cameras at the passing buildings, but they almost seem to be a repeating design, and she can't see anything that would indicate the technologies on her list.

"Is this the way your entire civilization is constructed, or are there differences from city to city?"

"Oh, we have so much diversity in architecture and culture. We have cities that are like this, and on other continents, we have cities like that on your base. We even have people who choose to live in simple structures made from compacted mud or handmade brick."

"That's so interesting how both our civilizations are so different but the same."

"Yes, I think the only difference other than appearances is we have not lost our history and continued technologically. Your civilization lost your history and had to relearn. Of course, some of our people broke our laws and helped from time to time, but for the most part, you have done much of it again on your own."

"So you look at us almost like your children?"

"In the past we have sometimes referred to you in that way, but now you are advancing so quickly. It won't be long before you are caught up."

Aros commands the vehicle with either a direct link to his mind or wherever he currently looks to fly above the city so Carter can get a better view. As they rise higher, she starts to see the inner curvature of the land. She looks up at the artificial sun, and even though it is not as bright as the real sun, it's still difficult to see the land beyond it.

"Can we fly to the other side of the sun and see the rest of the continents?"

"If you wish, but it is nighttime on that side."

Aros increases the vehicles speed towards the artificial sun. The vehicle speed is difficult to judge from her point of view, but the sun grows larger very quickly as they race towards it. The automatic tinting windows adjust to protect their eyes, and after a few minutes of flying, they pass to the night side of Agartha. She looks back at the sun and sees, for the first time, the floating nightshade. It's a black hemisphere, hundreds of miles in diameter that covers one-half of the sun.

"So the shade orbits the sun every twenty-four hours?"

"Actually we decided long ago that our day should be longer. We have a forty-hour day in Agartha. Our agriculture benefits greatly from the increased time in the light because our artificial sun is not as bright as the real one."

She presses her head against the window, looking down at the continents on the nighttime side of Agartha. From this altitude, no details of cities are visible except lights on most of the landmasses.

"So these other races you have here, are they all descendants of those who were part of the exodus from the surface?"

"We have some races, or species that are actually not from this planet. I'm sure you are aware of this, being in the TTRC."

"No, I'm not familiar with that. Are you talking about aliens?"

"Perhaps I have said something I should not have. Since I have, I will not try to deceive you. Yes, your people are also aware of our refugees. I will let your superiors tell you about that, as our treaty forbids me from disclosing those details with you."

Carter is extremely curious now, but one thing she has been accustomed to since she began working at the TTRC is to not press for answers to questions that are above her pay grade. She decides to table the question and ask something else.

"Aros, what do your people think about us at the TTRC?"

She suddenly feels that she just made a mistake by asking him that question. Her mission, as far as she can tell, is a failure. The long list of information she is supposed to be gathering intelligence on has been a complete bust. Nothing on the list has been visible. The only way she is going to get the necessary answers is if she asks for them.

"You are referring to time travel? Well, at first we were slightly concerned about your people altering the past and affecting our own civilization. However, we had already had made a treaty with you of non-interference before you discovered time travel. So when we discovered that your time devices could not enter Agartha, we realized it was harmless to us."

Surprised that Aros knew the pods couldn't come into Agartha, she presses on with the big question. "Why can't the time machines enter Agartha?"

Aros laughs for a few seconds until he looks at her and realizes she really doesn't know. "Oh, that's right, you are a computer operator, why would they tell you. The reason is because of our artificial sun."

"What do you mean?"

"Our sun is suppressed from expanding in an energy field that is similar to the device you call a phase generator. If we were to shut off the shield, the sun would expand and destroy the entire planet. So as long as our sun is being suspended in the field, no other fields can enter. The tremendous energy needed to contain the sun extends its influence far beyond our land. It penetrates deep into the crust of our side of the planet. The only way to have another phase field active is to be outside or inside of the influence of the field. Two fields, however, cannot pass through each other. We would have to release our sun to allow you to use those machines to enter here. Why do you think we had to ride the transit tube? It would be much more convenient to have one of your machines to save time."

Carter realizes the mission is over. With no conceivable way to shut off the Agarthan shield without killing everyone on the planet, there is no point in continuing the mission. She realizes she needs to get back to base and tell Bill.

"Aros, your world is incredible. I wish the rest of our people could travel here to enjoy it."

"One day, when things have evolved enough, I'm confident they will see it. We are very proud of what we have accomplished."

"Why exactly do you prevent us from knowing about Agartha?"

"War!" He says with a stern voice. "We have watched your people for thousands of years wage war against yourselves over matters that we consider to be insignificant."

"So, you have no war? You never had war?"

"We have not engaged in battle amongst ourselves since thousands of years before exodus. When we left, those who stayed behind suffered greatly after the planet recovered from the solar flare damage. Your people emerged from poorly shielded caves to find a world on the surface devoid of the things you took for granted. I have heard your people refer to it as the Stone Age."

"So, forgive me for being so blunt, but why didn't your people help?"

"You have to understand that we begged those who stayed behind to follow us down. For years, we pleaded and warned that once we were below, there would be no second chances. If people chose to stay on the surface they would never be able to rejoin us."

"So you're saying because they made a wrong choice to stay, even after they realized it was a wrong decision, you withheld aid ? They were suffering; don't you think that was cruel?"

"Miss Carter, it was a very long time ago. I was not even born. My ancestors thought differently than we do today. If I was faced with the choice to let you back in, I would."

"So why don't you?"

"First, there are a lot more of you now then when we originally left. Our society might be able to absorb a few million people, but with our ability to grow food and provide shelter as it is, we would not be able to accommodate more than a small fraction of your population. And second, your world is once again livable, so there isn't even a need to try."

She slumps in her seat with her arms folded across her chest, looking through the window as they pass over a large mountain protruding from the Agarthan cloud cover. *The ancient people of Agartha were wrong to lock themselves away while everyone still on the surface suffered,* she thinks.

"Miss Carter, I know it sounds heartless, but please understand how uncertain our survival was when we entered Agartha."

"I do understand. I just wonder what might have happened had the people on the surface received more help from you after."

They circle around the artificial sun and go back towards the capitol city, where Aros takes her to his home, a small single level house on stilts. The house is a flat rectangle with curved windows which form its walls. The house sticks out from the side of a hill with twenty foot stilts supporting it on one side.

"You live alone?"

"Yes, it's just me here."

Aros lands the car on the roof. A door in the flat rooftop opens revealing a staircase, which they walk down. Carter gingerly descends the stairs ahead of Aros, wondering what she's getting herself into. Is this where he rapes her, then erases her memory with some sort of Agarthan rape pill?

When she reaches the bottom, she stops and makes a show of looking at her watch. "They're expecting me back at 11 p.m. for a meeting."

"Yes, you mentioned that earlier. We have plenty of time for a meal, and to converse a little. Are you feeling uncomfortable? Would you like to go back early?"

She pauses as she looks into Aros's eyes as she tries to get a sense of his intentions. "No, supper sounds nice. Thank you."

Aros prepares for her a traditional Agarti meal. She has actually enjoyed the day with him and feels that the fears she had earlier were completely unfounded. However, she's not taking any chances by coming clean with him.

After dinner, they walk to a long sofa that has a view out the window overlooking the capitol. He brings her a glass of wine and sits a foot or so away on the sofa. She decides for her own information before she leaves to find out why his people find women who look like her appealing.

"Aros, there's a rumor on base that Agarthi men prefer women from the surface who look a certain way. Is that true?"

Aros seems embarrassed by the question, laughing uncomfortably. "There are some more traditional men here in our culture who feel that way. Women on the surface who have certain features match those of Agarthan women from our history as the origin of intellect, as well as the teachers of science and technology. Remember, we once looked similar to your people." Aros casually places his elbow on the sofa seat back, draping his hand over her shoulder. "However, you do have a very close resemblance to one of our most beloved historical figures. That is really all it is, just nostalgia for those of us who hold our culture close to their hearts."

She instinctively wants to flinch against his touch, but resists. "Um, tell me more about the Agarthans you called criminals for entering the surface."

"From the beginning there were many who also felt as you do—that the ones who remained should be helped. At first, travel to the surface was permitted to a few who went on humanitarian missions. After a few hundred years, we saw the Earth started to recover, so we stopped going. At that point, many on the surface did not know their own history any longer, and our appearance upset the natural progression of rebuilding society."

"So you're saying Agartha *did* help, but then stopped?"

"Precisely, when we had not appeared on the surface for so long, many forgot about us. It was feared that if we suddenly showed up with advanced technology and rendered assistance, then the people above would grow dependent on us."

"So how did it become a crime?"

"Well, we didn't just fear they would become dependent, I should have said we saw them become that way. At some point Agarthans were mistaken for saviors, or prophets, and sometimes even for gods. So when we saw this mistaken identity occur we began to cloak ourselves and simply gave supplies anonymously."

Carter, touched by the compassion, places her hand on Aros's. "I'm sorry I rushed to judgment earlier. I prejudged your people without knowing the facts."

"I understand. So as you can imagine, the idea of being a god can be appealing to some who are of lesser character, hence the origin of the criminals you inquired about."

She smiles, which Aros takes as a personal connection between them. She feels his hand start to slide downward until his fingers reach her breast.

She corrects his indiscretion. "Aros, I don't want to give you the wrong impression." She moves his hand away.

"My apologies, it must be the wine. I assure you it was an accident." Aros stands and steps back from the sofa. Aros's robe doesn't do much in the way of concealing his excitement.

He'd been a complete gentleman for most of the day. With the exception of copping a cheap feel, he made sure she was entertained, well fed, and back at the transport tube by 10:30 p.m.

When Carter gets back to the base, she immediately drives to TTRC headquarters, where the General and the rest of Carter's team are waiting in the lounge drinking coffee.

Carter runs right past the lounge, not noticing they were all waiting for her inside.

Bill jumps up when he sees her dart by. "Carter!"

She stops and her rubber-soled sneakers make an audible squeak which echoes down the hall. All four of them meet in the middle of the hall.

Bill puts his hands on her shoulders. "Are you OK? Why were you running, did he hurt you?"

"I'm fine, I just was anxious to get back and give you the information."

Sue looks at Bill, realizing this is not just a supervisor being concerned. She could see all day that he'd been pacing, waiting for Carter's return.

Carter pulls out her cell phone and hands it to Sue. "I recorded from the time I got off the transport to the time I got back on. I'm sure there's information you'll be interested in that I may not have realized was important, but I think the biggest question we had is the most pressing."

General Wilson asks, "The shield?"

"Yes, sir, the shield is the sun."

Bill and the General look at each other, realizing there's no way they're ever getting into Agartha.

Bill shoots Carter a confused look. "So what you're saying is, the only way to shut off the shield is to shut off the *sun*?"

"Yes, and not only that, if the sun shuts off, the reaction is released and it will expand. From what I gathered, something like that happening wouldn't be good for anyone inside or on the surface of Earth. You'll hear on the tape, after we got back to his home I asked him what happens if the shield fails on its own. He told me the sun supplies the power that keeps the shield going, so the only way the shield would fail is if the reaction that keeps the sun going fails. It's a failsafe design so their Earth would never be in danger. If the sun died, they could start another one. The sun is over four hundred thousand years in operation, and they expect it to go for billions more years. If we somehow disabled the shield, everyone dies, everywhere."

General Wilson tosses his empty Styrofoam coffee cup on the ground and walks a few feet down the hall with his hands on his hips. Sue connects Carter's phone to a workstation.

"He took you to his house?" Bill asks Carter.

"Relax, nothing happened."

"Oh, OK, good."

"He touched my tit."

"I'll kick his ass."

"He claims he slipped."

"Sure, he did."

Bill and Carter join Sue over at the video terminal reviewing the footage. The General comes over from the hallway after cooling off for a few minutes.

"Miss Carter, is there anything else you saw that would suggest any weaknesses in their perimeter?"

"Not that I saw, but from what I heard from Aros, the field generator that contains the sun prevents them from having time travel technology. I suppose they're not worried about anything we can do, because when they first made their pilgrimage to the center, there would have been nothing of value for us to travel back and do prior to them turning on their artificial sun. I think they're confident that the damage we could do to them is pretty limited."

"That's what I was afraid of."

"General, forgive me for asking, but from what I've seen, these people—with the exception of a few bad apples— are an advanced, peaceful race and they have no need or even interest in coming back to the surface. We don't even have anything they want. So why are we so intent on finding a weakness in their defenses?"

General Wilson doesn't answer, just stares at Carter for a few seconds. He looks at Bill, who shrugs his shoulder as if to say, *'do what you want'*.

"Carter, I don't want to upset you, so I'm not going to go into detail. Let's just say, we may need a place to hide in the near future."

The General lowers his head and walks past Carter, touching her shoulder. She now knows why there's so much urgency. She doesn't know the how or the when, but the question of if has been answered.

"Bill, what's going to happen?"

"Not tonight, let's just go home."

Carter stands firm. "Tell me!"

"There's going to be an extinction soon."

"What do you mean? How do you know?"

"We went forward and saw it. It's going to be bad."

"How bad?"

"It's the end of all life."

"What!?"

"Come on, let's go."

***

Carter doesn't say anything as Bill walks her up to her apartment door.

Before she swipes her card on the lock, she turns to him. "Stay with me tonight."

"Are you sure?"

"Not for sex, just be with me."

"Of course."

They both get into Carters bed, where she lays her head against his shoulder. "So what's going to happen?"

"The same thing that happened to the Agarthans—a sun flare. It goes through cycles, and it's our turn."

"So what, everyone's going to die?"

"Not if I can help it. We asked the Agarthans if they had room for us, and they said no. They told us that they have population controls in place, and our ancestors who stayed behind the first time agreed never to try and enter. It may seem unfair, but we as their descendants are expected to honor the agreement our ancestors made close to a half a million years ago."

"So all this, the collecting of ancient technology, looking for weaknesses in the shield, was for us to invade them?"

Bill sighs as he looks up at the ceiling. "What would you do? We have seven billion people who'll die if we do nothing. When the Agarthans made their escape, their technology was already centuries beyond our own, and they'd already found the hiding place. We have no place to go, and we don't have the same technology that gave them the fighting chance."

Carter sits up in bed. "You went forward in time—did anyone make it?"

"Look when we found out what happened, scientists immediately started checking data to see if it had happened before. So we went back before the Agarthans, and saw it was a cycle. It was happening between 400,000 and 475,000 years in repeating cycles. Sometimes the Earth got lucky and the sun shot and missed. This time, when the activity starts on the sun, it'll shoot off these massive flares every few weeks for about a year straight before it calms down. Some of them hit lightly and sometimes they'll hit repeatedly with lingering radiation."

"So you went forward in time and saw the next one? When is it?"

"In eighty years."

Carter stops and stares at Bill. She slaps him on his arm repeatedly. "You asshole, I thought it was going to happen soon, like next week or something."

Bill is a bit taken back because he has been living with this knowledge for two years now, and he had taken the news much differently than Carter. "Carter, next week or eighty years, what's the difference? We still get wiped out. Everything not made of marble or granite gets vaporized. The oceans boil and almost everything on Earth goes extinct."

"Are you a pessimist?"

"I'm a realist."

"Look, we're here now right? We stayed behind 400,000 years ago. We hid in caves, and we found a way to survive and rebuild. There are millions of species of life that survived. The oceans are full of fish and coral; they survived. The trees, the grass, the flowers. They all survived."

She sits up in bed, puts her hands on Bill, and presses down. "We did it before, why do you think we can't do it again? And now we have something that the Agarthans didn't have—we can travel through time; we can find a way to do something about it this time. Instead of just putting our head in the sand and leaving those who can't hide or are unwilling to hide behind. Besides, let's say we find a way to invade Agartha. Do we conquer them? Do we kill them all and live in their houses? What happens in 400,000 years when the new species on Earth comes to conquer us? This isn't the way humans are. We *solve* problems, not push them off for future generations."

Bill looks into Carters eyes, seeing her passion. He takes her hand with both of his and squeezes it. "Carter, you're amazing."

"Our mission is over Bill."

"What mission?"

"The mission you've been on for two years, looking for a way in to Agartha. Tomorrow we start a new mission, and that's to find a way to protect the planet."

"Carter, I can't just change the mission."

"Why not, you're the senior officer in charge of field operations. Talk to Wilson, get him on board. We'll find a way to fix this."

"I can try, but there's no guarantee he'll listen."

"We'll make them listen. We just have to put our minds to it. Or what's the purpose of living if we don't even try to live?"

Her optimism is palpable and it's something he has never felt before. It makes him feel hope for the first time in the years he has known about the future. "Okay, let's get some sleep, we have a new mission starting tomorrow."

CHAPTER 11: DAWN

On Tuesday morning, Bill wakes up at 5 a.m. Normally he sleeps until 7 a.m., but he slept harder than he had in recent history, which seemed to throw off his internal clock. After years of tossing and turning, he finds that he's held Carter in the same position the entire night. She's asleep with her arm draped over his chest.

He looks at her and realizes today is different. The daylight bulbs outside the window seem different. The scent of her shampoo soothes him. He wonders if he's fallen in love. He's only had a small number of women in his life, less than a dozen, exempting his hookups after a night at the karaoke bar.

Bill glances at the alarm clock next to the bed. He has two hours before he officially needs to get up. Should he wait? Should he wake Carter and make breakfast? Should he make love to her? He lays silently, thinking about these things, but also about the conversation he needs to have with General Wilson.

The General knows there's no chance of invading, but will he listen to the sound logic Bill has yet to form into a sentence? Bill is good at being an officer; he is good at following orders. But the real question is, is he good at convincing the entire chain of command to abandon the mission on the word of a couple of people whose only argument is the word hope. Can he walk into the General's office and say the right combination of words which might change the mission's path?

How can he, a simple Colonel, convince a General to abandon a mission to invade which has been building up for years? Even before the higher-ups learned Earth was doomed, they coveted Agartha. They wanted the technology, they wanted the safety, and they wanted the life of 400,000 years of peace. However, they wanted this all with the intention of using war to get it.

Bill looks at Carter. She's almost magical, so optimistic, so loving. So beautiful and filled with hope. He sees his future now, and it's not what he saw from the window of the pod when he made the trip forward in time. Bill puts his hands on Carter and carefully feels her skin. He doesn't want to disturb her, but he feels the urge to take her, and it becomes overwhelming.

Carter opens her eyes, but doesn't say anything. She's been awake for a few minutes, waiting for him to do something, but since he hasn't, she reaches down under the covers and makes it happen.

"It's only five, we have time."

"Yes Ma'am."

At six, they finally get out of bed. "Well, Bill, It's a new dawn and the mission needs a rewrite if we want to save the world."

Bill sits on the edge of the bed, putting his shoes on. "Save the world, what a set of words. They're not words that are combined all that often." It sounds so simple.

Carter dresses in her uniform after a hot shower. Bill left to shower and change in his apartment. It's now two days in a row they've shown up together at work. Not that Sue would say anything or General Wilson would even notice, but they'd agreed to keep it out of work.

When Bill arrives back at Carters door. "Ready?"

"Let's go."

At the TTRC headquarters, Sue sits in the control room with the control panel removed and a bunch of computer hardware wired into the main board. A large bundle of cables stretches from the control room to their pod, and presents a tripping hazard as Bill and Carter walk into the hangar bay.

"Sue what the heck is all this?" Bill steps over the tangled mess.

"Sorry, sir, I got to the root of the software bug."

"Have you got it fixed?"

"Yes, sir. I guarantee no more random phase-ins."

Bill starts walking towards the pod. "Pod One muster inside."

Carter looks at Sue. "Did he say mustard?"

"It means Bill wants to have a meeting."

"*Mustard?*"

They get inside the pod, where Bill already occupies Carter's seat. "Carter, shut the door."

She does and stands next to Sue by the control panel.

"OK, our mission is over. We're no longer on a mission to enter Agartha. Our new mission is to stop the world from extinction. Specifically, from solar flares. Sue; I want you to do research on solar flares and find out what causes them, and what blocks them."

"Yes, sir."

"Carter, we need to get as much help as we can. Call on Ambassador Dennia and let him know we're facing the same fate as his people faced. Find out if his people have developed any technology that can help us prevent or block a solar flare. It's been 400,000 years since the last solar cycle, and his people must have given this some thought."

Carter glows with excitement, her eyes glazing from the energy she feels from Bill's command over the situation. "Got it."

Bill stands up. "I'm going to see the General, and inform him of our mission change. I want options in seventy-two hours from both of you. I'll get the General to order the rest of the base to make this a priority. I'll make him get the full support of the President and the rest of the world's leaders."

Bill and Sue head out of the pod while Carter sits in her seat and thinks of a way to approach the Ambassador again. She's already met with him once under false pretenses and lied about what she does at the TTRC.

She steps out of the pod and walks down the hallway towards the elevators. As she passes General Wilson's office, she finds Bill standing in front of the General's desk. The glassed door is closed, so she can't hear what he is saying to him. The General sees Carter walking past when he tells Bill to bring her in.

Bill opens the door. "Carter, can you come in here, please?"

She turns back and goes in. Wilson points to the two chairs in front of his desk. "Please, sit."

Bill and Carter look at each other as they take their seats. Carter doesn't know where in the conversation Bill has already been with the General, so she waits for a cue.

"Miss Carter, the Colonel is saying that you advised him, after your mission to Agartha, that there's no hope of the Agarthans allowing us entry into their land. Before you say anything, I want you to know I agree. I also agree that the only option we have left is exactly what Bill is proposing, and that's we need to change tactics and move from trying to infiltrate to trying to cooperate. Now I'm going to the President this afternoon because I didn't sleep at all last night, and I came to the same conclusions the two of you did. From now on, your team is on point. I want you to head up this new mission. Colonel, I will get you the resources you need to accelerate the program."

The General leans in and puts his arms on his large wood desk. "Carter, Bill tells me the Ambassador has taken a liking to you. Now, I know you're not a diplomat, and I don't want to suggest anything inappropriate, but do you think you can create a trust between our two peoples through him?"

"General, I lied to him about what I did here, and that's going to come out eventually. My idea is to just reveal that we had ulterior motives and come clean with exactly what we want."

The General pauses. "That'll be risky; we could violate the treaty from that."

"Yes, but unless we can find a way without their help, we have nothing left to lose."

"Agreed."

Dismissed, Bill and Carter head into the hall. Bill says to Carter as they're walking towards the elevator, "Do you have any ideas yet?"

"Well, I sort of have an idea, but it's just a hunch at this point. I definitely need to find out some more information from the Agarthans before I'm sure. There's a part of the Agarthan story that's missing and I need to find out the truth."

"What's this hunch?"

"It's something that Aros said when we were at his house. He mentioned the difference between his people and ours is that we lost our historical record after the solar flares, but they managed to keep theirs. I need to see those records because there's a missing part that I don't even think *they* know about."

"Well, you're definitely better at spotting a story than me. Let me know if you need my help."

"I will."

Carter stops at the elevator and watches as Bill gets in. After the doors close, she turns and walks back down the hall to archives, where Sue sits at a computer compiling data on solar flares.

"Hey Sue, how goes the search?"

"It's pretty easy to find information about the sun, but no one has really ever written about ways to block a solar flare. Solar flares that could wipe out the Earth are not usually small enough where a device we place in orbit could do us any good. These things are massive." Sue pulls out a blank sheet of paper and draws a circle on it about the size of a green pea. "Let's say that's the Earth."

"Okay."

Sue then draws a shape similar to a tear drop, where the widest part is the size of an orange. "The Earth-killing solar flare could be as big in scale as this, or even bigger. Our magnetic field surrounding the Earth would do us no good in a flare that size. Sure, some life would survive, but we'd face the same civilization reset as the Agarthans did." Sue looks around the archive room to see if anyone else is there, then whispers, "Come here and look at my screen. This is the video Bill and I made when we went forward eighty years to the next flare."

Carter hesitantly walks around the table Sue's computer sits on. Sue opens the video file, and it begins with an image from about two million miles away from the Earth. The moon and Earth are visible, and Carter watches Earth rotate in space. Suddenly there's a flash of bright red light from off screen. Then a wave of red and orange plasma hundreds of times wider than the Earth engulfs the entire screen. As the plasma gets closer and closer, Earth seems unaffected, until suddenly the plasma strikes from behind and swirls as the Earth's magnetic field tries to protect it. The atmosphere instantly starts moving, causing the clouds to vanish in less than a second.

Only seconds pass and the atmosphere is completely gone. The entire surface of the Earth glows from fire. The oceans steam. The flare passes away from Earth and impacts the moon, which gets smoother but doesn't catch fire.

Carter watches in horror as the boiling oceans give off steam that blankets the whole planet. "Shut it off." Her voice cracks from sudden, overwhelming emotion.

"Sorry, I should have warned you how violent it was."

Carter falls back into a rolling chair and slaps her hands on her head as if trying to stop her head from exploding.

Sue pulls Carters chair closer so they're hidden behind the computer monitor. "Shhh. Don't make any noise."

"Sorry." Carter sniffs and wipes her eyes. "So who survives?"

Sue puts her hands on Carters knees. "No one. This one will end everything. It's the biggest we've seen in Earth's history."

"So did you go forward to see if life comes back to Earth?"

"It never does."

"Oh my god!"

They squeeze each other's hands.

"What about Agartha?" Carter asks.

"We don't know if they survive or not. We know the shield they have survives because no matter how far in the future we went, we couldn't phase in to their city. We went all the way to the end of the sun's life and never got an answer. With the oceans boiled off it's not likely they survived since the internal ocean and the one on the surface are shared."

Carter takes a deep breath and lets it out slowly. She looks at Sue and smiles as if to say *thank you*. She slaps her legs to cause enough pain to divert her emotions, then asks about what she had originally came in to the archive to do.

"I wanted to find out what we have as far as the Agarthan history."

"Well, not much after they went underground, but we watched them make the five-year journey. After they were mostly underground, their shield prevented us from knowing anything until 1947. The Agarthans provided us with a very limited history. Mostly information on the kings and queens."

"Show me what we have."

"Sounds like you've something cooking."

"I do, but I don't want to speculate until I know the full story."

Sue logs into the computer and shows Carter how to do basic searches to access the database. Carter sits at the computer for hours reading everything they have on the ancient people who formed Agartha. She completely misses lunch and at around 8 p.m., Bill walks into the archive room with a couple cups of coffee and sandwiches.

"Carter?" Then louder: "Carter?"

She's so lost in the writings and video footage, she doesn't hear Bill. He puts the coffee cup in front of her face, startling her. She jerks the headphones behind her head and rests them around her neck.

"What?" She snaps, until she sees who's disturbed her.

"Take a break."

"Bill! Sorry. What time is it?"

He puts her cup of coffee and sandwich on the table next to her computer. "It's time to eat and take a break."

She takes the headphones off. Reaching up with both arms above her head, she stretches out her back muscles. "My back is killing me."

Bill takes the chair Sue had been sitting in earlier.

"Where did Sue go?"

"She went home hours ago. She called me to check up on you. When you didn't answer your phone or your doorbell, I tracked your phone here."

She takes a few large bites from her sandwich, not even realizing how hungry she is until the first bite hits her throat. She drinks about half the cup of coffee in one long sip.

"So what are you working on?"

She wipes her mouth with her jumpsuit sleeve and turns back to the computer. "Look, before the people of Agartha left the surface, they lived in a somewhat advanced civilization. They had decent architecture, sort of like they have now, they had air and land transportation but no space flight."

"So what?"

"So everything! If they didn't have space flight, and we never found any of their satellites in orbit, then how did they know the sun was about to wipe them out?"

Bill stops eating.

Carter starts playing a video from one of Bill's missions to 400,433 BC. "Look, the footage you shot from right before they went in the Earth."

Bill leans toward the computer screen. "Yeah, that was the ancient power plant, but we couldn't get inside."

"Exactly, and why not?"

"Our pods couldn't pass through an energy fluctuation that surrounded the power plant walls."

She stares at him encouragingly, waiting for him to realize what he just said.

"I don't get where you're going with this."

Carter slaps Bill on the side of the head. "The artificial sun, you dummy."

"I still don't get it."

She takes the sandwich out of his hand and puts it on the table. "Aros told me the artificial sun was contained in the energy field to prevent it from expanding. In your video, the power plant had the same fail-safe protection. Unlike our own nuclear power plants, if *their* power plant gives off dangerous radiation, the shield protects the population. To me that means it's not the same type of nuclear as ours. So I did a little research, and what I realized is the power plant was a reactor, but not like what we use now."

"So they invented a different type of reaction that powers the shield."

"Exactly, they have been using the same technology for over 400,000 years and have adapted it to act as their sun light source."

"OK, well, that's great, but what does that have to do with them not having a space program?"

"I'll get to that in a minute. So, I called engineering and spoke to someone named Gene who knows about how our phase generators work. He told me that there's plutonium in the engine core, and it generates the phase field around our pod. Thanks, by the way, for warning me about the radioactive core that's literally right under my chair in the pod."

Bill picks up his sandwich, smiling as if to say 'oops.'

"So I asked Gene, how much plutonium would be needed to make a phase field seven hundred miles wide like the Agartha sun has. He said it's not physically possible to put that much plutonium in the same place. It's more than what he called critical mass. It would just explode like a nuclear bomb."

"So that means they're using an element that's more stable and capable of fusion that will last for billions of years!"

"Exactly!" She slaps his legs repeatedly like bongo drums.

"So we need to find out what that element is, then."

"Yes, and I know just the skinny bald guy to ask."

"Wait a second, what are we going to do with the element once we get it?"

She stares incredulously because he just can't see the big picture. "Bill, sweetie, we're going to build a shield around the Earth that's capable of blocking a solar flare."

Bill stands up quickly, still holding his sandwich. "Carter! You're a genius!"

Carter stands up and Bill hugs her tight.

"We have to go see the General right now." He drops his sandwich on the table and they run out of the archive room and down to the General's office. When they get there, the General is on the phone.

"Yes Mr. President. I'll let you know in forty-eight hours of our plan. Yes, sir, yes Sir. Goodnight, sir."

He hangs up and waves Bill and Carter through the door. "That went better than I thought. He only screamed at me for one hour." The General reaches into his pocket for a handkerchief and dries the sweat from the long phone call off his ear. "What are you both still doing here?"

"General, Carter figured out how to save the Earth."

The General walks to the coat rack, pulling his hat and jacket off. "Colonel, it's late, I haven't slept in more than twenty-four hours, and I'm in no mood for jokes."

"General it's not a joke I assure you," Carter says as she takes a step towards him.

Bill puts his hand on Carter's shoulder. "Break it down quickly for him."

The General looks at his watch and starts walking out the door. "Yes Miss Carter, please make it quick."

"Sir, the Agarthan artificial sun is powered by an element the Agarthans have. That element provides the power to the Agarthan shield that contains the sun. I believe if we were to acquire this element from the Agarthans, we can create our own reactor and generate a similar shield to protect the entire planet from the solar flare." Carter turns to Bill as the General gets a few steps from the elevator. "Was that quick enough?"

General Wilson stops walking and turns around. "My God, that's brilliant. It might just work. In my office, both of you."

They go into the General's office, where Carter spends about twenty minutes laying out the research she'd done that brought her to this conclusion.

The General calls the President back, and after it ends, the General looks back at Bill and Carter. "Have a mission plan for the acquisition of the element on my desk by the end of the day tomorrow."

They both say in unison, "Yes sir."

As the General walks out of his office, he turns back to Carter. "You've become an invaluable asset to this operation, and I'm very glad you chose to join us. I couldn't be more impressed by your performance so far."

"Thank you, sir."

"Oh and Carter, you have mustard on your shoulders and your back. Please try and maintain a clean uniform. Goodnight Carter, Colonel."

When the elevator doors close in front of the General, Carter turns to Bill and jumps up and down in front of him, letting little screams. Bill smiles as he watches her revel in her moment of excitement. She leaps up one last time, and Bill catches her as she wraps her legs around his waist. They quickly kiss, then remember there are cameras everywhere, so he puts her down. Composing themselves, they walk to the elevator. Bill thinks, *He could explain it as simple excitement and celebration if anyone asks.*

They decide to go out to the club and have some drinks, a decent dinner and play a little pool. At the end of the evening, they wind up back at Carter's apartment and spend the night together for the third night in a row.

CHAPTER 12: LITTLE PURPLE ROCKS

The next morning, Bill and Carter get ready to start their mission plan. Carter grabs the first shower and then while Bill takes his, she makes them another one of her to-go breakfasts—this time, a pancake sausage wrap with a couple foamy cappuccinos.

Carter's doorbell chimes unexpectedly. Not sure who it is, she looks through the view port in the door. It's Sue. Carter starts to panic and decides to open the door and tell Sue she's just on her way out, so as not to broadcast Bill's presence. She grabs her breakfast bag and opens the door, standing firm so Sue doesn't come in.

"Hey girl, I was just on my way out the door."

"Good morning, great I was just coming down to see if you were OK. I left last night and you were still hard at work, and I was worried about you."

"Yeah, I'm doing good now. I got a lot of work done and we may have a mission plan by the end of the day. Let's go in together."

Sue steps back, making room for Carter to move past. Carter closes the door and starts walking down the hall. She looks back at Sue, who is still stands at her apartment door.

"You coming?"

"Sure, but don't you want to wait for Bill to get out of the shower?"

Carter stops, and turns back to Sue with a bowed head.

"Listen, I'm your teammate; we don't keep secrets from each other about this type of stuff."

Carter feels bad. Sue has been so nice to her since day one and she obviously cares for Bill. "I'm sorry. Bill and I thought we should just keep it at the apartment and not risk causing any problems at work."

"I said we shouldn't keep secrets about this type of things from each other, I didn't say we shouldn't keep it a secret from the *General.*"

Carter realizes what a great friend Sue can actually be. She swipes her card and goes back inside with Sue. "You want a sausage pancake wrap?"

"Sure, thanks."

Just then, the shower shuts off and Bill comes out wearing a small towel around his waist. He walks into the kitchen and picks up the cup of coffee Carter had left on the counter for him.

He gives her a kiss. "Thanks babe, I'm going to go get dressed."

Bill completely misses the fact that Sue is sitting on the couch, until she says, "Good idea, sexy man."

He turns and sees Sue sitting there with a big smile on her face. "Sue? Oh, crap!"

"Relax, I'm on your team, remember?"

Bill puts the coffee cup down in front of his towel as if it would block any unintended wardrobe malfunctions. "I'll be quick."

Sue laughs. "Not *too* quick, I hope, for Carter's sake."

Carter laughs loud as Bill hurries in to the bedroom and shuts the door.

"So how did you figure it out?" She asks Sue.

"Come on, I have multiple PhD's and degrees. I have a genius IQ and have spent many hours in the field observing many cultures. Oh, and I heard the shower when you opened the door."

"Yeah, that was probably a dead giveaway."

"Look, I know what it's like to fall in love with someone you work with. Maybe I can help you not make the same mistake I made."

"What was that?"

"I told General Wilson about it."

"Good tip."

"I have no problem with it. I worked better with Steve when we were dating than before. We used to spend days in Andromeda staring at stars and planets looking for a sign of life. If we didn't have the occasional romp on the pod floor we probably would have gone crazy just staring at each other."

"Oh, you only have two people in deep space pods?"

"Yeah, it's all instrument recordings and simple photos, we didn't need any fancy photography."

"So you two had sex on the pod floor? How was that? Was that comfortable?"

"We had sex on the pod floor, on the pod seats, in the pod shower. When we were out of gravitational pulls of stars and planets we would have zero G sex, which is a lot harder to do than you would think." Sue can tell Carter's mind is racing. "Don't worry, I'll call in sick or take a walk every once in a while for you."

Carter laughs as she puts her hands in front of her face to hide her blush. Bill walks out in his uniform, holding his coffee. He looks at Sue, then averts his eyes from embarrassment. He looks at Carter. "You OK? Why is your face red?"

Sue chimes in. "You'll find out."

Bill looks confused but he doesn't want to say anything until he figures out how Sue will take the news.

They all head out with Sue leading the way. Carter leans into Bill as they walk through the door from the apartment. "Don't worry Bill, she won't say anything."

Bill looks at Sue, who is a few feet ahead. "Thanks, Sue."

"You're welcome."

***

Later, at the ready room, Carter makes print outs of her research and discusses the nuclear reactor idea with Sue.

Sue has a difficult time figuring out how the mysterious element could possibly provide this much energy for billions of years like a star does without needing either electrical input or constant balancing of the element.

"Obviously the reactor works, Bill and I saw many of them prior to the exodus and you saw the artificial star. However, my knowledge of physics is apparently child's play or just completely wrong when it comes to figuring out how to make it work. At least not without an actual sample of the element."

"That's why I'm going to call Aros and arrange another meeting. If I can explain what's coming and convince him to share the technology, then we can work together to create a big enough reactor to form a shield."

Bill stands at the podium reading the treaty between the Agarthans and surface humans. "Our treaty strictly forbids any trade in technology."

"That treaty was written so each of our civilizations could live without the interference of the other, correct?"

"Yup." Bill closes the file folder.

"Well the treaty won't mean a damn thing if the Earth is scorched dry and the oceans stop flowing from our side into theirs."

"We have no way of knowing if the ocean on their side will be affected. For all we know, they'll live long past five billion years from now when the sun dies. They're a city in a bottle." He sits next to Carter and Sue.

Just then General Wilson walks into the ready room. He immediately says, "As you were," to prevent Bill and Sue from following military protocol of standing at attention when the commanding officer enters a room. "Team, how are things progressing?"

"General, my team and I are still developing a plan to acquire the element. We're working on a method of getting the Agarthans to share it with us."

"Good, Colonel. I hate to say this, but it's still business as usual, and we have our case load backing up from the software glitch of the last four days."

Bill looks frustrated. "General, I thought the President was onboard?"

"He is, Colonel, but as you know the oversight committee is not aware of the solar flare extinction, and they want regular results from the TTRC. We have missions that may seem pointless right now, but if we want to maintain our uninterrupted support from congress, we need to keep on schedule."

Bill walks over to the podium, shaking his head. He tries to hide his disdain for the congress but the utterance of the word *'fuck'* can be heard clearly multiple times coming from him.

"Believe me, Colonel, I dropped the F bomb a dozen times just walking down the hall to come and talk to you.

Orders are orders. Remember who keeps us wearing these uniforms."

"I understand."

"Colonel, I'm distributing Pod One's mission list among the other pods, but you still have two missions that if you bang them out you can be done by the end of business on Thursday."

"Yes sir." Bill takes the two mission folders.

The General turns and walks out of the ready room, clearly as upset with the ignorance of Washington as Bill is.

Bill opens the mission folder and reads for a few seconds while standing next to the ready room chairs. "Looks like we got a collection mission and a surveillance mission. Which do you want to do first?"

"Either is fine," Sue replies.

Carter sees Bill just wants to get them done, so she figures the faster the better. "Might as well do the collection first, we can leave the longer mission for last. What are we supposed to collect?"

Bill looks down at the collection mission folder. He stares at the mission plan, then shuts the folder and walks out of the ready room.

"Should we come with you?" Carter calls after him.

Sue grabs Carter's arm and shakes her head no. Bill walks down the hall to the Generals open office.

"Come in, Colonel," General Wilson says to Bill's knock.

Bill shuts the door behind him. "General...sir. I wanted to talk to you about the missions."

"Colonel, do you have a problem following orders?"

"Sir, no not following orders. Sir, I have concerns that my team is not being utilized by the TTRC properly. This mission is a collections operation to get a missing stone from the original construction of the White House so the President can place it on a shelf, and the surveillance mission is to watch an entire forty-eight hours to see if anyone drops a ring shaped like a watch into some coffin in 15th century China. Sir, these are hardly priority missions for the team when..."

"Colonel, I'll stop you right there." General leans forward and snatches the two mission folders out of Bills hands. "I'll give these to Major Daniels' team." He places them on his desk, and goes back to reading something on his computer screen. "Colonel, is there anything else?"

"Sir, am I in trouble?"

"Colonel, you will be if you don't find that element, and figure out how to use it."

Bill stands at attention, snapping his feet on the floor. "Yes sir." He heads back to the hangar bay. When he gets to there, he stops and stands in the doorway.

Bill had advanced to the rank of Colonel quickly because of his ability to follow orders accurately and without question. During his time as a combat pilot, he relied on his strict adherence to the chain of command and his ability to follow orders. These were key aspects in his personality that not only sped up his movement through the ranks as an officer, but also kept himself and his fellow squadron pilots alive during combat.

For Bill, it was out of the ordinary to question orders, but his gut told him that time was important in finding the solution to the shield problem, and if he lost focus, it could cost the world its very survival.

Back in the hangar bay, Carter immediately notices Bill no longer has the folders with him. "What happened?"

He walks over to the coffee pot and pours himself a cup in an extra-large mug that has an F-16 airplane painted on the side. His hands shake as he fills his mug.

"Now we get back to work and save the world."

They all sit down at a table near the front of the room. Bill lays down a small touch screen tablet and begins the mission-planning meeting.

"Carter, did the Ambassador tell you what the name of the element was that they used for their artificial sun?"

"No, we didn't talk about how the sun is powered, only that the shield is powered by the sun."

"OK, so that's the first thing we need to find out. Call the Ambassador now and see if he'll tell you more about the power source."

Carter reaches into her pocket and takes out her phone. She calls Aros's direct line and a woman answers.

"Ambassador Dennia's office."

"Hi, this is Evelyn Carter, I was looking to speak to the Ambassador, if that's possible?"

"Miss Carter, I have your name on my list of calls to put through, but I'm sorry, the Ambassador is home right now, and there is a do not disturb until Friday."

"Well, maybe you can help me."

"I will do my best. What is it you need?"

"Well, the Ambassador was giving me a tour the other day of his home town in Agartha's capitol city, and he was telling me about the artificial star."

"Yes, the Ambassador is very proud of the achievements of Agartha."

"Yes, it was a fascinating tour. But I can't remember the word he used describing the power source of the artificial star."

"Oh, you are referring to the plumestones."

"Plumestones, that's what it was. Is there any way I can get more information on the plumestones? I'm working on a project here on base and I mentioned it to my supervisor who was interested in the technology."

"I'm sorry Miss Carter, plumestones are not available any longer. All of them where used when we built our sun. They were gathered from all over our past civilization well before the exodus and stockpiled."

"Well, that's disappointing. You seem to know a lot about the history of the plumestones, is there anything in the Agarthan historical record I could read about on the subject?"

"Yes, look in the Agarthan exodus writings that were shared with your people under royal jewels. There is the part when the purple crystals that made up the royal crown early in the exodus where removed in sacrifice to power the new sun. The Queens crown was the largest of the plumestones we had."

"Thank you, you've been helpful. I'll read the section right away."

"Goodbye Miss Carter, I will let the Ambassador know you called."

"Have a good day."

Carter ends the call. "Looks like we need to find out where these plumestones came from."

The three of them sit for a few hours in the archive room going through the Agarthan historical documents. The Agarthans are a very proud civilization, and the historical record had been written in a pompous and egotistical manner, describing how they overcame eons of suffering and rose to be masters of the world.

Carter scans through the documents referring to thousands of years of kings and queens who ruled various tribes of what would later be the nation of Agartha.

She flips page after page on her computer screen looking for images or words that would indicate royalty or the royal crown. The archive is surprisingly large, but the

Agarthans had been very careful not to reveal how any of their technology works.

It becomes more and more frustrating until Carter stops at a page which shows a drawing in pastel colors of a woman wearing a crown. "Guys, look. It's a crown with little purple stones."

Bill and Sue look at the Queen of the ancient Agarthans on the screen. She stands at the top of a staircase, waving at thousands of people below her. The section of the text is titled *The Queen of the Fifty-Second Order.*

"That's it!" Bill exclaims. "Now we just have to go there and get those little purple rocks."

Sue puts her hands on her hips as she analyzes the image. "Yeah, but when was the fifty-second order?"

Bill says, "Well, we'll just have to wait for Dennia to call back on Friday and ask him."

Carter lightly slaps Bill on the shoulder with the back of her hand. "What's that big metal bell-shaped thing sitting out there in the hangar bay?"

"See, that's why I need you. We'll just go back and ask them personally. I need to get permission to phase in first. This may not happen today, so why don't you both head on out for the night, and I'll go see the General to get authorization."

Carter and Sue walk with Bill down the hall to the General's door. As Bill turns into the office, Carter gives him a wink, then remembers that was a big no-no, so she salutes him as she walks backwards with a smile. He instinctively salutes her back.

"Calling it a day, Colonel?"

"No, sir. I mean, that depends on my request for a phase in."

"Phase in to when?"

"Sir, we determined that the ancient Agarti crown is encrusted with the element we need to build the shield."

"So, you're going to steal the crown?"

"Well, sir, I thought we would borrow it, or maybe just borrow a single crystal from the crown so we can analyze it and determine what it's made from."

Bill's nerves tingle. Never before has a collection mission been authorized without the express written permission of the Congress. In this case, the Congress cannot be told because the mission is top secret.

The General sits still for a moment, and then issues the order. "Colonel, I'll inform the President and call you as soon as we're cleared to go."

"Yes sir, should I assemble my team now?"

"No, take the evening to relax. We'll schedule the mission for first light."

"Yes sir, goodnight, sir."

Bill rides the elevator to the lobby, where Carter and Sue wait for him. Carter sees him exit the elevator and walks towards him. "So are we going now?"

"No, we need to wait for the President to authorize this as an off-the-books mission."

"So now what do we do?"

"Well, my suggestion is we get some crab legs. I'm dying for some hot buttered crab legs."

"And karaoke!" Sue adds.

"Bingo," Bill replies.

Sue pulls out her phone and calls her husband Steve. "Hey, Bill is singing tonight, are you in?" She looks at Bill and gives him the "OK" sign with her hand.

The three take Carter's car to the club, where she meets Steve in the parking lot of Hangout 18.

"Hi, Evelyn." Steve takes Carters hand.

Sue leans in and tells Steve, "Just call her Carter, she prefers that."

"Sorry...Carter."

"No problem, Sue's told me a lot about you."

Steve smiles and they all walk into the club. Sarah the club server sees Bill and gives him a big wave from behind the bar. She grabs four menus and brings them over to the booth that Carter and Bill had sat in a few nights ago.

"Beers all around?"

Carter says, "You have any single malt scotch?"

Bill reaches under the table and gives her thigh a firm rub. "Single malt, I'm impressed."

"Sure, but normally it's reserved for 05's and above, but since you're with Bill, I'll just put his name on it," Sarah says in a conspiratorial tone.

"I think we all want the same thing, so if you could bring us all a big bucket of steamed crab legs and lots of melted butter, that would be great."

"Sure, be right out with the drinks."

The drinks arrive and Steve looks at Carter. "So, you're a former independent journalist?"

"Well I wouldn't say *journalist*. I never actually reported or wrote a story, but I try and give the anchors video that tells the story they can narrate over."

Steve drinks about half his beer as he nods. "I gotcha. Well, I know that in the time division, your job is crucial to the mission. I bet Bill is glad to finally have someone who knows what they're doing with a camera on his team."

"I couldn't be happier. Carter's an expert at seeing the story. She has the eye for capturing what's important."

Carter blushes, and feels an overwhelming sense of being needed. "You know this is a much better job than I had before. I feel so much more at home and relaxed. I've never been on a team before either, with the exception of a short time working with another photographer; I've pretty much been on my own for ten years since I was seventeen."

"Well, Sue says you and Bill make a great team, I'm glad to see you two are banging."

Carter's eyes widen and Bill spits a little beer out of his mouth. Sue immediately interrupts. *"Banging* as in working well together, is what he meant to say."

"So Steve," Carter says, "Sue tells me you're charting the galaxy for planets for us to live on?"

"Yeah but not specifically to live on, just a basic cataloging of habitable worlds. Really the mission is to see if anyone else is out there other than us, and then determine potential contact if they exist."

"So, like aliens? Have you found any yet?"

"Well, that depends on what you mean by aliens. We have charted a number of habitable planets with life, but so far the life is mostly bacteria on the small end, and sea life on the larger end of the spectrum. Intelligent life like humans is still undiscovered."

"Wow, that's interesting. How long have we been looking?"

"Sue and I started two years ago in the Andromeda galaxy and we worked for about eight months. After she moved to time division, I kept at it."

"So after all that time, not one smart alien?"

"In Andromeda no, but we have pods in our galaxy as well, so you never know what will be found."

"What interesting things have you found in Andromeda?" Carter asks.

"We haven't found intelligent life yet, but we've found a number of planets that are in the stage of development that Earth was before man. Some planets that are almost the same size and atmosphere that have millions of species of life. One planet we're studying has such a similar ecosystem that if you went there you wouldn't realize you were on another planet unless you looked up and saw the three moons."

"Oh wow. Is that something that'll be released to the public?"

"Probably not. The mandate of planetary exploration keeps findings classified until the public needs to know. If for some reason we ever need to leave Earth, that would be a potential destination."

Carter looks at Bill as if she has just figured out the solution to the coming catastrophe. He realizes what she is thinking and interjects an important fact.

"Steve knows it would take a hundred years to load six people at a time in the pods and transport them to another planet. Not to mention all the things we'd need to bring with us that wouldn't fit in the pods."

Steve nods in agreement. "Bill's right. We have it as an option. We're finding lots of stars that are similar to ours, but the planets in their solar systems are not in the habitable zone. They're either too close or too far from the sun. It's amazing how rare it is to find a solar system where a planet is in just the right place for life. It's a shame, too, because some of these solar systems are almost perfect. One that we just cataloged is particularly fascinating. It's a young star with a very low UV index. It has no asteroid belts or cloud of comets due to fifteen large gas giants in the outer section of the solar system. There's also a very wide habitable zone, but no planets in the zone. We find a lot of that."

Carter can't help but try to come up with a way to move the people of the Earth to another planet. She doesn't know what the population of Agartha is, but she does the math in her head of how long each trip would take and how many people she could save over the next eighty years. She knows there has to be a way.

After they finish dinner, the DJ goes up on the stage. He has a nametag on his shirt that says Eddy, but he put some numbers on it so it reads '87Eddy 80'.

Carter notices the odd nametag and asks Bill, "What do the numbers mean on his name tag?"

Bill points to Sue to give the answer.

"His name is Eddy Stern; he's a crowd favorite because he sounds like the lead singer of Queen. He's also a physicist in the TTRC applied physics lab. The numbers on his name tag are a joke from the periodic table of elements. The 87 is the symbol 'FR', then his name Eddy and then the number 80 which is the number for Mercury."

Carter laughs, "Oh I get it, very clever."

Science jokes and plays on words seem to be part of the culture on base. As the music plays, more and more people pour into the club. Karaoke night is very popular, and always draws big crowds.

The four of them sit at the table drinking and eating chips and salsa.

"Where are you putting all that scotch?" Bill asks after Carter tosses back her third glass.

"You have those pills, so I'm not too worried," Carter says, a little too loud.

Bill laughs, but doesn't tell Carter he forgot to bring the anti-intoxicants with him. One of the guys from the advanced weapons lab three buildings down from the TTRC gets up on stage and sings a killer rendition of Billy Joel's 'Captain Jack' which gets the whole club singing along. Eddy does his regular two song set of 'Bohemian Rhapsody' and 'Somebody to Love'. After an hour of listening from the table, Carter grows uncomfortable from sitting. Bill takes notice and gets up to let her slide out.

Eddy sees Bill stand and goes up to the microphone. "Bill's up next!"

The crowd turns to look at Bill as Eddy starts chanting "Bill, Bill, Bill."

Bill walks over to the piano on the edge of the stage. Almost everyone who sings on karaoke night uses the programmed music on the karaoke machine, but Bill is classically trained on the piano and whenever he gets a chance, he comes to the club just to play.

"Bill is a big Styx fan, wait till you hear his singing voice." Sue says to Carter.

Carter smiles, watching the crowd cheer.

He sits at the piano and pulls the microphone over. "OK troops, here's one I've been thinking about all day. It's called 'The Best of Times' by the best band in the world— Styx."

His voice is amazing, and Carter is shocked. As he sings, Carter, who isn't familiar with the song, listens closely. She's a little buzzed, but stands back by the booth holding her drink.

The lyrics make so much sense to the dire situation they're facing. It's so prophetic to their upcoming mission. She feels her mouth get dry and her throat close up.

As Bill finishes the song, he looks over to Carter and sees her face is red and her eyes are puffy. He stands up, about to go over and console her, but the crowd starts chanting his name again. Carter waves him on to do another song.

He mouths *are you sure?*

She nods and smiles.

He looks out at the crowd and says, "Another one?" to loud applause. "This is another one by STYX called 'Come Sail Away.'"

Bill plays the piano beautifully and matches the original like he had recorded it himself. This time Carter's emotions move to hope and happiness as she listens. The whole club sings along, and they cheer loudly when he finishes and steps off the stage and makes his way back to the booth.

Steve leans into Bill. "You do know Carter has a thing for you, don't you?"

Bill looks at Steve with a certain amount of hesitation. "Really?"

"It's OK if you want to ask her to dance, she's not military."

Bill stops, frozen in thought, thinking back to his officer training, and for the life of him, he can't remember any rule about fraternizing with civilians under his command. "Maybe I *will* ask her to dance."

At this point, Carter's feeling of desire is overpowering as she heads back toward the booth. She feels as if the entire room can hear her heart beating.

"Would you care to dance?" Bill asks as she approaches.

"Oh my god, yes."

Sue and Steve lean into each other and smile.

Bill takes Carter by the hand and leads her to the middle of the dance floor. One of the guys from the NRO office takes the stage and starts singing Five for Fighting's 'World'. Carter looks into his eyes and sees for the first time, he has a sense of hope for the future. They dance without breaking eye contact, both silent, and the people around them are blurs in their peripheral vision. She wants to speak, but she can't. He wants to say something clever, but his voice is locked and dry.

She regains control over her voice and says the first thing she can think of.

"Take me."

CHAPTER 13: A VERY LONG SCAN

Bill wakes up to Carters alarm clock and reaches over her to shut it off.

"Carter," Bill whispers into her ear then kisses her on the cheek. She smiles as she stretches and puts her arm over his chest. "Come on, it's time to save the world."

She kisses him, gazes into his eyes.

Bill puts his hand on her cheek. "What?"

She hesitates like she's finding the right words. "Let's go save the world." It's not what she's intended to say, though. She wanted to say *'I love you.'*

They both roll out of bed at the same time and stare at each other for a few seconds as both fight the urge to jump back in. After a quick breakfast and a large cup of coffee, they drive to headquarters.

Bill goes straight to General Wilson's office. "Good morning, General, have we got a go on the mission?"

"Yes, Colonel, the President authorized me from this point forward to do whatever it takes to accomplish the mission last night."

Bill smiles, but then looks confused. "You should have called me sir; we were ready to go last night."

"I figured your crew deserved a night of rest before the mission."

Bill knows not much rest had been had, but he keeps quiet about it, saluting the General and heading to the hangar bay.

When he arrives at the ready room, Bill has no folder to grab from the mission tray. He walks to the podium, looking at Carter as she smiles from the front row. Sue arrives and sits next to her.

"Well, we know what our mission is, and we're going to play it by ear from here on out. We need to get at least one of these purple crystals. Let's get straight to the pod and figure out where these things are."

Sue and Carter follow Bill into the gear room. Bill goes over to the wardrobe rack and starts looking for appropriate costumes. "The clothes that the Agarti wore in that drawing with the queen were just simple robes, right?"

"From what I saw, yes, but I'd say we should also bring other types just in case."

Bill pulls about a dozen different styles off the rack and hands them to Carter. He opens the weapons locker and grabs a couple tranquilizer dart guns. Sue picks up a metal case from the tool locker and places it on the table.

Carter walks over to take a look. "What's that?"

"This is a portable version of the mining particle beam that we adapted for collections. The one on the pod can hold an object up to the size of a house. This one is for smaller objects. So if we need to collect something that's too small for the pod to phase into, then we can carry one of these in by hand and collect the object with it." Next to the portable collection device which looks like an oversized hand gun are some extra parts. "These square things are basically the equivalent to memory cards. If we're collecting something and run out of storage space, we can swap out the storage cubes and collect multiple items without having to carry more than one collector gun."

"So how much can each of the memory cubes store?"

"Each cube will hold about the size of a car. If we find the source of these crystals, and it's, let's say, embedded in the ground or is just not possible to pick up and carry, we can transport out a part of it just like we're mining a hole in it. Then when we get back to headquarters, we can flip this switch and that reverses it. Pretty cool device, I got to use it many times in missions. I can target exactly what I want to take."

"Is this a technology *we* invented, or is it Agarthan?"

Sue places the collection gun back in the case and closes the lid. "It's Agarthan; it was found in a tunnel they dug before their exodus. One of a few pieces of technology we found over the years. They were a bit more careless with leaving tools around before they went to the center."

Carter walks with Bill and Sue to the pod. When he gets inside, he checks the pods supplies.

"We have seven days of food and water, costumes, survival gear, collections equipment and defense gear. Looks like we're ready. Let's go. Wheels up, shall we?"

"Hold on I forgot the tablet." Carter goes to the archives room where a portable touch screen tablet sits next to the computer terminal she used the previous night. She disconnects the cable connecting it to the computer and races back to the pod with the tablet in hand.

Bill notices her climb aboard with the tablet. "What's the tablet for?"

"I put the ancient Agarthan history book on the tablet last night so I could study it further. I figured we could use it to identify the location based on the drawings."

"Smart thinking. Close the door and take your station. I know we're not doing any documenting for this mission but I put a handheld camera in the gear storage locker for you anyway. Maybe you can make a video for posterity. Who knows, maybe you'll get another Pulitzer." Bill types in the coordinates in the navigation computer and locks in the destination. "I'm bringing us to a point where there's a large population center of pre-Agarti people living on the surface. 402,198 BC in what will eventually be Germany."

"Why this particular location?"

"Sue and I were here before. The power station from our mission video is nearby. I figured we could narrow our search for the royal crown by first going to a place where we know these stones are currently in use. The power station is the best place to start. If we can find some here, then maybe we can use that data to track down ones not in use."

The pod arrives near the power station Bill and Sue had previously visited. Carter looks out the window, amazed to see extremely familiar architecture.

"Guys, this looks identical to the city Aros took me to in Agartha. The same building style, even the layout of the streets are the same as modern-day Agartha. I thought they advanced for nearly a half million years from this time in their history?"

"I never got to go to Agartha, so I'll take your word for it. After Sue and I saw this time period, I think we both assumed they would have advanced more, as well. Maybe they're sentimental, so they stuck with the design."

Sue activates the pod's onboard scanners, looking for unusual energy signatures. "Colonel, there's no radiological or magnetic signatures coming from the power plant below us. I don't think it's nuclear or electromagnetic. There's a strong radio frequency though that's being broadcast from the power plant. It might be worth taking a better look."

Bill mirrors Sue's display on his console. "Looks like a fifteen megahertz radio wave, but it's really strong. Let's go to ground level and see if we can penetrate the outer wall of the power facility."

He flies down and slowly moves forward toward the power station. The pod skims about four feet above the grass-covered field surrounding the facility. There are many people walking about the area outside the building. As the pod gets closer to the outside wall of the building, the floor starts to vibrate.

Carter grabs the camera rail to steady herself. "Is this safe?"

Bill keeps his eyes on the screen. "I think so, the phase generator is keeping us out of sync, but the frequencies from the power station shield is causing our phase converter to fluctuate a bit."

The pod suddenly slams into something and comes to a stop about fifteen feet from the wall of the power plant. Carter jolts forward, falling against the pod window, smacking her forehead on the glass. As she regains her stance by grabbing the camera slide rail above her, she lifts herself up and notices the people outside the pod who shouldn't see it are looking directly at it.

"Bill, they see us!"

Bill slaps both hands on the console surface. "I thought you fixed the cloak, Sue?"

Sue looks at the phase cloak panel. "We're still cloaked; the impact caused a plasma discharge for a second. They can't see us." She scrolls back the phase activity log on her screen.

"All right, I'm going to back us off and look for a safe place to phase in. The only way we're getting in that power plant is on foot. There are two entrances and they don't seem to be guarded. Maybe we can just walk in."

Bill flies the pod a half mile away and hides the pod in a building that looks like it's under construction. The pod passes through the walls of the structure and lands inside.

"This looks like a safe place."

Carter and Bill get up and open the equipment locker. She pulls out two costumes that look similar to the clothes she saw on the people near the power plant; a lightweight robe tied with a simple rope as a belt. Very similar to what people currently wear in modern-day Egypt. Carter slides the metal case that contains the collection gun out of the locker.

"We don't need the collector, Carter. We don't know what we're looking for yet, and we have no way of hiding that gun in our robes."

Sue swivels her chair around. "Colonel, do you want me to phase out after you leave the pod and position the ship outside the power station door?"

"No, stay here and monitor our channel remotely. I'll put it on VOX. "

"What is VOX?" Carter asks Bill.

"It means the radio will transmit our voices to the pod when we speak. It's automatic so we don't get caught holding the microphone in our hands."

Sue leans back in her chair. "Yeah, so no talking about the stuff you guys do in bed, I don't need to hear that while I'm sitting here by myself."

Carter smiles and gives her a wink. They both take off their jumpsuits and put on their costumes. Carter wraps herself in a tunic with a string belt dusted with gold leaf. Bill wears a longer robe with a white rope belt.

"Nice legs, sir. I think you need more time in the sun tower," Sue jokes.

As soon as Bill closes the door, Sue phases out.

"OK Carter, you ready?"

"Yes, but should we keep our names, or call each other something different?"

"I say we just stick with our names for now. If someone gives us a hard time, we can adapt."

They walk through the empty building towards the exit a few feet away. As they open the door, they notice how hot it is outside. The sun is bright and there's a slight breeze. They can hear the sounds of a busy city, sounds you might expect in the 21st century. There are regular internal combustion vehicles driving around, and they see the streaks in the sky from aircraft.

They're only a fifteen-minute walk from the power plant, but there's so many things to see on the way over. Carter notices they're passing by shops and restaurants.

"Bill, look! We can eat some ancient food!"

"We don't have any money, and we don't even know what language they speak!"

"I know, but this is amazing."

"Remember, this is all about to get destroyed."

They continue walking along the ancient yet very high-tech city streets, towards the building they suspect has plumestones inside. They hear people they pass speaking to each other.

Carter whispers to Bill, "That's the same language that they speak in modern day Agartha."

Bill nods. "What a beautiful day, if it weren't for knowing without a doubt what these people were about to face with the coming solar activity, I wouldn't suspect anything was wrong."

"It's sad to think that all this is going to be destroyed soon."

"Keep looking forward, you look like a tourist. Just walk at the same rate that everyone else is walking, don't make eye contact or facial expressions with anyone."

"Sorry, what if people stop us and want to know who we are?"

"We'll deal with that when the time comes."

Up ahead, across a beautifully landscaped field, they see the power plant. It's a round building with a domed roof. The outside is pure white, and has a brushed aluminum support lattice which forms a geometric exoskeleton around the building. They follow the sidewalk towards an opening in the side of the building.

Carter keeps her eyes on the entrance as she leans closer to Bill. "So what, there are no guards? It looks like we can just walk right in."

"Sometimes it's easy, sometimes it's hard. We may just get lucky today," Bill replies with a grin.

They enter through an arched doorway and walk slowly into the building.

"It's completely hollow in here!"

"Keep your voice down."

The entire structure is a shell. In the center of the steel grated floor is a metal pole four feet in diameter that goes all the way to the roof of the dome. About halfway up is a five-foot gap in the pole, and suspended between the gap is a small glowing orb which swirls and pulsates.

Carter gazes up at the brilliant blue sphere of energy. "That's the same color as the phase field from the pod."

Bill turns his back to the energy ball and stands close to Carter so they're face to face. "The plumestone is suspended in the middle of the energy orb. Now we have to figure out how we're going to track down more. If I can get a reading on the stone, we'll be able to track them down easily."

He lifts his arm to reveal a small scanning device he has strapped to his wrist. He slides his sleeve back and presses the scan button on his wrist device. On the device's screen, a series of numbers start to appear. The numbers lock onto a spectrum frequency. He slowly aims the scanner around the room to focus in on where the signal is originating.

"Looks like the stone is generating a frequency."

"Where is it coming from?"

"It looks like it's inside the energy sphere."

"So how do we get it out?"

"I don't think we're getting this one. I have the frequency now, so I can find others that might not be actively connected to the power plant. Maybe we can scan for that queen's crown."

He covers up the scanner on his wrist and guides Carter back towards the exit. They casually walk out without saying anything.

"Bill, those are the same people who witnessed the phase fluctuation earlier when we bumped the power plant."

"I know, just look straight ahead and keep walking."

A dozen or so men with handheld scanners take readings in the location where the pod had bumped into the outer shield. As Bill and Carter walk past, one of the men's scanners starts beeping.

Bill hears the ancient scanner make a progressively louder beeping as they approach. After they get further away down the sidewalk, the beeping returned to a slower, softer volume. Realizing there's something wrong, Bill walks faster and puts his hand on Carters elbow to accelerate her pace.

"Don't look back, just keep going. Those scanners are pinging on us."

Carter keeps up with Bill. She hears the men behind them call out in Agarti, and one voice speaks English.

"Stop!"

Carter turns her head and makes eye contact with the man who called, and he and his fellows walk quickly towards Bill and Carter.

"Bill, he said stop...in English!"

"I heard him, but we gotta go!"

He grabs her wrist, running towards the landing site, and calls out to Sue over the VOX. "Sue we're coming in hot!"

"Copy, Colonel, do you want me to come and pick you up?"

"Affirmative!"

Bill and Carter are nearly halfway to the landing zone, running out of breath.

Sue jumps into Bill's seat and pushes the control sticks forward. The pod passes through and out of the building's exterior wall as she guides the pod directly down the middle of the street.

"I have visual on you now, Colonel." She can see Carter and Bill running towards her and brings the pod to a stop in the street, rotating it around so the door faces them. She phases in the door then gets up to open it.

Carter and Bill see the door opening appear in the street.

"There are three men chasing us, and they're only a few feet behind. Target them with the stunner."

The men giving chase speak in Agarti to someone on their own radios.

"Sue, try and jam their communication."

"Jamming now, sir."

One of the Agarthans behind Carter reaches out, grabbing hold of Carter's ponytail.

"Bill!"

He stops to look back. One of the men has Carter held tight from behind in his arms while the other two men run towards Bill.

"Sue, Fire!"

Sue had already targeted the Agarthans. An invisible pulse blasts from the pod, making an ultra-low-pitched sound. To those listening on the street, it sounds like a large bass drum. The two Agarthans drop in their tracks, their momentum causing them to skid across the cobblestone road.

Bill had ducked, hands over his ears when the shock wave blasted over his head. He stands, seeing that Sue couldn't target the man who restrains Carter because her body had acted as a shield.

"I got this last one, Sue." Bill runs over to the man who bear hugs Carter. Her arms are pinned at her side, and no matter how she struggles, the man is too strong for her to break free.

"Carter, duck!"

She snaps her head down just as Bill throws a punch at the remaining Agarthan's face. The punch lands with a satisfying smack and definite broken nose that immediately starts dripping blood.

Carter drops to the ground when the man releases her.

"Get in the pod!" Bill yells.

She begins running before she is even fully back upright on her feet. The Agarthan Bill punched holds his nose, which gushes blood. Bill readies his stance to strike again, when Sue fires the third stunner blast. It knocks the Agarthan backward.

Down the street, more Agarthans run at full speed towards them.

"I guess they got the call for more back up," Bill says to himself.

Carter runs towards the pod and jumps into the open door. She tucks and rolls across the floor and crashes into the swivel mount of the chair she normally sits in. Sue stands off to the side, hand on the door handle as Bill jumps in and slides into Carter. Sue slams the door shut.

Outside, the Agarthans watch the doorway disappear as the pod phases out. One of the men scans for the pod while the other two feel around the empty air, trying to touch the pod.

"You okay, Carter?"

Carter and Bill lay on the floor of the pod, trying to catch their breath. "I'm fine, just a bit out of practice with running. I need to find a gym on base."

They remove their costumes. Carter looks out the window and sees a crowd gathering around the street.

"I'm going to get us out of here. If they can scan us, they might be able to disable us." Bill sits in his seat and flies the pod one thousand feet above the city. Carter goes to the supply cabinet, pulls out three bottles of water, and hands them out.

"Bill, that guy said *stop* in English—how is that even possible?"

Bill locks in the pod's altitude on the navigation screen and pivots his chair around. "I don't know; I've never heard it spoken before the 11th century. It's possible they invented it, and it didn't resurface until later."

Carter drinks half of her bottle of water. "Maybe it was brought up to the surface by one of those god imitators."

"That's a good possibility. There are lots of Agarthan con men and criminals who made their mark throughout history. It wouldn't surprise me if that was the case."

Bill removes the scanning device from his wrist and hands it to Sue. "This scan should help us locate some more of those plumestones. Plug that in and let's do a scan of the area."

"Yes, sir." Sue takes the portable scanner and connects a cable to it.

Bill flies slowly over the surface of the city. "Any readings yet, Lieutenant?

"Scanning now, Colonel."

Carter turns to Sue. "How long will it take to find more stones?"

"It might take a while; this signal you recorded inside the power plant has a bandwidth that's very narrow."

"So...like an hour?"

Sue laughs. "It won't be that fast, the sensor in the pod is going to have to pass directly over a stone because this signal is so narrow. It's sort of like looking for an invisible laser beam. We have to pass directly over it to even catch it."

Carter sits back in her chair, feeling suddenly bored.

Bill looks over at her and laughs. "I warned you, this job can go for long boring hours, just waiting for something to happen."

"Yeah, I know, but you got my heart pumping and my adrenalin going, and now I just have to sit and wait."

Sue leans over to Carter. "I'd step out and let you work off your energy on Bill, but I think he wants these scans to continue."

She and Sue giggle like two teenage girls.

"What are you ladies laughing about?"

"Nothing."

"Back to work then, we have a civilization to save, you know."

Carter puts her hand on Bill's leg. "Sorry, Colonel." She picks up a three ring binder under the control panel console and fans herself with it.

"I can turn the temperature in the pod down if you want," Sue offers.

"No, I just need to stop sweating."

"Well, you're not needed for this part of the mission, go take a shower."

Carter gets up and walks to the door to the head. She peeks inside and examines the fold-up toilet and sink. "So what, you just fold it all back and stand in the middle?"

"Yeah, there's a recirculation water supply, and little bottles of soap in the wall panel."

Carter gets undressed and steps into the cramped shower stall, closing the door behind her. She presses a button that says *on* and water starts pumping out of a showerhead directly above her head.

"Wow, it's surprising that the water is just the right temperature and pressure."

Sue looks over at Bill. "That's some woman you got there."

Bill smiles at the closed shower door. "Thanks for being a good friend, Sue."

"I've never seen you happier. I told Carter at her apartment that I was OK with it."

"That means a lot, especially considering what you had to do because of you and Steve."

"Steve and I are fine with it. Sure, it was nice working together, but we're both officers and that's against the rules. I don't know how the General will look at you and Carter, but as far as I'm concerned, everything is fine."

"Well, Carter and I do enjoy being together, but we agreed to keep it off of missions and out of headquarters. If the General knows or finds out, I'll deal with it."

"She really is beautiful," Sue says in an almost jealous tone.

"I know, I was in a trance since the day I saw her photo in the file during candidate selection. It was hard to look past her appearance and focus on her skills. Then when we saw her in action at the fire, I knew she was the right one for the job. Everything else was just icing on the cake."

Carter finishes up her shower, and shuts off the water. "Bill!" she calls out.

"Yes?"

"Do you have a towel?"

"Just press the dry button. It's like a big hand dryer. We don't have an onboard laundry."

She presses it, and a rush of warm air starts blowing from multiple directions. She uses her hands to ring out her hair and leans her head into one of the blower nozzles. She steps out of the shower and puts back on her jumpsuit. Carter catches Bill watching and gives him a smile. "Sue, do you have a brush?"

"There's one in my personal item drawer in the locker."

Carter grabs the brush and sits back down, brushing her hair. "Any signals yet?"

"Nothing. I only scanned one tenth of one percent of the city."

Carter puts the brush down and ties her hair into a ponytail. "Too bad we don't have a satellite map of where all the stones are."

Sue looks at Carter, but doesn't say anything, staring at her for a few seconds.

"What is it?"

"Carter, Bill was right about you. You're a frigging genius."

Carter looks perplexed, but smiles. "I know. What did I say?"

"We can use a satellite in a polar orbit to scan the planet. Just the way they map the world, one strip at a time."

"Yeah, but won't that take just as long?"

Sue swings her chair around to face Carter. "It'll take a long time, probably years to find every single stone. Who knows how much of this stuff it's going to take to make a shield big enough surround the whole Earth. I suggest get a satellite, bring it back in time, launch it, and then jump forward. Then when we arrive back, right before the Agarthan exodus, we can download the data from it and find out exactly where all of the stones are and how much is available."

Bill looks at Carter and Sue. "So we need a satellite that we can launch from the pod. It needs a scanning unit installed on it, and it needs to be able to maintain an orbit for at least how long?"

"Well the best I think we can do is a few thousand years, but if we sent up regular maintenance missions to prevent orbital decay, we could prolong that indefinitely. I could have Steve and his teams do multiple missions to stabilize a satellite and make sure we kept it flying."

"OK, let's head back to base. Sue, organize with the other pod captains for maintenance checkups on the satellite. I'll call my buddy over at space surveillance and see what kind of hardware they can supply us. Carter, you go to engineering with the portable scanner and tell them we need a full-time data collection unit made that will fit inside a satellite."

Bill brings the pod back to the base and everyone goes off and works on their mission objectives. Carter heads to engineering with the wrist data recorder, and Sue goes to

Hangar Bay Two to organize a maintenance schedule with Steve and the other pod captains.

Bill drives over to space surveillance command headquarters about ten miles north of the TTRC. The SSC is a small building made totally of glass. Ironic that passersby can see everything inside a building that creates spy satellites. He arrives at Lieutenant Colonel Stennmeyer's workshop.

"Hey Stenny, what's new in the spy world?"

"Colonel! It's great to see you. Oh, there are some good things happening. We just got this new camera that can see in infrared through the roof of a house from orbit."

"That sounds creepy. Listen, I hate to just come in and start asking for something, but we're on a mission right now, and we need a satellite."

Stenny walks over to his workbench where there's an array of different electronic components laid out on the table. "Sure, what are you looking for?"

"I need to scan a very narrow bandwidth for a mineral. I have to do a pole-to-pole orbit so I can map the whole planet over a long period."

"How many years do you want the craft to orbit?"

"That's the thing, we're not sure. We're sending it back to pretty much the beginning of the Earth, and then we're going to check it periodically for data changes in the locations of these minerals."

"That's a tall order."

"So you don't think it can happen?"

"No, I didn't say that. I have this prototype, but we've never flight tested it. Right now, it's just an empty system. It only has a navigational and propulsion system. "

"Is there room in there for our scanner?"

Stenny and Bill head to a closed door. Stenny swipes his ID card and brings Bill into the prototype room.

"That's it, right there." Stenny points to the odd-looking satellite.

They approach a five-foot long two-foot wide solid black satellite with many facets facing in all directions.

"It has stealth plating?"

"Yes, it's radar invisible, has active scattering of laser and other detection methods. There's a solar and nuclear power plant that drives the electronics, and a new type of microwave propulsion system."

"How long will it last?"

"That's a good question. There are so many things in space; just about anything can take out a satellite. We've been experimenting with a phase generator similar to what you guys use. The phase generator draws power from the plutonium core and provides a shield. Theoretically, it should survive pretty much anything, and the shield will provide protection from EMP and solar flares. The half-life of the plutonium is twenty-four thousand years, so you can do a core change around then."

Bill lifts one end of the satellite. "Boy, it's lightweight."

"Yes, it's only ninety pounds."

"I'll call General Wilson and get him to arrange the procurement."

"Bill, this baby isn't on the procurement list yet. You're going to need permission from much higher up than your base commander."

Bill pulls out his cell phone and smiles at Stenny. "Give me a minute." He speaks momentarily to someone on the phone then hands it to Stenny.

Stenny hesitantly takes the phone, looking nervous. "This is Lieutenant Colonel Stennmeyer, how can I help you, sir or ma'am?" He listens for a few seconds. "Yes, sir. I will, sir.... Thank you, Mr. President." He hands the phone back.

"Bill, what the hell are you guys into? Wait, I don't want to know. You want me to load this in your car for you?"

"No, I'll send a couple airmen to pick it up in an hour. Thanks buddy, this is really important."

"Anytime. If the President orders me to do it, it's got to be super priority. Hey, we should go shoot some pool soon."

"Right after this mission is over, dinner and drinks are on me."

Bill leaves the building and goes back to TTRC headquarters. Carter and Sue have already completed their tasks and are waiting in the hangar bay as Bill walks in.

"Sue, go over to engineering and get a phase generator from one of the distress beacons."

"Yes, sir. What are we doing with the phase generator?"

"I want you to fit it inside the satellite and modulate it to act as a shield. Also, take this schedule to Steve so he can do the required power core swap outs at these intervals."

Sue takes the schedule and looks at it. "Colonel, this is only thirty changes."

"I know, we're going to place the satellite at 250,000 years before Agartha, and let it run until current time today. That way we can go up right now and download about 750,000 years of data."

"Copy, Colonel." Sue leaves the hangar.

"Carter, how long before my scanner is ready?"

"The engineers were able to make one, but they're waiting on the satellite so they know how big to make the enclosure."

Just as Carter says that, the two airmen Bill had sent to pick up the satellite walk in, wheeling it in on a large metal table. The satellite is strapped down with large yellow bungee cords. As Carter watches the airmen untangle the satellite, Bill takes the cordless drill mounted to the side of the table and removes the bolts from the component chamber's cover plate.

"Carter, call the techs in here so they can take the measurements of this cargo chamber."

"I'll run down and get them."

***

About three hours later, Bill, Sue and Carter are in the ready room waiting for the technicians to inform them that the satellite with its new shield and scanner is ready for launch. Bill stands next to the coffee pot, staring at the bulletin board. Carter and Sue are both on their phones, playing scrabble with each other.

The lead technician walks in the ready room. "Colonel, you're all set. If you want to send your engineer out, I'll go over the launch instructions."

Sue follows the technician out to the hangar bay.

Bill walks over to Carter and sits down next to her. "Well this is it. We're in the home stretch."

She smiles and puts her hand on his. "So after we launch the satellite, how long before we get the data?"

"Steve said his crew will take about an hour for each core change, so it won't be until tomorrow when they get back."

"So why can't we just go forward to the present right after we launch it in the past?"

"That's just the way the laws of time travel work. If we leave the base before Steve completes his mission and arrives back, the timeline won't have changed, and we'd arrive to a long dead satellite."

"Right, right, because his mission wouldn't have even happened, and we'd be in a different timeline."

"Exactly. Don't worry, this timeline stuff gets easier the longer you do it."

220

They head into the hangar bay, where airmen load the satellite inside the pod.

"How are we supposed to launch the satellite from inside the pod?" Carter asks.

"The phase shield allows us to pass it through the shield from the inside, but will keep the vacuum of space from affecting us."

After the satellite is loaded, Bill, Sue and Carter board the pod. The satellite lies flat on the pod floor, one side facing the door, and the other right under Carter's chair. The technicians installed a set of rollers on the floor so the satellite will easily roll out.

"Shut the door Sue, and let's get this baby launched."

Carter looks at the satellite sitting below her feet as she sits in her chair. "You know, before they launch a ship, they usually give it a name."

Bill looks at the large angled facets and protruding anti-radar sections of the spy satellite. "It kind of looks like something Batman would have."

"Then we'll call it the 'Black Knight.'" Carter reaches into the console storage drawer and pulls out a white wax pencil used for marking maps. She writes *Black Knight* on the side of the satellite.

"Sounds like a fitting name." He brings the pod into a polar orbit around the Earth 750,000 years in the past.

Carter stands and looks down at the Earth. "The air is so clear and the continents look close to the way they do in the present. Sue, by having the satellite orbit around the Earth from pole-to-pole, does that make the scan more accurate?"

"It not only makes it more accurate, it also takes less time to completely map the Earth. If the plumestone mineral is there, we'll get a ping on the instrumentation, and the next time around, if the ping moves, we can see the track it took. Sort of like the way the GPS works on your phone."

"So how long is each orbit?"

"Roughly one hundred minutes."

Bill locks in the pod's speed. "I'm setting the orbital speed to the proper velocity to insert the satellite." He moves over to the door and swings it open. "The phase shield prevents the harsh environment of space from entering the pod's interior."

Sue leans over the satellite with a handheld system status monitor. "The satellite is powered up and operating properly Bill, we're a go for release."

Bill releases the locks on the wheels and gives the satellite a gentle push towards the door. As it slides through the doorway, the shield glows with a blue plasma discharge, indicating the satellite is penetrating it. Within seconds, the satellite is clear of the pod and in orbit around the poles of the Earth for its three quarter million-year scan.

Carter watches the Black Knight slowly disappear into the night side of the Earth. "So now we jump back to base and wait?"

Bill pulls the door shut and latches it. "Yes, as soon as we get back I'll let Steve know to begin the thirty power core changes, and when he gets back from those, we can leave and retrieve the data."

"Do you think we should jump forward a few years from here and just check to see if the satellite is working properly?"

"Good call. Jumping forward one thousand years now." Bill turns the dial on the control panel and jumps the pod ahead a full millennium. "Sue, locate the satellites secure transponder signal."

Sue taps out the signal frequency on her computer. "Signal located. I'm sending the coordinates to your station."

Bill moves the pod in range of the satellite, which now has one thousand years of data stored in its memory banks. "We're in range, you can begin the data retrieval now."

"Yes, sir. Data link is confirmed and download in progress." Sue watches as the data is transferred to her computer.

Bill and Carter look over Sue's shoulder and see the map of Earth on her monitor. Sue starts a playback of the data on a day-by-day basis. The map shows small red dots that indicate a hit on the scanners sensor.

"What am I looking at here? I know the dots indicate sensor hits, but the hits are increasing in places that previously had shown nothing on past satellite passes."

"I think the reason these areas showed no indication of the mineral, then suddenly did on later passes is because the plumestones are landing on the planet's surface."

Carter puts her finger on the screen. "So, plumestones are meteorites?"

"Precisely. From the data, it looks like they're arriving slowly. This means they're not in a large clump of asteroids in space that arrived at one time. They're spread out over a very large area of space, and impacting the planet extremely slow."

Bill faces the door to the pods storage locker, thinks for a few seconds, and scratches the side of his face. "How much of this stuff is on Earth right now?"

"Let me calculate it." Sue moves the sensor log forward to the end of the data stream. "The computer confirms its approximately forty grams combined."

"And how much do we need?"

"That's still an unknown factor. Once the element is in use, like in the power plant or in the Agarthan artificial sun, it's not possible to scan for the amount used. We need to get a decent sized sample to test and then we can calculate the amount needed to generate an Earth sized shield."

"What would you consider a decent size?"

"Um…, maybe about the size of an egg, or larger."

Bill sits back down. Both women can sense Bill's enthusiasm is fading and his frustration is rising.

"I'd hoped we'd find enough of the rocks to accomplish our mission right now, but this might be harder than I thought. All right, we'll just have to hope that there will be a sufficient amount of accumulation over time. Let's get back home and let Steve know he can get on with the core changes."

"Well, I'm happy we got some results," Carter tells Bill.

"I'm glad it worked, I just had higher expectations on the quantity we'd find." Bill steps out of the pod in the hangar bay and calls Steve. "Steve, you can begin core change missions now."

After he hangs up, Carter walks with him down the hallway to update the General on the successful deployment of the satellite.

"Bill, don't worry, we'll get this done." She tries to keep pace with him.

"I know, it's just that I expected the mineral to be everywhere, and it just took me by surprise."

"Didn't you say some missions were easy and others were hard? You didn't think we could save the world before lunch, did you?"

Bill stops walking and looks into her eyes. "Remind me to kiss you later."

"You can count on it."

CHAPTER 14: A ROYAL AND A PROPHET

After getting back to her apartment that evening, Bill and Carter decide it's time to introduce his two flat-faced chubby pugs to her fluffy white cat. Bill brings the dogs in her front door and releases them from their leashes. They immediately see Mayonnaise sitting on the couch and go up to greet her.

"I've spent too much time away from my puppies. It looks like they're getting along with Mayonnaise."

"What are their names?"

"That's Snort, and that one with his nose jammed up against your cat's butt is Sniff."

"Where do they sleep?"

"Pretty much anywhere they want. I got them dog beds once, but they just ripped them apart, so now I usually find them at the foot of the bed each morning."

***

When Carter wakes up the next morning, she finds a couple of loud snoring dogs sleeping between her and Bill. At the foot of the bed, a very confused cat sits, staring silently. Mayonnaise has a heavily matted patch of fur on her head, as if something had spent a few hours licking it. Which pug is the cat hair stylist is unclear.

"Mayo, I can see you're plotting revenge, aren't you?"

Amazingly, there are no broken plants or signs of animal disagreements in the middle of the night.

"I want to take you over to see a friend of mine." Bill says later at the breakfast table over pancakes.

"Sure, I guess we have a little time before Steve finishes the core changes. Who is it?"

"His name is Jim, and he's an advanced tactical training officer."

"Because of me getting grabbed yesterday?"

"The hold that Agarthan had you in is actually easy to escape from if you know the moves. I just think with the number of phase-ins we might be doing, it'd be a good idea to prepare a little more."

"Aww, you're worried about me."

"I am. I don't want to see you get injured."

"Is there a gym nearby?"

"Yeah, about fifty, the only thing on base there's more of is places to get coffee."

When they arrive, Bill introduces Carter to one of the gym's personal trainers. "This is Petty Officer Jim Spencer, a current Navy Seal."

"Jim. It's nice to meet you! You've obviously seen your share of hand-to-hand combat...or is it from brutal bar fights?"

"You too, Miss Carter. Yeah, I've got quite a tapestry of knife, bullet and general beating marks from head to toe. What are we working on today?"

Bill leans in. "Carter and I were just on a mission and we sort of were running for our lives, so I wanted to make sure Carter could defend herself if she got caught."

"I can handle myself!"

Jim looks Carter up and down. "You seem physically fit, but what happens if someone grabs you like this?" Jim reaches out for her arm and pulls her towards him, spinning her around so her back is against his chest. Jim reaches his arms under Carter's and places his palms with fingers interlaced behind her head. "This is a full nelson in wrestling."

Jim's strength is more than Carter expected. He tightens his grip until she gasps. Carter starts to struggle, and Jim's grip gets firmer the more she resists. He waits for her to figure out the movement to release her from the hold.

Jim whispers in her ear, "Hands up, then drop to your knees."

Carter raises her hands and bends her knees, dropping through his hold.

"Finish me with your elbow."

"You mean in the nuts?"

"Don't worry, I'll be fine."

She swings her elbow back at full force. Jim, already prepared for the impact, has done a tuck back on his most vulnerable region. "Good, you didn't hesitate, now we need to make it second nature—no command is required." Jim offers his hand and pulls her back to her feet.

"I have to say, that was extremely satisfying."

"Good, confidence is the difference between being subdued and being free. If you're not ready to react, then you're ready to die."

Bill follows Carter throughout the day, helping with Jim's instruction on self-defense and evasion tactics.

"Carter's an excellent student and learns quickly," Jim says at the end of the session.

"Well, it looks like she's ready for a fight. Thanks for your help today."

On the way back to the car, she taunts Bill playfully with her newfound skills. "Come on bub, you wanna piece of me?"

"By *a piece*, I'm assuming you mean a fight?"

"We can start with a fight and see where it goes from there."

On the drive, Bills phone rings.

"The core swaps are complete and Steve and his team are back." Sue says.

"Thanks, we just finished at the gym, so we'll be back in an hour." He hangs up. "Time to put your hair up."

She looks at him with a slight confusion. "Right here in the car?"

"Right here in the car what?"

"You want to have sex?"

Bill laughs. "No—I mean, yes. What I was saying is, that was Sue letting me know Steve's back, and we can go retrieve the data from the Black Knight."

"Oh." She puts her arm on the door as she looks out the window watching as they pass by all the buildings on the way home. "Now that you said that, I want to have sex."

"Me too, but not while I'm driving."

After a quick stop at the apartment to shower and get changed, they meet up with Sue, who's already at headquarters in the control room.

"Lieutenant, is the pod ready for departure?"

"Yes, sir. I also have our gear from our last mission refreshed and stowed in the pod in case we need to go into the field again."

"Excellent L.T. Let's get aboard."

They take their stations inside and Bill brings them up into orbit. "Okay LT, get me a location on our satellite."

"On your screen now."

"Carter, look!" Bill says.

Carter looks out the pod window. "Oh! It's the International Space Station."

"Yup, here, let me fly us closer." Bill brings the pod about fifteen feet from the ISS.

"I can see in the window. Can they see us?"

"Hang on. I'll phase us in so we can say hi."

"Wait, are we in the present?" Carter asks.

"Yes, it's safe for them to see us." Bill picks up the radio transmitter microphone. "ISS, this is TTRC Time Ship One, do you read?"

One of the ISS crew comes to the big window. "Copy that, TTRC vessel, nice to see you folks up here."

"You as well ISS, sorry for the interruption, we were just passing by and wanted to extend our salutations."

"Much appreciated TTRC vessel, ISS out."

"Wow, I know we're in space, but it's really cool to see the ISS."

Bill flies the pod close to the Black Knight and puts it about two hundred feet in front of the pod in the same polar orbit. "OK Sue, connect to the data feed and download the entire stream."

"Yes, sir. Connection complete, stream downloading now."

"ETA for completion?"

"We're at five hours for complete data retrieval."

Bill swivels his chair around to Carter. "You didn't happen to pack a deck of cards did you?"

Carter rolls her eyes upon realizing they are in for a long wait. "Too bad we can't just leave the pod here and go get some dinner on the ISS."

"They do have better food and a cappuccino machine."

Sue swivels her chair around and stretches out her legs. "Coffee would be great."

Carter gets up, goes to the supply locker, and pulls out the shelf with the MRE's. "Well, there's a pack of instant coffee in each meal, so I guess we can take a dinner break while we wait?"

Bill leans back in his chair. "Sounds good, see if there's lasagna in there for me."

"Lasagna, lasagna....here it is." She tosses the bag of military field rations over to him.

"Sue, what are you up for tonight?" Carter asks.

"Um... I'll take pasta as well; spaghetti and meatballs are in there if I remembered to pack it."

"Yep, here ya go." Carter flips through the brown packets of food. "Ah meat loaf and gravy. Just like mom used to make."

Sue laughs. "I hope mom didn't make it like this."

"I actually kinda like these MRE's."

Sue turns to Bill. "Boy, you better take her out for an expensive dinner when this is all over. That girl needs to expand her palette."

They eat and Carter gets some hot water from the dispenser to make instant coffee using the coffee packets. As she sips her coffee, she puts on her headphones and slumps in her chair, waiting for the scan to finish. She sits quietly, listening to her playlist, currently Cyndi Lauper's 'I Drove All Night'. Ever since Bill reminded her of sex, she's been thinking about it all day. She stares at him with a lustful smirk.

With about three and a half hours remaining in the download of satellite data, Sue taps Carter on the shoulder.

Carter pulls her headphones down around her neck. "What's up?"

"You and I haven't spent a lot of girl time together. Bill seems to be filling up most of your free time."

"Yeah, we've been having fun."

"So I've been curious about why you decided to be a stringer at seventeen?"

Carter sips on her coffee, contemplating saying she didn't want to talk about her childhood, but realizes Sue isn't interrogating her.

"OK, sure. Well, I finished high school a year early because I skipped seventh grade. My parents told me to apply to college, but I wasn't even driving yet, and all my friends were off doing their own thing and had their freedom."

Bill listens but doesn't interrupt.

Sue leans forward in her chair. "So you wanted to take a break for a year to catch up on everyone else's age before starting your first year of school?"

"I didn't want to go to school at all. I know this sounds stupid; I wanted to make funny videos on the internet." She laughs and pauses to sip her coffee. "When my friends went off to school, I had no one to do it with anymore, so I just had my camera and lots of ideas."

"So did you make money with the videos?"

"A little, but without my friends to act out my ideas with, I tried doing a vlog on my own, but no one really liked me just talking to the camera. So I decided to take the camera out with me wherever I went, and started filming interesting things. You know, nature stuff, people on the streets. Then there were problems with my parents fighting, so I just took off one day and became a stringer by accident. I guess lots of people find their jobs by accident." Carter finishes her coffee and puts the cup in the storage locker.

Sue watches Carter sit back down. She puts her hand on Carter's thigh. "I didn't mean to bring up bad memories."

"No, it's no big deal. My relationship with my parents is good now and they don't fight anymore."

Bill knows that this is a sensitive area for Carter, and probably something she prefers not to discuss. Bill reaches over to give her back a rub.

"Really, it's okay Bill. My relationship with my parents is fine. I just try and not dwell on the past."

They wait until the data stream download has completed, and then Sue uses the computer to create another visual map to show the last 750,000 years of plumestone locations.

"Sir, the data is compiled, come take a look."

Bill and Carter stand behind Sue's chair as she plays the data back over a map of the world. They watch the hits appear on the map, and then suddenly see a spike of hits appear all in one spot near northern Europe. Then all the hits suddenly disappear.

"Pause it there, back it up to right before the hits all vanished. What did we just see happen?"

"Sir, it looks like this is a few years before the Agarthan exodus into the Earth's center. Watch, I'll slow it down for you. See the mineral signatures were collected from the entire planet and show up here, in current day Turkey. Then you can see it all heads up to the North Pole and disappears. They must have realized they needed a large quantity for the creation of the artificial star and literally swept the entire planet for every last ounce."

Bill looks at the map, which is now empty of mineral hit markers. "Move forward to our current day."

Sue speeds up the playback, stopping at the end of the data file.

Bill leans in and stares at the map. "Not a single hit after the collection, how can that even be possible?"

Sue pauses for a few seconds. "Well, it's possible that the element was in a large asteroid field that stretched out its impacts with the Earth over a large period of time, and then moved out of the solar system. Alternatively, just ended up being pulled into the sun. Let me back it up to before the collection."

Sue restarts the data stream playback and leans her head in closer to see the smaller hits as the minerals were deposited by meteor impacts. She rolls the playback forward and back multiple times while Bill and Carter watched over her shoulders.

"There, this is the time when new hits stopped appearing. This is about fifty thousand years before exodus date."

Bill stands up straight and walks back to his work station. "They got every last bit of it and brought it all with them into Agartha?"

"It would appear so."

"Go back to the point when the entire supply was massed in the one spot and calculate how much it was."

"Yes, sir, give me a few seconds to run the calculations."

Carter, quiet throughout the analysis, grows concerned at Bill's obvious dissatisfaction with the results. "What does this all mean?"

"It means we need to find out how much of this stuff they used, and how much is still down in Agartha."

"So we still need to go into Agartha and try and get some from them?"

Sue interrupts. "Sir, the calculation shows this mass is equal to roughly one ton, or about the size of a three-foot square block. But we still don't know how much was used to create the artificial star."

Bill walks back over to Sue and leans on her console with both hands. "How much of a sample did you say you needed to experiment with?"

"About egg-sized."

"Roll the data file back and see if you can find one that size."

Sue scans the data file for a few minutes. "There, right in this location there's one that size."

"OK, what year is that?"

"Looks like it's one thousand years before exodus. It's located in what looks like an island off the coast of Spain."

Bill sits down. "Send that to my console."

"Coordinates transferred, sir."

"Let's go get a sample, shall we?"

Carter looks out the window as Bill phases the pod into the past and arrives in the pre-Agarthan city near Spain. They hover at night one thousand feet above the new location. As Carter leans towards the window, she can see the lights of the city below her.

"The city lights are beautiful! It looks like the city is a bunch of circles from up here."

Bill looks out the window. "This is a new one for me. This island isn't on our maps. I've never been here or seen this one before." He sits back down and looks over at Sue. "Start a scan for the sample we need to collect. This island isn't that big, we should be able to locate it pretty quickly."

Sue starts her scan, and in a few seconds, she finds the signal. "Sending the coordinates to your station now."

"Well that was easy, looks like it's dead center in the middle of the island."

Carter looks out the window as Bill lowers the pod closer to the surface. "This city is a little different from the last one we were at; it looks more like the architecture of ancient Greece with technological features added on."

"Yeah, most of the ancient cities I've seen were all pretty modern-looking. This city looks really old underneath, like they decided to just build onto the original structures." Bill brings the pod to a stop on the ground next to a tower in the center of the city.

"Maybe after this is all over we can come back and take a tour of the place during the day time, and some dinner," Carter whispers.

"Sure, it's a date."

Bill goes to the locker, pulls out a costume, and begins to put it on.

Carter puts her hand on her hip and taps her foot on the pod floor. "You're not going in there alone."

"It's a quick grab, the stone can't be that difficult to find."

"You're just worried if something *does* happen, I won't be able to protect myself."

"It's not that."

"Then it's because we're screwing?"

Sue glances over. "She's right, Bill."

Bill stops getting dressed and stands silently looking at Carter. He exhales as he grabs the other costume from the locker and hands it over. "You're right."

"I'm not going to get hurt, trust me. I have enough training. Besides, these people are peaceful; they don't want to hurt us." She puts one hand on his shoulder, leaning in a few inches from his face. She pretends to go in for a kiss, but suddenly lifts her knee up and stops right before it makes contact with his groin. "If someone *does* touch me, I'll kick them in the balls."

Bill flinches as an adrenalin rush goes quickly through his body. "I know you will."

They finish dressing and step out of the cloaked pod onto a stone walkway that leads into the island's center tower, where they had picked up the signal. Bill closes the pod door and checks his communication with Sue. "Com check, one, two."

"I read you, Colonel."

"Copy, radio silence until my next."

Carter and Bill, wearing the same robes they had on in the previous mission, walk up the pathway towards the tower entrance. No one is visible along the way, but the tower is high on a hill and they can see down to the rest of the city, which thrums with activity and people.

"Bill, is this weird to you?"

"What do you mean?"

"Well, the stone's in *this* tower, but no one's here guarding it. I mean, there aren't even people just walking around, but down there it looks like New York City on a Friday night."

"I guess, but you know what they say about looking a gift horse in the mouth."

"Yeah, I also know what they say about things being too good to be true."

"You're right, it does seem strange. Just keep an eye out, if we see anyone, we need to find a place to hide. We can't blend in if no one's supposed to be here."

They enter through an open passage in the side of the tower and see a very old-looking spiral staircase.

"This looks like an old castle. What is this place?"

"I don't know yet, but your voice is echoing, so keep it low."

They head to the stairs and walk up almost one hundred feet. When they reach the top, they enter a room that looks like a royal museum, with display cases holding artifacts and jewelry throughout the round room.

"That's it, there's the crown you saw in the Agarthan history book. Let me see the tablet so we can be sure," Bill says.

Carter reaches under her robe and pulls out the tablet. She swipes through the pages to the image of the queen. "Here you go."

Bill looks at the image and compares it to the crown. "This is it."

The crown is a solid piece of quartz, shaped into a large ring. Embedded around the outside are various gems—green emeralds, red rubies, and in the center, a purple stone.

Bill lifts the glass lid to the display case. "Good, it's not locked."

Carter pulls out the crown and rubs the purple stone. "This *has* to be the plumestone. I don't think I've ever seen a purple that iridescent before. It looks like a big purple pearl, the way the grain of the stone swirls around. Looks like there's something inside, like a metallic object."

"Let's get it back to the pod." Bill reaches for his radio. "Sue, we've acquired the stone, prepare for departure."

"Copy, Colonel."

Bill takes the crown and puts it in a green canvas bag under his robe. They descend the winding stairs all the way back down and walk out the door to the stone path. Suddenly, a piercing noise goes off, echoing through the city. Floodlights emit from all directions.

"Shit, not again. Carter, run!"

Carter sprints down the path towards the landing zone. Sue swings open the door. Carter reaches it first and stops, but doesn't get in. Bill runs slower, his legs banging against the canvas bag under his robe. About fifty feet from the pod, a bright red beam streams in from the left side of the pathway, striking Bill in the back. He stumbles and falls face-first.

Just then, a dozen men appear out of the darkness and converge on top of him. Carter instinctively starts to move towards Bill, but Sue has already gotten a firm grip on the back of Carter's robe.

Carter feels the tug on her robe from behind and looks back. "What are you doing? Let me go, I have to help him!"

"No, he's caught, you can't help him now." Sue pulls back on the robe with all her strength. Carter falls backwards into the pod. Sue reaches down and grabs Carter's leg, which hangs out the door, and yanks it hard enough to flip Carter onto her stomach. Sue swings the door closed, which makes the pod once again completely cloaked.

"Sue! What the fuck are you doing? They shot him!"

Sue jumps into Bill's chair and grabs the flight sticks, pulling the pod up about fifty feet.

"Go back down, we have to save him!"

"That isn't the procedure."

"Fuck the procedure, Bill's down there!" Carter runs to the window. "He's hurt! Bring me back, I can help him." She watches as the guards put wrist and leg restraints on Bill. A vehicle arrives next to the guards, and they pick up an unconscious Bill and place him in the rear of the vehicle. "They're taking him, Sue!"

Sue presses buttons, ignoring Carter. A new screen appears, and on its display is a blinking red light and a green set of concentric circles.

Carter looks down at the screen, wiping tears from her eyes. "What is that?"

"That's Bill's implanted transmitter."

"What, you can track him?"

"I told you, we have procedures."

Carter drops to her knees on the floor behind Sue and covers her face with her torn robe, wiping her tears dry. "Why didn't you just tell me you had a plan?"

"There wasn't time to explain. I had to activate the transmitter remotely, it has a limited activation distance of one hundred feet, and there's only a five-hour battery life. I needed to get us to a safe distance in case they tried to scan for us again, and get the transmitter activated at the same time, not to mention pull you back in the pod."

Carter takes off her robe. She goes to the bathroom and turns on the faucet, washing her face with some cold water. She goes back to her seat and sits, watching Sue follow Bills signal.

"It looks like they're taking Bill underground. They're heading down that tunnel."

"Can we follow?"

Sue pushes the flight sticks forward and moves the pod down to the road . "Already doing that."

Sue follows the vehicle, a white pill shaped car, down the tunnel into an underground facility. They watch as four men dressed in robes remove Bill from the back.

"Does he look alive to you?" Carter asks, a nervous waver in her voice.

"His vitals are displayed here on the screen." Sue points to the top right corner of her display.

"Oh good, OK good, good."

Carter hands shake as she holds the camera rail above her head. Out the window, they watch as the men put Bill on a rolling stretcher and wheel him in through a set of auto opening doors. Sue moves the pod through the doors and follows down a long hallway. At the end of the hall, they bring him into a room that looks like a medical facility. Sue stops a few feet away.

"Sue, turn the pod door towards Bill and I'll pull him in."

"Hang on, we don't know what they shot him with, he might just be knocked out. I need to make sure we can wake him up on our own before we take him."

Carter bites her fingernails. Some other men and women who appear to be medical personnel come into the room. One goes to Bill, holding a small handheld device that he places over Bill's head. The man presses a button on the handle, releasing a flash of light.

Bill starts to wake, restrained and unable to sit up. "Where am I? Where's Carter?"

Two of the medical personnel speak to each other in what Carter recognizes as Agarti. They gesture to a woman over by the door, and she comes over to stand beside Bill.

"You are in our city," she says in a kind, soothing voice. "You can understand me?"

"Yes, your language is old, but we are familiar with it."

"Where's my friend, the woman?"

The woman speaks momentarily to one of the guards who had apprehended Bill for a few seconds, then turns back to Bill. "Your companion is not here. She disappeared right after you were captured trying to steal the royal crown."

Bill relaxes, leaning his head against the padded stretcher. "Good."

The woman walks to his other side and smiles pleasantly. "Please, why did you take the crown? What reason do you have for this?"

"I don't know, I just wanted it."

"What is your name?"

"Bill."

"Bill, I'm sorry, but this is not allowed under the Queen's law."

"I'm sorry, I don't know your rules. Please let me go and I won't bother you anymore."

One medical worker walks over with a different handheld device and places it over Bill's head. Another flash of light fills the room.

"What was that?"

"That is your punishment."

"What punishment, I said I was sorry. Let me just leave."

Carter stands at the pod window, gripping the camera rail with both hands. "What the fuck did they just do to Bill?"

"I don't know," Sue answers.

The woman leans into Bill. "For taking the crown means death."

"No!" Carter runs to the pod door, kicking it open. Sue doesn't have time to react and misses grabbing Carter as she jumps out.

She runs up to Bill and grabs his arm. "Please, don't kill him, he's trying to save you all."

"Carter no, get out of here!"

The woman motions to a guard, who immediately grabs Carter. "Who are you?"

Carter grabs the guard's arm and twists it, causing the guard to let go of her. He drops to his knees while she tightens her grip on his wrist.

"I'm his friend, and he was trying to save your people with the plumestone."

"You know of the stone's powers?"

"Yes, and if you don't let us help, your whole planet is going to die."

Bill struggles in the restraints. "Carter, shut up!"

"No, Bill, this is what I was saying before. I know what I'm doing."

"What are you talking about?"

Carter pulls out the tablet with the Agarthan history and hands it to the English-speaking woman. "Look, this is your history, your future history."

The woman takes the tablet and swipes through the pages. She looks at it for a few seconds, and then shows Carter the image of the queen. "What kind of trick is this? Our queen is not an old woman."

Bill starts to feel drowsy, having trouble keeping his eyes open. "Carter, stop. Just go home."

Carter takes the tablet. "This is from your future, and we're here to save you. We're from the future."

The woman takes back the tablet, swiping page after page, reading very quickly. She stops and looks up at one of her fellow workers. "Call the queen!"

Carter runs over to Bill, who's fading in and out. "Please don't let him die, please, please."

The woman grabs the device and places it back over Bill's head, flashing him yet again.

Bill opens his dilated eyes and squints at the bright room light. "Carter? What happened?"

"You're fine, I'm getting you out of here."

"Carter, what were you talking about before?"

She smiles. "It was a suspicion I had, but now I know it's true."

"What are you talking about?"

"Bill, they have no space program. They have no satellites."

"So what, what are you trying to say?"

"How do you think they knew to move their whole civilization to the center of the Earth? How do you think they knew the sun was about to scorch the planet?"

Bills, eyes still adjusting, stares at Carter in complete confusion. "I don't understand."

Just then, a woman in her mid-thirties dressed in fancy robes walks in, holding the crown that they had just tried to steal. "You are the ones who tried to take my property?"

Carter turns to the Queen. "Yes Queen, and I'm sorry, but we did it to try and save your planet."

The Queen is handed Carters tablet by the English-speaking woman, who points out a few pages. The Queen's face shows shock. "Explain this to me, how are you from our future?"

"We traveled from the future to warn you about the sun. Very soon, as you can see in the history book, all life on this planet will burn. You need to start preparing now so your people can survive, and in return, we can live in the future. That book will show you what you need to know, so please keep it, but we need something in return for this foreknowledge. We need the purple stone."

"These stones are worthless; we only use them for energy; why would you need them?"

"These stones, when combined with others, will give you power to make a new sun. They'll give you a shield that will protect you from the coming solar storms. There's enough on this planet to give you everything you see in the history book when you move your people to the center of the Earth."

"How did you know about that, no one knows about the center of the Earth space yet. We just recently discovered it."

"As I said, we're from the future. We know of all of this."

The Queen walks over to Bill, looks at him briefly, then walks to the other side of the room. "So why do you need my stone, why not get some from your own time. They're everywhere."

"After your people move to the center of the Earth, you take all the stones and use them to make a new sun. No more stones fall from space ever again. We need to experiment with this stone so we know how much we need to find in order to make another shield.

In the future, there are many more people on this planet. The ones in the center, who lived there for 400,000 years, and the ones who are on the surface. Now there are too many people in the future to all fit in the center of the Earth under the protection of the old shield. We need to build a bigger shield to protect everyone. The problem we have is the technology of how to make the shield is lost to history. We needed to come back to your time and use this one big stone to do our tests."

"So why come here, to this time? Why don't you just gather all the stones before we find them and build your shield?"

"If we take the stones that you need now, then we'll never be born, because you'll die in the solar storm."

The Queen walks over to Carter and stands face-to-face with her. She's taller than Carter and looks down into her eyes, reaching for Carters hand without saying another word.

She places the crown in Carter's hand. "Your story is too incredible to be false, and this crown is ugly anyway. If you are truthful with me, then we owe you our lives. If you are not truthful, then you only got an ugly crown for your troubles."

"Queen, we *will* bring back the crown, I promise. You'll need to wear it in the future for that drawing in your history book."

"When you have finished with the stone, please come back and see me again." She turns and walks out the door, motioning for the guards to release Bill.

Bill gets up and grabs Carter, giving her a strong hug. "How did you do that?"

Sue turns the pod around so they can see the open door. The Queen stops and watches as they climb through the pod door, which from her point of view is just a hole in the middle of the room.

Bill closes the door then sits in his chair. "Now would you please explain to me what just happened?"

Carter sits beside him. "Remember I mentioned about how they had no space program? Well, I was thinking about what you told me, about things that disappear from history. That's why we're allowed to go on missions to collect them. People think the reason those things disappeared in the first place was probably like a mini-paradox, because we collected them."

"No, I understand that part, but how could you possibly have known that you were supposed to tell them about the solar flares and Agartha?"

"Aros told me the people of his culture were fascinated by dark-haired women who look like me. You noticed that most of the people we saw here are blonde or redheaded, but no one, from either time we visited the pre-exodus, had black hair. Aros told me a woman who looked surprisingly like me was a very important historical figure. I never asked him why she was important, but when I was looking at the history book, I realized that without a space program, they would never have been able to predict the solar flares without satellites. That meant someone had to tell them it was coming. Anyone who told them something that ended up saving their entire civilization would be a pretty important historical figure."

Bill tilts his head. "That's a pretty big stretch, you know?"

"Yes, I know, but regardless of what the truth might be, we left them the history book and now they have a path to follow. If we go back to our own time and something's wrong, we'll know it before we phase back in."

"I trust you, and you're right, we can undo it if we have to. I just hate having to worry about crossing our own timeline. It can get tricky."

Before Bill can turn his seat around to the control panel, she jumps into his lap and kisses him. Sue smiles as Carter and Bill kiss as if they hadn't seen each other in a month.

After a brief reunion, Bill brings the pod back to the hangar bay. Carter's theory turned out to be correct, and after a radio check and a pod-to-base computer validation signal verified the timeline was intact, they phase in and bring the crown down to the physics lab for testing.

The three of them stand over Dr. Madison, who manages to pop the stone out. When it hits the metal table, it creates an electrical discharge similar to an old Tesla coil. The spark takes everyone by surprise, arcing from the table to the fluorescent light in the ceiling above their heads.

Dr. Madison looks at them. "Guys, this might take a while."

Bill puts his hands on Carter and Sue's shoulders. "Come on troops, let's give the man some space."

Sue stands firm. "I'd like to stay and learn what I can."

"Sure thing, Lieutenant."

***

Later at the diner, Bill looks up at Carter, across the table, eating pancakes and sausage. "I'm exhausted."

"Well, a few hours ago, you were almost dead, so yeah, I can see that. We've been awake for a good twenty-four hours with the time in orbit and our evening encounter with the Agarthan Queen."

Bill eats his last pancake. "You want to go back and get some sleep?"

Carter still feels the effects of the multiple adrenalin rushes from the past few hours. "No, I need to talk to Aros about the history book. I need to find out if I was right."

"Are you sure that's a good idea?"

"I'll be subtle. I won't reveal anything if it doesn't look like I'm right."

"Well, I'm coming with you then."

***

Carter and Bill finish up then they drive over to the Agarthan Embassy office.

"What if he doesn't know, or they just don't want to tell you?"

"I have to ask, because if I'm right and they already knew who I was, then that changes the whole game between us and them."

"You're right; it'd be a game-changer."

They pull into the parking lot at the embassy and ask to see Aros at the reception desk. A few minutes later, the elevator door opens and Aros comes out smiling.

"Miss Carter, what a wonderful surprise. I received your message but when I attempted to phone you, I could not connect."

"Hello Aros, this is my coworker, Colonel Adams."

Aros extends his lanky hand to Bill, who gives Aros an extra firm handshake and a fake smile. Carter notices the look of jealousy on Bill's face, and while she doesn't want Bill and Aros to be at odds with each other, she feels special for it.

"Sorry Aros, I was out of cell range for a couple days, and I didn't see any messages from you."

"It is not a big deal as your phrase goes, I understand."

"Aros, the Colonel and I aren't actually here on a social call. We came to ask you a question."

Aros extends his arm towards the embassy lounge. "Please, let us sit and converse about anything you would like." Aros brings them into a small room with some pillowed chairs and a small coffee table. "May I offer you some refreshments?"

"No thank you, we just came from breakfast," Carter replies.

They sit in the chairs, Bill uncomfortably rigid with his palms on his legs.

"So, what did you need to ask me, Miss Carter?"

"Well, this may sound odd, but I'd like to know if you know who I am."

Aros smiles, slightly amused by the question. "Of course, you are Evelyn Carter, and you are an information technology employee for the TTRC."

"That's not entirely accurate; I do work for the TTRC, but not in the computer room."

Aros pauses as he looks at Carter, eyes growing glassy. "It *is* you then. I told them it was you and they did not believe me."

Carter's jaw drops as Aros confirms her suspicion. She glances at Bill, then back at Aros. "So it's true then, the reason your people have a thing for women who look like me."

Aros closes the door, then walks over to Carter and kneels before her. He takes her hand and holds it with both of his. "Miss Carter, my people have been waiting for you for nearly a half a million years. You are the unknown prophet."

Bill leans forward. "Ambassador, you knew about us all this time? Why is this the first time we're hearing about this?"

"Colonel, Miss Carter. When was your time travel mission to visit our Queen?"

"It was today, just a few hours ago."

Aros turns to Bill. "And Colonel, your first name is Bill?"

"Yes, how did you know?"

Aros stands and clasps his hands together loosely. "Because you told us your name when we revived you." Aros goes back to his seat, his eyes beginning to water. "It was your warning and the gift of the digital history record that saved our entire civilization. Our queen kept the meeting between you a secret until she could confirm your story was true. It was not until after the entire civilization had survived the solar activity that the truth was released to the rest of the Agarthan civilization. However, only those in our government were told that you were time travelers from our own future. To the rest of our society, Miss Carter was simply referred to as the Prophet. Mysterious visitors sent by the gods, or as some grew to believe, extraterrestrial beings of highly advanced technology."

Carter laughs aloud. "HA! They thought we were aliens!"

"We knew that we must allow time to play out as your own history and the history you provided to us had been written, or we would face the possibility of a paradox, that could prevent your mission in the first place."

Bill interrupts, "So is that why you never developed your own time travel?"

"Exactly, its research was banned immediately after the exodus, even though we had sound theories on how to do it. We simply could not allow it out of fear of corrupting the timeline and endangering our own existence."

Carter asks, "So did they take a photo of me? Is that how people came to admire women like me?"

"There were photos taken, but the Queen hid them and described you to our historians. She admired your beauty. She told the tale for many years of the dark-haired prophet who saved us, and over time, images were created based on her description. It was decided to not share the images with you when we gave you our history books so that we would not influence your own selection as a time traveler. No images or names of the prophet were to ever be shared with the people who stayed on the surface. That was the decree of the queen before her passing."

"Aros, what does this mean for our two people's relationship now?" Bill asks.

"This indeed *does* change our treaty. Now we must have our two delegations meet and disclose why we were so secretive. Miss Carter, I knew with every fiber of my being when I saw you in the café it had to be you. The description of your appearance was so close. Your TTRC badge showing your last name, and, of course, your unrivaled beauty. I just knew it."

Carter blushes, smiling.

Bill clears his throat loudly. "Did Carter tell you we are dating?"

Aros seems taken by surprise for a moment. "My apologies, Miss Carter, for any indiscretion on my part."

Carter smiles at Bill, then at Aros. "No problem Aros, you didn't know."

"Yeah, no problem Ambassador," Bill adds reluctantly.

Aros stands and walks them to the lobby. "It appears we are in uncharted waters now. I no longer have a guide book for my Omni, as you might say."

Carter stops and looks at Bill then turns back to Aros. "Aros, the plumestone the Queen gave us. We don't know how to use it."

"Ah, yes, I almost forgot about that. Of course, I will have our scientists contact your technicians so you know how to use them."

"That's good, but we have another problem: we only have the one stone. And we think we'll need more—a lot more."

"Yes, the Queen wrote that you could not find any more in the future. We found that the origin of the stones was from space rocks."

"Yes we found the same thing, but we need help finding more of them in space."

"I will inform our scientists to also bring you all data we have researched on them. This will be delivered to your headquarters as soon as I contact my superiors back home."

"Thank you, Aros, we look forward to it."

"It once again has been a pleasure, and now it is truly an honor to finally confirm who you really are, Miss Carter."

Bill and Carter leave the Embassy and get back in their car.

He sits in the driver's seat and rubs his face with his hands. "I'm blown away."

"I kinda am, too." She rolls down the window. "I was starting to think I was wrong and it was just my imagination running wild, but when Aros confirmed it, I sort of went numb."

"You went numb? I've been having sex with an alien slash prophet, think how I feel."

They both laugh loudly.

CHAPTER 15: ORIGINS

At 5 p.m. that evening, Bill and Carter are catching up on some missed sleep when his phone rings. He grabs it before the second ring and walks into Carter's kitchen so he doesn't wake her.

"Yes, General, sir."

"Colonel, what the hell is going on? Can you explain why every general and admiral from the entire United States Armed Forces is sitting in my ready room and why the Secretary of Defense, the joint chiefs, and the Secretary of State are flying in as we speak?"

"Well, sir, I was going to tell you but we got hung up on some base business and—"

"Colonel, you and your team better be in my office in the next ten minutes, or I'm going to send some MP's and drag you down here."

"Yes, sir, we're leaving now."

Bill hangs up the phone, and calls Sue. "Sue, get to the General's office immediately. I'll meet you there in five minutes."

He disconnects. "Carter, get up, we're in trouble."

She sits up from a sound sleep and whips the comforter off so forcefully that it spins in the air and hits the bedroom floor. "What's wrong, what is it?"

"I don't know for sure, babe, but the General's fuming. It probably has something to do with us paying Aros a visit before getting permission."

They put on their jumpsuits and rush down to the car. When they arrive at the TTRC, they run to the General's office, where Sue already stands at the door, smiling.

General Wilson gets up from his desk, walks past them, and barks out "Follow me!"

They double-time down the hallway and follow the General to the hangar bay. When they arrive in the ready room, every chair is occupied, and about thirty generals stand against the wall.

"What's going on?" Carter asks.

Bill shakes his head, looking at the largest gathering of generals he has ever seen.

General Wilson escorts the team to the front of the room next to the podium. "Ladies and gentlemen, allow me to introduce the crew of Time Ship One."

The entire room erupts in applause as the three of them stand there stunned by the unexpected ovation. General Wilson reaches to Carter and motions for her to stand next to him.

"This is Evelyn Carter, she's the one you've all come here to meet. Miss Carter, please stand at the podium."

The crowd begins another round of applause, and all of the generals, who'd been sitting, stand up. Carter, feeling overwhelmed and confused, reluctantly moves up to the podium and looks at the crowd with a nervous smile. Just as she feels the situation can't get any more uncomfortable, a delegation of Agarthans, including Aros, walk into the room. Behind them is the President's joint chiefs and the President of the United States himself.

General Wilson calls out, "Attention!"

Everyone rises and stands at attention as the President makes his way to the front of the room next to Carter.

President James Bradford reaches out to shake her hand. "It's a pleasure to meet you, Evelyn."

"Thank you Mr. President," Carter replies with a momentary stutter.

Carter steps to the side of the podium as the President moves in. "May I introduce the King of Agartha, His Highness King Solla."

The Agarthan King, who doesn't stand out from the rest of the delegation, walks up to the podium. His robes and appearance show no sign of status. He is very tall, about six feet five inches, with short blonde hair and pale skin. On his hand he wears a gold bracelet Carter notices when he extends his hand to the President.

The President continues, "Today is a turning point between all the people of Earth. Just a few hours ago, King Solla informed me that the restrictions in our treaty regarding trade, technology and travel are officially lifted. We are now a singular civilization who shares this planet equally."

The generals applaud again. Carter looks over at Bill, amazed. He responds with the same expression.

The President shakes the Kings hand and guides him to stand next to him. "King Solla has requested to meet our time ship crew who made the journey just last night. These three crew members fulfilled an historic Agarthan prophecy that made this new union possible. King, if you please, allow me to introduce ship Commander Colonel William Adams, Engineer Lieutenant Susan Philips, and Documentarian Evelyn Carter."

The King shakes Bill and Sue's hands, then as the President steps aside, King Solla approaches Carter. She smiles and lifts her hand to the King's. Solla immediately drops to his knee and places her knuckles on his forehead.

When the King stands back up and looks into Carters eyes, Carter finds he's crying, overwhelmed by the moment. "Please don't cry," she says in a soft voice.

"Imagine if you had just held the hand of your savior."

He lets go of her hand and pulls a cloth from his robe to dry his eyes. As he turns back towards the President, he puts his hand on the President's shoulder. "Thank you Mr. President." He turns toward the audience. "May our future together be one of peace, joy, and millennia together." He steps down from the podium and rejoins his delegation.

The President steps back to the podium and puts his arm around Carter pulling her close to his side. "They told me to call you Carter, so Carter, let me say that this mission has made the relationship between our two peoples an open one, and one of hope and peace."

"Thank you, sir."

The President shakes Carter's hand as a photographer snaps some photos. After a few minutes of meeting some of the generals and more of the Agarthan delegation, Bill, Carter and Sue step out of the ready room and walk across the hangar to their pod.

"Wow, I thought we were in trouble for the unauthorized disclosure of future events," he says.

"You know, had I not seen the history books or had conversations with Aros, I don't know if I would have done the things I did to try and save you. Sue was calling the shots in your rescue."

"Well, it's a good thing you did."

Sue holds up a tablet and shows it to them. "One of the Agarthan delegates gave me this in the ready room. It has all the relevant data on the plumestones from the Agarthan database."

Bill takes the tablet. "Let's get this over to Dr. Madison and figure out how much of the mineral we need."

They start heading out the hangar bay and walk down the hall when Carter, about to say something to Bill, notices he is not in the hall with them. "Bill?"

Bill stands next to the pedestal that the Times Square time capsule hovers over. "Guys, come look at this."

Carter and Sue walk back in the hangar and look at the capsule. "What about it?" Carter asks.

"The countdown timer is different from when we left. It should say there are still a couple years left, but the timer says fourteen days," Bill says in a whisper.

"Why are you whispering?"

Sue leans in. "I should have noticed this when we got back from collecting the crown—we must have changed something in the past."

"Is that bad?"

"I don't know, the base computer and the pod computer synced the random code that's generated on every departure to ensure the timeline wasn't disrupted. When we came back, the codes checked out, otherwise we would have gotten an alarm not to phase in. Should we ask someone if they noticed the countdown timer change?" Sue asks Bill.

"Not directly, let's try and ask someone without letting them know there's a possible paradox first."

They leave the hangar bay and head to Dr. Madison's lab. When they arrive, Madison is running tests on the sample they pulled. Bill approaches and hands him the tablet Sue received from the Agarthans. "Doctor, here's the data on the stones."

Madison takes the tablet and sits down on his lab stool. He swipes through page after page, looking for specific formulas.

Sue sits down next to Madison. "Do you see anything, Doctor?"

"This formula shows how to start the reaction, which looks like a type of fusion, and this one," he swipes the pages on the tablet rapidly forward, "this one here shows how to create the phase shield strength, size and shape manipulation."

Bill watches as Sue and Madison speak in what he considers tech jargon. "How much do we need?"

They both pull out scientific calculators and start working out their answers. They chatter back and forth, verifying they are following the proper steps.

"How much?" Bill says in a loud annoyed voice.

Sue shows her calculator to Madison and he does the same. "Four tons," they reply.

"Four tons, huh? That seems like a lot."

Sue puts her calculator away. "Well considering how much of it fell to Earth over three quarters of a million years, yeah, it's a lot. However, you have to take into consideration that wherever this mineral originated, it had to be in much higher concentrations. Even the asteroid field that the Earth was making contact with wouldn't have deposited more than a few percent of its entire volume. Not to mention the amount under the oceans that we have no way yet of detecting."

"All I want to know is can we find that amount?"

"Yes, but I think we'll need to bring in some help. I suggest we get Steve to help us track back the asteroid field to its origin so we can find the bigger asteroids. He has the experience with deep space flight and can assist in tracking the trajectories."

"Right, why scoop up thousands of small rocks when you can get one big one," Carter says.

"Exactly."

Bill slaps his hands together and rubs them vigorously. "Perfect! Sue, go get Steve. Carter and I will prep the pod for departure."

"Yes, sir."

As they start walking out the door, Bill stops and asks Madison, "Doc, do you think you and the Lieutenant can put this thing together before the timer runs out on the original time capsule?"

Dr. Madison looks at Bill strangely. "You mean in two years? I can probably get something made in a few days. What does making the shield have to do with the capsule?"

Bill had only made that up off the top of his head to see if Madison knew about the countdown timer change. "Oh, I just wanted to make sure we would be done before that."

"Oh."

The crew walks out of the lab.

"Real smooth, Bill," Carter says with a smile.

"Yeah, I didn't really think that one through. It sounded better in my head, but the reality is the timer changed after we phased in, so the mission didn't have a paradox. Now I'm just as concerned because the countdown timer was affected by something else."

"What if the countdown changed after we confronted Aros?" Carter asks.

"That would be a first, normally we don't have changes that occur after a phase in," Sue says. She splits off from the group as they pass Hangar Bay Two. "I'll see you guys later, Steve should be back soon."

As Bill and Carter get closer to General Wilson's office, Bill starts heading towards his door.

"Are you going to tell the General about the countdown timer?" she asks.

"Yes, now that we know it was not us, he needs to know." He knocks on the door and pokes his head inside. "General, are you busy?"

"Colonel, Carter, of course not, what can I do for you?"

"Sir, we were just in the hangar after the meeting and I noticed the countdown timer on the original time machine capsule has changed."

"What do you mean?"

"Sir, it says fourteen days now. At first we thought there might have been a paradox from our mission to get the royal crown, but we double checked, and the synchronization was accurate."

"Thank you Colonel, I'll get the science team down there to see what's going on."

"Yes, sir. Also, we've determined the amount of the mineral we'll need, and are preparing a deep space mission along with Lieutenant Colonel Philips to backtrack the path the original asteroids traveled. Sue feels we can locate the entire amount we need in one large rock by traveling to the source."

"Normally I'd deny the request to have Sue and Steve together on a pod again, but under these circumstances I see no problem."

"Yes, sir. I'll let you know when the mission plan is complete."

"Thank you, Colonel. Oh and Carter, good job on the last mission, I just hope your next is as successful, or we won't be around to enjoy our new relationship with the Agarthans."

"Thank you, sir. I won't let you down."

"I have no doubt about that, Carter."

They leave the Generals office, and Bill looks at his watch. "Well it's 19:00. Do you want to call it a day, as short as it was? Maybe get some dinner?"

"That sounds good; I'm starving but my sleep routine is all messed up after sleeping all day."

"Well, tomorrow you'll be suffering from too much sleep."

"You think we'll get sleep tonight?"

"Well, if we want to get back on schedule, we should probably hit the rack at regular time tonight."

"Bill, think about what I just said."

He continues walking with Carter towards the elevator. When they get in and he presses the button, he finally realizes what she meant.

CHAPTER 16: PACK AN EXTRA LUNCH

The next morning, Carter and Bill arrive at the hangar bay, where Sue and Steve are prepping the pod for the mission.

Bill extends his hand to Steve. "Thanks for coming with us on this one, we will definitely need your experience in deep space."

Steve, pushing a rolling gear table towards the pod, stops to shake Bill's hand. "No problem Colonel, I'm excited to track these asteroids down. I've done a few track backs before, and they can get tricky."

"So how did you react to the sudden rush of classified information that just got dumped on you?"

"I always knew something was going on with your pod, but I never anticipated something this big."

Bill looks over the table of extra gear. "How many matter containment modules are we bringing?"

Sue replies, "I'm packing three of the large capacity pod based modules and I have a few of the smaller modules that go in the handheld unit just in case."

Bill picks up one of the pod modules and inspects it, a heavy cube-shaped digital storage device with a textured surface and a data port on one side. In his head, he calculates their combined storage size. "That's more than four times the capacity we need."

"It is, but we don't want to have to go back for more if we miscalculate our phase shield or damage the mineral."

"Good thinking, Lieutenant."

"How long will we be out there? This is a lot of supplies," Carter comments.

"Steve, how long do you estimate?" Bill asks.

"I've spent weeks tracking asteroids. If the asteroid is being directed by the gravity of just stars and planets, we can plot straight paths from one to the next. If the asteroids change path because of collisions, then they could be bouncing around all over the place. That can take a while to locate the impact points and recalculate the trajectories. So there are some quick straight jumps, and then some instances where I'm reversing time very slowly as I calculate deflection points."

"So, Carter, I'd pack some extra food and personal items if I were you," Bill says.

Steve points under the rolling table. "I already loaded up about one hundred MRE's. I've also installed the deep space equipment package on the pod. The DSEP gives us an extra oxygen generator, a larger water supply and longer lasting urine forward osmosis filter. Plus, I packed a few other things I found are helpful for these longer, boring missions."

"Well, it sounds like you have your shit together." Carter laughs.

"No, that gets collected and converted to soap." Steve pushes the cart over to the pod.

"Carter, he's joking about the soap," Bill whispers.

"Ya think?"

After loading the extra supplies, the four of them board the pod that is now stuffed with almost too much equipment. It's cramped, and Carter looks around, trying to figure out how they're going to manage for a week or more.

"Oh look, Steve installed an extra command chair behind mine. Great, less room to sleep," Carter jokes.

"Sorry to steal your seat, Carter."

"No, it's fine, you men love to do the driving on long trips."

"HA." Sue laughs, then snorts loudly. "Steve hates driving when we go out. I'm always doing the long drive to Tucson when we go home."

Bill closes the pod door and hops in his chair. "Ready, troops? Let's wrangle up some asteroids."

"Yee-haw!" Carter pauses for a few awkward seconds. "Sorry, that sounded dumber than I thought it would."

Bill powers up, and phases out the pod. They arrive in space above the Earth.

Carter looks out at the Earth. "When are we?"

Steve answers, "We're one hour before impact of the large plumestone that eventually becomes the queens crown embedment. I used the data from the Black Knight survey recording. I'm going to locate that asteroid before it impacts Earth, and use it as a tracking point to find its origin. Sue, can you start the scan?"

Sue taps her screen. "Scanning now, honey."

Bill turns around, puts his hand on Carters knee, and gives her a smile. "This is it Carter, if it weren't for you we wouldn't be here."

She smiles back and holds his hand.

Sue's console starts flashing and beeping. "Got the signal. It's one hundred miles off our starboard bow. I'm sending the coordinates to navigation."

Steve moves the pod into visual range. "Colonel, begin your time reversal now, and I'll see if I can get a track on its origin point."

"Reversing at normal speed, let me know when you want me to speed it up."

Bill and Steve continue tracking the asteroid back in time along its path. As they go back in time, they move further away from Earth. The Earth and Sun get smaller and smaller in the window until they are so far away they can't see them.

They move faster and faster backward through time, keeping the single plumestone asteroid on their scanner.

"Well Carter, you may be in luck, so far the trajectory is pretty straight," Steve says.

The pod moves deeper and deeper into the galaxy, passing multiple stars and planets. For three days, they pass through beautiful gas nebulas, past stars and planets of all sizes and colors.

***

"Bill, wake up Carter, she might want to take a look out the aft window on the door," Sue says.

Bill stands and steps over Carter, who is sleeping on the pod floor, and looks out the rear window. He smiles, bends down, and lightly moves the hair off Carter's face.

"Carter."

She opens her eyes. "What?"

"Come look at this."

She sits up and rubs her face to shake off the sleep. Bill points out the window. As her eyes adjust, she stands and looks through the window. "Oh my god, it's beautiful. Is that ours?"

"Yup, it's the Milky Way galaxy. We're far enough away to see its shape."

"There are galaxies all over the place; why are they so close together?"

Sue turns to Carter. "We're far enough back in time that stellar drift hasn't spread the galaxies apart that much yet."

Carter grabs her camera from the gear locker and presses the rubber lens shade against the window. "Has anyone seen this before?"

"No babe, you're the first to record it." Bill holds her waist from behind and kisses the back of her head.

"My God, I can see the rotation. It's backward, but I can fix that in post."

"Normally you'd never be able to perceive the rotation, but we're moving backwards through time so quickly that the Milky Way is rotating once every thirteen minutes," Steve says.

"Oh look, those other two galaxies are about to join together!"

"Actually, they already *did* join, remember they're in reverse," Steve replies.

The two oval shaped galaxies get closer until they blend in Carter's camera viewfinder. The billions of stars from each galaxy splash together and spin in all directions.

"They're dancing!"

"They are indeed," Bill whispers.

"Now they're separating again, and the two galaxies are rounder and flatter, like a disc."

A few hours later, after Carter finishes documenting the galactic movements, they sit waiting for the sensors to find the larger grouping of plumestones.

"Bill, did you bring anything to do? Like maybe a game or something?" Carter asks.

"Steve installed a portable digital video player with movies and TV shows to keep everyone from going crazy from boredom."

"Cool, what videos do we have, Steve?"

"I brought the entire *Doctor Who* series from 2005 on."

"Seen them. Anything else? Maybe not time-travel themed."

"Sue brought some chick flicks you guys can watch."

"Carter, if you're bored, why don't you and Bill take a shower?" Sue suggests.

"Come on, let's try it." Carter grabs Bills collar and guides him into the shower.

***

Twenty minutes later Sue turns to Steve. "Sleeping arrangements are a little bit uncomfortable with four people in the pod, and Bill snores. Maybe we should take the remaining days in shifts?"

"That's fine, it looks like there is a signal ahead."

"Yeah, I see it. It's big too."

"Sue, go get Bill, it's time to go to work."

Sue gets up, walks to the door of the shower and presses her ear against it. She whispers, "I think they need a little more time." She listens and puts her hand over her mouth as she hears the muffled sounds. "Nope, they're done."

She tiptoes back to her seat just as Carter opens the door.

Steve looks back at her as she walks out. "Your hair's dry; did you even get wet in there?"

Sue smacks Steve on the arm. "None of your business, mister!" She turns to Bill. "We have a large target on sensors."

"Excellent, calculate the mass on it."

"It appears this is bigger than we need. It's about the size of a school bus. There's also lots of smaller fragments traveling with it."

"Ready the matter beam and let's scoop it and the fragments up except the original one."

Carter turns to Bill. "Why not take them all?"

"Because the Agarthans will be using this one for their artificial sun, and if we take it, we could alter the timeline."

Carter sits back in her chair. "Gotcha."

Sue beams in all the asteroids as per Bills command. "Ok we have them, and the first storage module is full." Sue Gets up and opens a panel next to her chair and pulls out the cube shaped storage device and replaces it with the second of three they brought onboard.

"OK let's continue tracking," Steve says to Bill.

They continue to follow the original asteroid back along its path for a few more hours. They once again come to a stop and pick up another giant asteroid made from the precious mineral.

"Sue, what do you think—is that enough? Bill asks.

"No, we still have enough storage left for two more that size. I say we go for the motherlode and collect as much as we can."

Bill looks down at his console, which shows the current year—seventeen billion years in the past. "Guys, I don't think anyone has ever been back this far."

Carter leans in. "How far back can we go?"

"I'm not sure. As far as we know, we're already farther back than astronomers thought possible. From the looks of things outside the window, it doesn't seem very hospitable. These stars look extremely volatile and shrouded in nebulas."

Steve turns to Bill. "I think we're safe. We're protected from everything by our phased shields, so I say we keep going."

Bill looks back at Carter. "What do you think?"

"Sue is the scientist; I'm just along for the ride."

"OK, let's fill her up then."

Bill and Steve continue going back in time, tracking multiple small asteroids. As they travel deeper into the past, the view outside the window becomes obscured by colorful gas nebula. They can no longer see the asteroids due to the diffused light from the nebula.

"Big one ahead on scanner, sir," Sue calls out, looking at her screen.

"Where is it?"

Sue taps on the control panel. "Sending it to your screen."

Bill slows the time reversal down and Steve maneuvers the pod into range.

Steve examines the sensor data on the screen. "Looks like it's actually multiple asteroids that just recently fractured."

Carter looks out the window as the house-sized asteroid comes into view. "Ha, it looks like it was almost perfectly round, like an apple before it split."

Bill looks over his shoulder. "Sue, that one looks too big, do you think we should skip it?"

"No, I think you should take it, we should have just enough storage space left."

"Okay, collect that split one and let me know what our storage is at."

Sue aims the matter beam at the giant split asteroid and beams it into the last storage module. "Done. We still have five percent capacity left if you want to fill it up completely."

Steve moves the pod as Bill continues reversing time. Suddenly, the pod emerges from the bright cloudy nebula into a dark region of black space.

Sue taps on her control panel. "This can't be right. Sir, I lost the signal. The target tracked asteroid is no longer on sensors."

Bill stops the time reversal. "How can we lose the signal? It was just right there."

Carter squeezes between Bill and Steve and leans into the window. "Guys...where are the stars?"

Everyone stops and looks out the window. Bill shuts off the interior lights so they can get rid of the reflection on the glass. The view is deep black with no stars or planets, not even the gas nebula they had just traveled through.

Sue sits down and starts scanning on all channels. "Sir, there's nothing out there. No radiation, nothing on infrared or any instrument. The time frequency readout says all zeros."

Carter looks at Sue. "How the hell is that even possible?"

"I don't know. According to my readings, it's just empty space."

Bill sits down and moves the pod forward in time. Slowly the years tick by on the digital readout, but the view remains the same. He speeds up the rate of time until over two billion years have passed, and still nothing. He brings the pod to a complete stop and just sits quietly, looking at the computer screen. He rolls the dial back and brings the pod to the seventeen-billion-year mark that they had just been at.

Carter stares at him, waiting for him to finish thinking through the problem, but he stays silent. "Bill!"

He looks up at Carter and she sees in his eyes that he has no answers. "This is extremely bad. I don't know, Carter."

Sue looks up at Steve, who still stares out the window. Her eyes move back and forth rapidly as she works out what has happened, until finally, she claps both hands over her mouth to contain her shriek. "I know what this is!"

Everyone looks at Sue, but Bill is the first to ask. "Just say it, Sue."

Sue looks at each one of their faces. "It's a causality loop."

Steve sits down, his hands on his head. "Of course!"

"What the fuck is a causality loop?" Carter says loudly.

"It's when a time traveler does something that affects the future, but until the time traveler does it, the future can't continue. It's like a self-fulfilling prophecy. They refer to it as the bootstrap paradox."

"A paradox!" Carter exclaims.

"Relax, we'll fix this." Bill pulls her back into her chair.

Sue leans in. "Bill, we can't fix this one. You already moved us through time two billion years. The universe is gone, it never existed."

"What do you mean it never existed, we were just in it a few minutes ago!" Bill yells.

"Everyone calm down. Let's just think this through," Steve interjects. "So we went back in time to before the universe existed, before the big bang or whatever created the universe. Then we went forward, but nothing was there. Maybe the instruments are off?"

Bill turns back to the console. The return button blinks on the screen. "So if the universe is gone, and I hit the return button, then we won't instantly travel back to base, right?" Bill hits the return button. There is the familiar flash of light, but once again, they're floating in space with nothing around them.

Carter slams her hands on the camera rail. "Fuck! Now what do we do?"

Sue stands up. "Bill, we have to go back again to where we just were. Go to the time and the location exactly when we realized everything was gone. I know what we have to do to fix this."

274

"You mind letting us in on your plan?" Bill brings the pod back to the origin point again.

Sue walks over to the wall panel where the matter storage unit is and pulls out the last of the three storage module cubes. She brings them over to a panel on the other side of the pod next to Bill's chair. She opens the panel, revealing the pod's emergency beacon, and slides the rectangular box beacon onto the floor.

"There's a cargo container inside the beacon. I can load up the matter storage modules and we can send them back to the base. Once they get them, they can build the Earth phase shield."

Bill slams his palm on the console. "Sue are you paying attention? We were just at headquarters; it doesn't exist anymore. How the hell will they get the beacon if we can't even go there?"

Steve turns to Bill. "Bill, what do you think caused the big bang?"

"I don't know, nobody knows!"

Carter realizes what Steve is saying. "Oh my god! *We* caused it?"

Bill gets up and walks to the other side of the pod. He turns around and crosses his arms, his face is red and his breathing is heavy. "No! How can that even be possible?"

Sue answers. "It's the causality loop. We were always meant to take all the steps we took to get to this point. Everything we've ever done as long as we've been alive was always going to happen and lead us to this point. Right here, right now, to do the next logical thing. The only way the universe can exist now is to introduce matter into it. When the matter enters the empty universe, it'll cause a reaction with the subatomic universe. That matter has to be us. Everything aboard this pod contains the building blocks for the universe. We have all the elements in the periodic table for all matter built into this pod."

Carter stands up. "Wait a minute, so we have to *die* to start the universe up? What the fuck? Bill, just launch the beacon, that'll be the same thing right?"

Bill looks over at Sue. "Sue?"

"No, that won't work. We only have one beacon. If the beacon gets destroyed, and it's not enough to start the universe again, then we'll have to destroy the pod anyway. We lose both, including all the plumestones we just collected. If we launch the beacon off the pod, then we phase in and send the beacon to the present, then the beacon with the plumestones will avoid the blast zone and appear on Earth. Everything will be reset, and the TTRC will have the plumestones."

Bill spins around and punches the door to the shower. "I don't believe in FATE!" He punches the door multiple times before Carter grabs him from behind and hugs him. Blood from his knuckles stains the white door. He drops his head against the door and stands silently while Carter sobs into the back of his jumpsuit.

Sue holds Steve's hand as they watch Bill and Carter dealing. Steve puts his hand on her cheek as he kisses her.

"Sue, what about a rescue mission? Can't we tell the General to send someone back, and then we transfer into another pod? The pod can still explode, but we can escape," Carter pleads.

"I think that's a bad idea. The matter in our bodies might be required to complete the periodic table of elements. The reaction when the pod explodes has to be exact for the timeline to be restored. We won't feel anything, Carter."

They all sit where they are for the next ten minutes. The four agree that the choice is a certainty. The universe is demanding the sacrifice. Carter continues to argue and propose different solutions, but eventually, she concedes.

Carter walks to the food storage panel. "Well, I guess before we do it, we have time for a last meal. I mean, even death row inmates get a last meal."

Carter opens the storage locker and pulls out the tray of MRE's. Over the next hour they sit and eat, sharing stories of their lives and laughing.

***

With only minutes remaining before they take the action to repair time, Sue stares at the data on her screen in a futile endeavor to find an alternate solution. Steve rummages through the gear in the back, trying to keep himself busy. Carter puts on her headphones and listens to some music, but shuts it off after listening to "Who Wants to Live Forever" by Queen. Bill, on the other hand, sits and stares at what everyone else is doing.

Bill reaches to Carter, grasps her hand and looks into her eyes. He clears his throat and issues an order to Sue.

"Prep the beacon for launch."

Carter leans forward and rests her head in his lap. Bill feels her body shake as he holds her.

Sue programs the beacon to phase in a few hours after they had originally left. As Sue writes the program into the beacon's computer, she thinks about leaving a message.

"Bill, I think we need to warn them not to attempt a rescue. If they come back to try and save us, it'll undo everything. In addition to the note, the last five hours of pod data, cockpit audio and video will automatically transfer into the beacon's memory bank, so they'll see what went wrong."

"That's fine, Sue."

"I think I have to program in some other stuff as well to complete the causality loop. I don't want this to be all for nothing. I just need a few more minutes."

Bill nods to Sue, then looks down at Carter's face, which is soaked with tears. He moves the stray hairs off her cheeks. "Don't worry."

Sue finishes programming the beacon and loads it with its precious cargo of digitized plumestone asteroids into the beacon launch tube. "Ready for launch, sir."

Carter sits back and wipes her face as Bill turns to the console and brings up the phase in controls on his screen. "I'm setting it to launch the beacon ten seconds before phase in. Right after the beacon launches, ten seconds later, we'll phase in and hopefully fix this mess."

He presses the start button and the countdown begins. Silently the numbers count backwards. Sue stares at Steve, who sits on the stack of extra equipment stored in the back by the pod door. Carter watches Bill through a steady stream of tears. The timer hits fifteen seconds, and she jumps out of her chair and hugs Bill tighter than she's ever hugged anyone in her life.

She pulls her head back and looks him in the eyes. "Bill, I love you."

Before he can reply, there's a flash of light.

Moments later, the beacon shoots out at incredible speed. The pod phases into the empty universe, creating a magnificent blue flash.

The chain reaction of matter entering a subatomic universe is spectacular. A wave of energy on a colossal scale blasts out from the blackness. Colors that no human has ever seen fill the empty space, and last for thousands of years. Shock waves emanate from the origin point, pushing the newly-formed matter in all directions. Over millions of years, the explosion known as the Big Bang settles, and matter condenses to form the stars and the galaxies.

Billions of years pass before the first formation of planets. Life once again takes root on the lucky ones. The universe continues to expand and plays out history, just as the crew of Pod One had intended and paid for with their lives.

Back at the TTRC, things exist just as it did an hour after Carter, Bill, Sue and Steve had left. To the people at the TTRC, nothing changed. Pod One's mission was a success; life went on.

CHAPTER 17: TIME'S UP

Airman Rodriguez is on watch in Hangar Bay One an hour after Pod One departed from their mission to collect the plumestones. He paces back and forth across the opening to the hangar bay door as he always does on watch. His M14 rifle is slung in ready position across his chest, an M9 Berretta sidearm on his belt. He loves working in the TTRC because the coffee machine has Kona beans, per General Wilson's request.

Rodriguez has been on base for about a year, guarding the hangar bay. He's the one airman who gives everyone a smile along with a salute as they enter and leave. When he's not on watch, he assists in any task the Air Force asks him to do.

Rodriguez marches back and forth until he hears the sound of a phase in. There is an electrical arc flash and the sound of a *thud*, like something metallic dropping. He turns to see what the noise is, but when he investigates, he doesn't see anything out of the ordinary from the pod arrival and departure spots.

"Hangar Bay One, security watch to control room."

"Go ahead, Hangar Bay One."

"Hangar Bay One reports all conditions *not* normal."

"Hangar Bay One, please describe situation."

"Evidence of a phasing in time ship, but no time ship arrived."

"Copy that, investigate further and report."

He walks over to investigate the sound coming from the pedestal area which supports the original Times Square pod. The cylinder is still there. He looks around the pedestal looking to see what caused the noise. Unable to locate the source, he radios his commander again.

"The sound came from the pedestal containing the time cylinder, but I can't see what made the sound." Suddenly he notices the cylinder is no longer hovering, and the phase field has deactivated. The timer on the cylinder says all zeros. "Belay my last. The Cylinder countdown has completed and the device is now unshielded and resting on the pedestal."

A few seconds later, a team of six security personnel and one Air Force security lieutenant arrive at the hangar bay after running down the hall.

Lieutenant Harris immediately calls out to Rodriguez. "Airman, did you touch the device?"

"Sir, no sir, it was like that when I found it, sir."

"Very well. All of you stand guard while I inform the General."

The seven armed airmen surround the pedestal with their rifles locked and loaded. Lieutenant Harris runs out of the hangar and down to the General's office.

"Yes Lieutenant, what can I do for you?"

"Sir, the time cylinder countdown has completed and dropped sir; it's no longer protected by the energy field."

General Wilson hangs up on whoever he was on the phone with. "That's three days early. What's going on with that timer?" He runs down to the hangar bay. "Science team, code one".

From every floor in the building, the sound of people running can be heard as the entire building rushes to the hangar bay.

When he arrives, he orders the airmen standing guard. "Step aside." He approaches the device and touches it.

"Sir, please don't endanger yourself, let me touch it first." Lieutenant Harris pleads.

"It's fine Harris, I'm OK."

The tech team rushes into the hangar bay, extremely excited to see the device now accessible. Doctors Stern and Madison rush to the pedestal and examine the device. Stern finds an access panel on the side of the cylinder that he immediately opens, revealing a storage compartment. When he opens it, he's stunned to find it containing matter collection device memory storage modules.

"General, these are our matter storage modules, how did they get in the device?"

"I have no clue, Doctor."

Madison removes the stack of modules. "General, this is a distress beacon from a time ship, but our beacons are square."

"Well, who sent it then?"

Stern looks in the compartment where the modules were stored. "Sir there is a piece of paper inside."

General Wilson reaches in, retrieves the folded paper, and reads it aloud. "Under no circumstances attempt a rescue mission for Pod One and its crew. We are trapped in a causality loop and cannot return to base. Enclosed are three storage modules all containing stored plumestone for the Earth phase shield. See embedded flight data recorder for details on mission. Signed, Lieutenant Sue Philips." General Wilson passes the note to Doctor Madison. "Doctor, how did a message from Pod One end up in a cylinder-shaped beacon when every single beacon our pods use is rectangular?"

"Sir, the only possible answer is this beacon is from an alternate timeline, an alternate reality."

"Take the beacon down to the lab and retrieve the flight data, call me if you see anything. Doctor Stern, I want those matter storage modules put under lock and key until we can bring them to an adequate location to reintegrate them, who knows how big they are."

Madison and Stern both take off to their respective labs. General Wilson walks over to the pedestal where the beacon had been sitting and places his hand on the cold hard surface.

"Godspeed Pod One, Godspeed." The crew of Pod One is lost and he wants to know how it happened. The General walks briskly over to the lab where Madison is retrieving the flight data.

When he walks in, Madison has already got a video cable connected to the beacon and is setting up a video monitor. "Almost done, sir."

Madison and the General sit and watch the video of the interior of the pod for a few hours. They listen to the crew as they worked out the situation and came to their final conclusion.

General Wilson stands up. "I've seen enough."

Madison pauses the video and then looks up at the General. "So they're dead, General? We can't launch a rescue mission?"

General Wilson, now feeling all stages of denial at the same time, quickly responds. "It's a causality loop Doctor, it had to go down this way. No matter what we do or did, this was always going to happen."

The General starts walking out of the lab. "Now I have to inform next of kin. This is the part of the job I hate the most."

After the General leaves, Madison continues watching the last two hours of the video. He watches the last hour of the crew enjoying their last meal and sharing stories. Madison is moved at how heroic the crew is, knowing they will be facing death so soon and so certainly. As he watches the last few minutes, he feels uneasy, about to witness their deaths. He's tempted to stop, but continues for the sake of science. He watches the thirty-second countdown begin and starts to become ill. He sees when Carter jumped to Bill for the final embrace. When she expressed her love for him, when that bright flash filled the pod.

Madison looks away from the monitor, stands up, and walks away to get a glass of water. As he fills his cup, he hears a voice coming from the video recording. He drops the cup to the floor and runs back, where he sees the pod interior but all the crew are gone, except Steve. Steve talks directly to the camera. Madison watches for a few seconds, then hits pause and runs out of the lab and down the hall screaming.

"General, stop! General stop!"

In his office, the General sits at his desk, looking at his phone. Wilson hears Madison's voice screaming in the hallway. He jumps up from his desk and hurries out to the hall just as Madison arrives at the door almost knocking the General over.

"What is it, Doctor?"

"Sir, they're alive."

"Doctor, what on earth are you talking about?"

"Sir, there was more on the video, you need to see it."

General Wilson quickly follows Madison back to the lab, where Madison rewinds the section of the video. It begins playing at the point when Bill starts the countdown timer. When Carter says "I love you", there is a flash of light that quickly messes with the camera's automatic iris, making it look like there was no more video, but as the camera readjusts, Steve is seen walking over to the timer, holding a portable matter gun in his hand. He pauses the countdown at eleven seconds.

"This is Lieutenant Colonel Steve Philips, aboard the United States Time Ship Pod One. Our pod is caught in a time causality loop and our only course of action to restore the timeline is to phase into the empty universe. It was determined by our pod engineer Lieutenant Sue Philips that the crew of the pod contained the necessary biomaterial to complete the entire periodic table of elements needed to restart the universe. I, acting on my own, have determined that the sacrifice of all four crew is unnecessary, and if the universe demands its pound of flesh, then mine would be sufficient. Therefore, I have captured the bodies of Colonel Adams, Evelyn Carter, and my wife Lieutenant Sue Philips in this portable matter collection unit. I am placing the memory module containing their living bodies in the pods distress beacon and sending them back to the present so they can be reintegrated."

General Wilson turns to Madison. "Get Doctor Stern and have him check for the memory module right now!"

"After I continue the countdown, the beacon will launch and this video will stop recording. I don't imagine I'll feel any pain, and hopefully I'll be successful in returning the crew of Pod One to their lives. To my wife Sue; I want you to know I love you, and please don't be mad at me for sacrificing myself to save all of you. It was the only solution to a hopeless situation. I'm sure you can agree with my logic, even if you don't like the outcome. Please continue traveling with your team."

Steve turns to the beacon and places the smaller memory cube in with the others. He walks to the control panel and presses the resume button on the console. The video cuts out one second after.

Doctor Madison comes running back in the room. "I can't find Stern, and the cabinet he put the memory modules in has a lock on it," Madison gasps.

General Wilson pushes past Stern and makes his way towards the lab. On the way down the hallway, he passes airman Rodriquez who holds an M4 rifle, and promptly snatches it from the airman's hands. Wilson barges into Doctor Stern's office, pulling the charging handle on the rifle, then takes aim at the lock on the cabinet. and in a single shot blasts the lock off without damaging anything inside.

The General tosses the rifle to Doctor Madison who followed him to the lab. Wilson reaches in the cabinet and grabs the smaller memory module and heads down to the hangar bay with it in his hand. He walks into the equipment room and slides a metal case off the shelf, kicking open the latch with his foot. He lifts up a portable matter collector from the case and swaps out the memory module for the one in his hand.

He brings the matter collector out into the hangar bay and aims it at the empty space where Pod One normally docks. Pressing the reintegrate button, he causes a bright beam of energy to scan back and forth along the floor, reintegrating Sue, Bill and Carter.

When the scan is complete, the first words said by the crew are from Bill. "I love you, too."

Bill still holds Carter's hand, looking into her eyes, unaware he's back in the TTRC hangar bay. His eyes have tunnel vision, fixed on Carter's face. Sue, on the other hand, immediately notices they are no longer on the pod and lets out a gasp, followed by confusion as she staggers backwards, falling onto her back.

Carter and Bill fall to the floor because the chairs they were sitting in have disappeared. Still disoriented, they look around and realize they are in the hangar bay.

General Wilson drops the matter collector to the ground and makes a grab for Bill and Carter while Doctor Madison lunges towards Sue.

Carter looks at the General's face in disbelief. "General? I don't understand. What happened?"

"Take it slow, Miss Carter, you're safe now." Wilson looks at Bill. "Colonel, welcome back. Welcome back to all of you."

Sue stands and walks over to Bill, Carter and General Wilson. "General, how did we get back home?"

Wilson knows he has to break the news that Steve was killed. "I'm sorry Sue, I have some bad news. Lieutenant Colonel Philips used a portable matter collector to store the three of you in the emergency beacon. He sacrificed himself so the three of you could survive."

Sue stands silent for a few seconds, processing the words. Carter immediately wells up as she looks at the blank look on Sue's face. Bill and Carter converge on Sue and hold her as she begins to lose her balance and her legs start to tremble.

Wilson stands, watching the three embrace. "Your husband is a hero Sue, and he left you a video message."

"Show me, I want to see!"

"Of course, follow me."

They walk to the lab and watch the video of Steve's selfless actions. Sue smiles and cries simultaneously, watching Steve take it upon himself to save everyone. After the video, Sue stares at the black screen. Both Carter and Bill have been holding Sue's hands during the entire time she watched. Sue turns to them, wipes her eyes, and tries to smile. "I think I need to get drunk. Will you come get drunk with me?"

Bill and Carter hug Sue, and General Wilson steps in close. "If the three of you want to be alone together, I'll leave you, but I would like to join in, if you let me."

Sue pats her hand on Wilson's cheek. "Of course General."

They go to the base bar and get extremely drunk as Sue tells stories of her and Steve's missions and their time together. Carter and Bill hold hands and keep constant physical contact throughout the evening, but don't make it obvious out of consideration to Sue's feelings.

Sue drinks way too much, but no one stops her. She's not usually a big drinker, but tonight she needs to get numb.

When Sue stumbles on her way to the bathroom and knocks over an artificial tree, Carter and Bill realize it's time to put her to bed. They bring her to her apartment, which is in the same building as theirs. Carter helps Sue wash up and get into bed safely.

***

Bill and Carter go to her apartment and get into bed. "I can't believe everything that just happened. It's like a dream right now. I thought for sure we were dead," she says as they hold each other under the covers.

"The part I don't get is how our emergency beacon, which was a square-ish type box, ended up being the tube-shaped time machine that you found in Manhattan."

Carter sits up on one arm and looks at Bill, stunned. "You're worried about the *shape* and not even at all blown away that the three of us have been inside that thing for years?"

"Well yeah, but also how did Sue know the loop involved the original time machine?"

Carter lies back down and they both stare at the ceiling.

CHAPTER 18: MELTDOWN

During the following two weeks, the crew of Pod One takes time off as mandatory leave. During that time, General Wilson held a memorial service in one of the sun towers for Lieutenant Colonel Philips. The entire TTRC command attended, as well as people who knew Steve and Sue from past assignments. Even the President came to pay his respects.

Sue met with counselors who cleared her for duty after she insisted she wanted to remain in service. Carter spent a few days with Sue after she had returned to the base from Steve's funeral back in his hometown in Tucson. During the time off, Carter also managed to see her parents for a weekend. Bill spent an evening with his brother and sister.

Since Pod One had been destroyed, General Wilson and Bill decided the replacement pod would be one of the larger experimental ships. The new pod, which is also designated as Pod One, is a newly developed time ship with updated features and a different appearance.

Upon returning from leave, the crew of Pod One gathered for breakfast at the café just down the street from the TTRC before starting their official first day back.

"Sue, you seem to be in good spirits," Bill says as they sit at the café table.

"I'm good, sir. It's weird though, I feel like the entire time Steve and I knew each other I was preparing myself for him to die."

"What, like you had a premonition?" Carter asks.

"Not a premonition; I guess I just knew that what we do is dangerous, and I prepared myself in the event it happened."

"I've been meaning to ask you about how you knew the capsule I recorded in New York was part of the loop paradox."

Sue nods while she chews. "It was the only possible solution. I figured if we were always meant to do what we did, that it had to be me that sent the Times Square capsule for you to find. Even if I was wrong, then there would be two arrivals that morning. Luckily I knew ahead of time everything I needed to make sure it arrived."

"What about the rectangular to cylinder shape change and the fluctuations in the countdown timer?" Bill asks.

"That one has me stumped. Not only can I not explain the change in shape, but also our countdown timers aren't external. There is no digital display on our beacons, and there's no backup field generator, either. Not to mention when we left, it was July, and now it's February."

"Well, after the cylinder dropped, Dr. Madison completely took it apart and said in future versions of our beacons; he thinks he will copy the design," Bill says.

"That's even creepier, so you're saying some future version of ourselves might find the square beacon, open it, take the cubes out, and put our digitally stored selves into the future beacon that hasn't even been built yet, so that I can find it in Times Square in the past?"

Sue and Bill stare at each other, as they both hadn't thought about that possibility. "Wow."

"Wow is right, so where the hell did the square beacon end up?" Carter waits for an answer, but Sue and Bill just shrug.

They sit and finish off their breakfast. The café server passes by the table, and Sue flags her down. "Can I get some more bacon and a couple more pancakes?"

They notice Sue has been eating a lot more than she normally does, and Bill is a bit worried that she's eating to mask her pain. Sue looks like she might have put on a couple pounds since the funeral.

"Well I'm stuffed, Sue, I don't know where you get your appetite."

Sue stabs her fork in the last bacon slice and swirls it around in the syrup. She swallows while nodding. "To be honest, I *have* been eating more than I normally do. I guess it's grief eating. I'll keep an eye on it so it doesn't make me fail my quarterly fitness test."

Bill puts his elbows on the table, interlacing his fingers. "Sue, I always knew you were 110%. You just do what makes you feel good."

After Sues' second order arrives, she stares at the plate for a few seconds, and then looks up at Bill and Carter. She takes a deep breath, then slides the plate towards the edge of the table.

Sue flinches at the sound of the plate as it scrapes the table's surface. There had been a slight ringing in her ears since she heard that Steve was dead. The ringing suddenly stopped at the sound of the plate sliding. The sound is louder than she thought it would be, the first real sound she has heard in two weeks. Every other sound up until now had been slightly muted. She'd shut out the world, but continued to interact as if everything was normal.

"You know, I'm full too." She sighs. "Let's get to work."

Bill smiles and places his hand on Sue's. "Don't worry, Sue. We're here for you."

Sue looks up to Carter and Bill, turning her palms up to grasp each of their hands. She smiles, a tear forming in her eye. "I'm glad I have friends like you." Sue squeezes both their hands.

They walk the short few blocks to headquarters. When they arrive in the hallway outside the hangar bay, Bill rushes in front of Sue and Carter and blocks the door with his body.

"Before you go in, I wanted to see the looks on your faces when you see the new pod. So close your eyes."

Carter looks at Sue; they both smile and close their eyes. Bill takes both their hands as he guides them through the door. He positions them in front of the new pod, and stands off to the side to watch.

"OK open your eyes!"

Sue's eyes get wide as she starts walking towards the pod and around the side, gently caressing the smooth black surface.

Carter stands where she is, and although impressed by the much larger size, she's not as easily impressed as Sue by these things.

Sue walks around the new pod, which is three times bigger than the original. The outside is a perfectly smooth black metal skin that is nearly seamless. It's triangular in shape with no sharp corners and stands twenty feet tall, flat on the top and bottom.

As Sue comes full circle, she wears a grin from ear to ear. "Why is it so big?"

Bill reaches into his pocket and pulls out a small remote, which he aims at the back of the pod. An automatic opening door begins hissing as a pneumatic piston pushes it open. The door is located in the middle, along the rear edge of the ship. It's similar to that of a private jet, and the door splits in the middle horizontally. The bottom folds down to form stairs, while the top swings upwards.

"The dual use of the pods has been a factor for a while. With a larger pod we can store more gear, bring more people, and now have real crew quarters that are better suited for longer missions."

Bill gestures for Sue and Carter to climb aboard. The interior is completely open, with a large, tinted curved window at the front. As soon as they enter, they see there is two levels. The bottom level is the crew quarters. There are eight bunks built into the walls, four bunks per wall, each with its own tinted window. To the left of the door is a larger bathroom. Directly to the right is a curved stairwell leading up to the command deck.

As Carter walks around the lower deck getting familiar with the crew quarters and all the features, Sue runs up to the command deck. The layout of the control console is the same as in the old pod—up in front are three chairs, the window is also curved and tinted, but unlike the old pod, there is a three hundred and sixty-degree view. The camera rail now stretches all the way around.

Sue sits at her station on the right side console and powers up her touch screen. Down on the crew deck, Bill shows Carter the new luxuries they have installed.

"This is incredible. I have a question. Remember the plutonium my chair sat over in the old pod?"

Bill laughs. "Yeah, what about it?"

"Well this ship is three times bigger, so how much radiation is my ass going to get now, sitting in that chair?"

"Relax, there's no plutonium or anything dangerous this time. This ship runs on plumestone."

She had almost forgotten the mission they almost all died on. "Right, of course. But don't we need it for the shield?"

Bill kneels down to the floor where a small panel is located. He pushes his thumb into a button and releases the lock on a deck plate labeled *Core*. He lifts the door panel and points to the plumestone.

"See, it's the size of a pea. We collected enough to make ten times the size shield we need. We have tons left over."

Carter looks inside the engine core. The pea-sized plumestone is mounted in a polished metal geometric cage. A purple glow fills the inner chamber from the stone's luminance. Bill stands up, using his foot to apply pressure on the panel door, which makes an audible *click* as it latches.

He brings her up to the command deck to join Sue, explaining to them what progress has been made since they went on leave.

"So other than this new pod, the other things that have happened in the last two weeks have been extraordinary."

Bill walks up to a large eight-foot long wood conference style table mounted in the middle of the command deck floor. There are eight swivel chairs mounted to the floor surrounding the oval table. Bill offers Carter a chair and sits next to her.

"Sue, can you join us so we can go over our mission plan?"

Sue is in full engineer mode, learning about the new pod's systems, but she manages to pull herself away from her workstation and sits across the table from Bill and Carter.

Bill opens a folder and pulls out an engineering schematic that he slides across the table to Sue. "The Agarthan engineers have been working with us for two weeks, preparing for the new shield generator. The plumestones we collected have all been reintegrated and are stored in a blimp hangar at the other end of the base."

Sue looks over the engineering drawings of the Agarthan phase generator. "So wait a second, if I'm reading this correctly, we need to generate the field in orbit?"

Bill walks to the rear wall panel where an instant coffee maker sits. He places a cup under the spout and presses the dispenser button. "That's correct; the plumestone powered phase generator needs to be activated in orbit. However, we didn't notice a new problem on our classified mission to the future." Bill takes his cup of coffee and sits back down in the chair. "When the coronal ejection hits in eighty years it doesn't just hit the Earth, it hits the moon as well."

Carter leans back in her chair and swivels it toward Bill. "So what, the moon is dead already, why would that be a problem?"

Sue interrupts before Bill can answer. "The mass of the solar ejection moved the moon didn't it?"

Bill points at Sue while looking towards Carter. "Bingo. The moon is nudged out of orbit with enough force that in five years after impact it's beyond Earth's gravity and becomes a minor planet. Of course, we all know that without the moon, life on Earth will struggle. So we need to protect the moon also."

Carter reaches over to Bills coffee cup and steals it from him. "OK, so what's the plan?"

"Well, it's a good thing we got so much extra mineral collected, because we are going to need seventy percent of it according to the Agarthan engineers."

"We need to generate a shield large enough to encompass the moon too?" Carter asks.

"That's right. First, we need to process the plumestone we have and get rid of the impurities. That means we need to melt it down. The Agarthans are going to help us out with that. We need to use the matter collector beam to place the mineral back in storage, and then haul it up into orbit. Once there, we reintegrate it in space. We have a new high-energy beam weapon on loan to us from Agartha, which we'll use to superheat the plumestone asteroids in space. The beam needs to stay active long enough so all the impurities burn off. Then, the molten plumestone will form into a natural sphere while it's floating in space. It's just like when you see astronauts playing with liquid in zero gravity. The molten blobs of plumestone will glob together, and then form a perfect sphere."

So after the plumestone cools down, we bring up the equipment for the phase generator and assemble it around the sphere we just created. After we activate the shield we should be home free and the mission will finally be finished."

Sue nods in agreement as she examines the generator diagram. Carter, however, looks skeptical.

"Do you see a problem with the plan, Carter?" Bill asks.

Carter folds her arms. "I don't know, I just feel like it's missing something."

Bill closes the folder and leans back in his chair. "What are you thinking?"

"See, I don't know. Ever since we decided to put the shield up in the first place, I felt like there was something I knew but I couldn't put my finger on it. Something just feels wrong. I'm not a scientist so it's probably going to work, but it's like when you leave the house and you suddenly stop outside your car thinking you left something, but when you check your pockets, you have everything. It's not until you get where you're going that you remember what you forgot."

Bill knows her instincts are usually spot on. "If you have something, tell me as soon as it comes to you. I think we've all learned to trust your judgment by this point in time."

Carter smiles and drinks more of her pilfered coffee. Bill stands up and lightly taps the folder on Carters knee.

"Alright troops, let's take our stations and phase the pod over to the hangar where the plumestones are stored."

They take their seats and Bill prepares for departure. Sue points to a new control button on the touch screen.

"Finally! An automatic door closer." Sue presses the button and the pod door closes on its own.

Bill enters the coordinates for the location and hits the phase button. The sound is different. Instead of an electrical discharge, there is a low hum, accompanied by the familiar flash of light outside the pod.

The pod arrives in the blimp hangar a moment later, and Bill phases the pod back in. The landing gear never retracted when they left the TTRC so he landed on the warehouse floor with gear down. Originally designed as a hangar for large dirigible airships, the warehouse is massive. Back in the 1950s, the Air Force had planned on storing Hindenburg-sized blimps large enough to carry nuclear weapons to near the edge of space. This is one of an undisclosed number of giant hangars built all over the country to store high altitude weapon platforms. But with the rocket age of the 1960s, the program never really got off the ground.

Outside the pod, in front of the cockpit window, the crew see four giant two-story house sized plumestone asteroids lying on the concrete floor. The concrete beneath them is crushed from their weight. Over to the left side of the large plumestones sits dozens of wooden pallets stacked with smaller samples which had been beamed into the matter collector along with the larger ones.

The three look out the window in awe at the bounty they had collected.

"Seeing the rocks on the ground next to that truck parked near them really changes the perspective of scale." Sue reaches over and presses the automatic door button. After a year of being the one to open and close the old pod door, she feels like she just got a new toy.

The three walk out into the warehouse and see people in lab coats working on a large piece of equipment a few feet away from where the pod had materialized.

As they approach the workers, they notice there are three Agarthan engineers and two base engineers.

One of the base technicians walks up to Bill and shakes his hand. "You must be Colonel Adams?"

Bill smiles at the engineer , giving him a firm hand shake. "Yes, and this is my crew, Lieutenant Philips and Miss Carter. The Lieutenant is our engineer."

Sue walks right past the technician and approaches the equipment. "Is this the energy beam weapon?"

An Agarthan who holds a small handheld electronic device shakes his head. "No, this is not a weapon, it is a tool."

Carter looks at Bill. "Sure looks like a big space cannon to me."

"Well Sue, why don't you get with these guys and get the *'tool'* mounted on the bottom of the pod. Carter and I are going to go and inspect the mineral samples."

"Yes, sir." Sue leers at the Agarthan engineer who corrected her.

Carter and Bill walk over to the four large plumestone space rocks on the concrete floor in a quad pattern. Bill walks between the four rocks and looks up at the surface of the stones. All four are encrusted with a black carbon coating, as if it had just passed through a tremendous heat source. As Carter walks around the outside, she notices the four large stones look like they had previously been one larger asteroid. The outside perimeter of the stones seems more rounded than the area where Bill walks between them.

"Was this all one giant asteroid?"

Bill pulls out his flashlight and aims it at the surface of all four stones, which stand about fifty feet tall. The matter collector deposited them in the same orientation as they were collected, and the crushed concrete floor had provided a sort of stand for them.

"It sure looks like it. I can see similar patterns of the fracture that match up on the inside like it should all fit together."

Carter continues walking around the four stones when she notices a translucent area that has been partially cleaned of the black carbon charring. She uses her sleeve to rub at the surface, revealing a light purple translucent crystal structure. Inside the purple, an object is embedded.

She takes out her flashlight. "Bill!"

"What?"

"Can you come here, please?"

Bill notices this is not a request, but a demand. He quickly runs out from between the four stones to where Carter is standing.

"What?"

"Look inside."

Bill holds up his flashlight, stares for a moment, then tilts his head. "No, it can't be."

"It's the pod door handle."

Bill's gaze sweeps across the warehouse, where Sue and the engineers bolt the energy beam under the pod between the three landing gear struts.

"Don't say anything, just forget you saw it," Bill says in a firm voice.

"Is Steve in there?" Carter claps her hands over her mouth.

"For all we know, it's just the handle. It must have happened during the phase in and got caught in the explosion."

"But that should have vaporized everything, shouldn't it have?"

"Obviously not."

They put away their flash lights and walk back to the pod.

"How goes the installation, Sue?"

Sue uses a large torque wrench to tighten the last mounting bolt. She pulls hard with both hands until the wrench clicks. "We're done."

Bill grabs the anodized flat black barrel of the nine-foot-long beam tool/weapon, and gives the entire assembly a good shake, something fighter pilots commonly do to the missiles or bombs mounted under the wings of military airplanes.

"Good job, Lieutenant." Bill gives Sue a light slap on the back.

Sue pulls a rag off the cart to wipe her hands of dirt and grease. "What were you guys looking at over there?"

"Oh, just looking at the impurities inside the crystal." Bill turns and starts walking towards the pod door stairs.

The Agarthan engineer turns to Sue. "The pod that created the plumestone is embedded in the crystal structure."

Bill stops dead in his tracks next to the rear landing gear. "Shit."

Sue looks at Bill, then at Carter.

"No, Sue." Carter reaches out with both hands to grab her.

Sue drops her rag and looks at the Agarthan technician. "What!?"

Sue darts past Carter, across the warehouse floor towards the asteroid.

Carter glares at the Agarthan. "You jackass, her husband died in that pod!"

The Agarthan's expression goes blank as he watches Carter turn and take chase after Sue. "I'm sorry, I did not know."

Sue, only twenty feet from the spot that Bill and Carter were looking at, trips as her leg muscles get weaker and weaker the closer she gets to the rock. She falls and her hands strike the rough concrete floor, leaving a streak of blood. She tries to get up, but continues stumbling until she runs into the surface of the plumestone. She slaps her hands on the section of crystal, seeing the pod handle that she had gripped so many times in the past. It's not connected to the door, just suspended and slightly melted in an encapsulation of purple crystal.

"Steve!"

Bill and Carter stop a few feet from Sue and stand over her, unsure of what to do or say. Carter sits with her back against the stone and puts her arm around Sue, hugging her tight.

"It'll be fine, sweetie." Carter presses Sue's cheek against her chest, stroking her hair.

Bill kneels on one knee, watching Carter try to console Sue.

For Sue, this is the first time she has let it all out since Steve died. She has cried, at the funeral and at night before falling asleep, but this is the first real emotional release she has had. The pain inside had been eating her up. She stares at the cuts on her hands through the rainbow-colored prism of her tear-filled eyes. Blood stains her uniform and her skin.

Bill reaches into his pocket and pulls out his handkerchief. "Come on, Sue. Let's take care of those cuts." He reaches under her arm and helps her stand.

Sue rises with the assistance of Bill and Carter, and they slowly make their way back to the pod. Bill sits Sue in a chair on the crew deck, then goes to the first aid locker and gets a small box out.

"Let me see those hands."

"I'm sorry, Colonel, I shouldn't have done that. I don't know what came over me."

Bill pulls out a small plastic container from the first aid box and opens the lid. Inside are some leaves from the mission they had collected the healing plant.

"Here, let me see if I remember how he did it."

Bill pinches a couple leaves between his fingers and lightly rubs them on both of Sue's palms. He puts a leaf in each palm and closes Sue's fingers around them. Sue squeezes the leaves and uses the backs of her hands to wipe her eyes. Carter goes to the bathroom to get a small hand towel and runs it under cold water.

"Here." Carter wipes the wet towel across Sue's face and forehead.

A knock sounds from the pod door, which is still open. It's the Agarthan engineer who had accidently spilled the beans about the pod. "Hello, may I enter?"

"What can I help you with?" Bill asks in an annoyed tone.

The Agarthan bows his head. "I just wanted to let you know that our staff scanned the interior of the plumestone, and there was no organic matter inside."

"Thank you. Anything else?"

"No, I am truly sorry for your loss, and for my error."

Bill slides his hand up to the door button mounted on the interior wall. "Thank you. That will be all." He presses the button to close the door.

Sue looks up at Bill and smiles. "You didn't need to be rude to him, he didn't know."

"Yes, I did. These Agarthans are jerks."

Carter stays silent, but thinks Bill is overreacting.

"Let's see those palms again." Bill leans over Sue.

Sue opens her hands, both stained with dried blood. Bill lifts off the leaves, and lightly wipes the wet towel across her out stretch palms. The scrapes have healed and Sue begins flexing her palms open and closed.

"It feels better sir, thank you."

"No problem. Do you want to take some more time off?"

"No, I want to work. I need to get back."

"That's my engineer." Bill pulls Sue to her feet.

"I'm just glad you didn't spit in my palms with the healing plant."

Carter throws her arms around Sue and they hug for a few seconds. Then she walks her up to the command deck, where they take their stations. Sue finishes cleaning her hands with the wet towel, then opens the matter collection screen on her console. The matter collection emitter extends from the lower front section of the pod in front of the forward landing gear. She targets three of the large asteroids, beaming them one at a time into the new larger memory storage modules.

"Asteroids are all collected, Colonel."

"Excellent, let's get to space, shall we?" Bill phases out the pod and puts it in a high orbit between the Earth and the Moon.

"Lieutenant, check our position and orbit speed, then release the asteroids ahead of us."

"Yes, sir. Coordinates and speed confirmed. Reintegrating now." Sue taps on the matter collection control screen and beams the three asteroids into space about one thousand feet ahead of the pod.

"So now we melt them down?" Carter asks.

"Correct, I'm targeting the Agarthan energy beam on them now. Once the beam gets them hot enough, they'll turn molten and join together under their own gravity. We'll keep the beam firing until the molten blob forms into a sphere, and then in a few hours it'll cool and solidify."

Sue fires the energy beam at the asteroids. The beam itself is not visible, but there is a bright blue targeting laser to indicate the beam is firing. The encrusted and charred asteroids emit gas as their temperature rises, and the purple color begins to show through. One by one, each asteroid takes on a more rounded shape, moving closer to each other as their mutual micro gravity causes them to coalesce. Two of the now brightly glowing purple orbs lightly touch and then suddenly merge. The rapid joining causes the new larger mass to undulate. The third and final asteroid sphere is pulled in, and the entire mass ripples in all directions, striving to form a perfect sphere. Over the next ten minutes, Sue keeps the heat on, monitoring the sphere's shape and vibration.

"How will we know when it's done?" Bill asks.

Sue keeps her eyes on the screen. "According to the Agarthan scientist, the more spherical the plumestone is, the more stable the energy output. Manipulating the projected phase shield to a specific geometric shape is important in the next phase of the operation. What I plan on doing is manipulating the lattice to form a thin shield between two spherical shield shapes."

Sue reaches over to Carter's screen and brings up a computer model of the shield shape she had designed. Bill and Carter lean into look at the animated demonstration. It starts with a computer generated rendering of the Earth and moon with the plumestone generator roughly midway between. The generator begins to project a cylinder-shaped shield which extends from the center towards Earth, the other side towards the moon. The mesh forms around Earth in a high orbit and does the same around the moon. The two connected spheres look like a lopsided barbell.

"So why can't we just use the fourth asteroid and just make a big sphere and shield both the Earth and Moon in a large ball?" Bill asks.

"We'd need about thirty samples that size to even come close to making a shield that large. This is much easier, and the only way to do it with the amount we collected."

Sue slowly reduces the power output. Because the plumestone is shock sensitive, reducing the temperature gradually prevents the frigid temperatures of space from cracking the structure. After about one hour of lowering the temperature, Sue shuts off the beam. "It's finished, sir."

"Good job, LT. Looks real pretty." Bill gazes out the window at the glass smooth forty-five-foot diameter purple and white swirled sphere.

Carter reaches out to give Sue a high-five. "So now what?"

Bill hits the return button and the pod phases back to the hangar bay. "Now we bring the phase generator up and activate it. Should be straightforward, we just need to give the engineers the final diameter so they can adjust the cage size to fit."

Carter nods but has an inquisitive look in her eyes. "Can we just jump forward and see how it works?"

"We will, but not until we actually turn it on. Remember, the events leading up to the completion of the shield have yet to happen. So until the thing is powered up, we would just go forward to the same orbiting plumestone we just placed up there."

"Right, temporal causality effect."

"Exactly."

Carter looks down at Bill's hands on her legs. "What do you think the temporal causality effect is of you rubbing my thighs like that, Colonel?"

Bill leans in close. "Let's go investigate that question."

CHAPTER 19: ABSOLUTE ZERO

Engineering needed an extra few days to complete the new space based phase generator. The team decided to relax for a day and then take advantage of the new open relationship with Agartha. The rest of the world still doesn't know Agartha exists, but travel to Agartha opened up to all authorized base personnel under the new treaty.

Carter sits with Mayo in her apartment when Bill calls.

"Carter, get in your prettiest dress, we just got invited to have dinner with the King of Agartha."

"When?"

"We have to be at the tube in two hours. Call Sue and let her know she's invited. I'm with Wilson at the hangar bay, and we'll meet you at the tube."

"Okay, I'll see you there."

Carter heads to her closet and rips through the unopened boxes the movers brought weeks ago. "Shit, I left that dress in New York at dickhead's place."

She runs out to the elevator and goes to Sues apartment. "Sue, help, I need your help."

Sue answers the door wearing a bra and panties. "What is it, what's wrong?"

"The King invited all of us to dinner down in Agartha, and we need dresses."

"Well, I have to wear my dress uniform, but I do have a dress you can use. Come in."

In the closet, Sue pulls out a slinky red number.

"That's a great dress, are you sure I can borrow it?"

"Yeah, try it on. I'm going to get my Class A uniform out of the dry cleaning bag."

Carter takes off her clothes and slides the dress over her head. Sue comes back from the walk-in closet with her uniform on a hanger and instantly starts laughing.

"Oh my God, girl, you are *not* fitting into that dress."

"I have to fit, zip me up."

"Carter, your tits are just too big, we're going to need to chop them off," Sue says in a strained voice as she risks breaking the zipper on the only dress in her closet.

"Well, that's not going to look very nice in this dress. I should just give those Agarthan men what they want and go topless. We can tell them it's the new style." Carter laughs in frustration. "If I stuff them in, it should close."

"Sweetie, I'm a small B cup, you're like five times bigger."

"Well, let's go to the dress shop."

"There *are* no dress shops on base, and the nearest one is eighty-seven miles away."

"The dinner is in two hours. What about Wal-Mart?"

"I love Wal-Mart as much as the next person, but you are *not* wearing a Wal-Mart dress to a royal dinner with the king." Sue unzips the dress and helps pull it off over Carters head. "The only thing I can suggest is we drive to town and pick one up. But even if we drove, it'd take us almost three hours. We don't have enough time. Why did it have to be a *formal* dinner? All they're going to wear are those robes." She pauses. "Actually, hang on, I have an idea."

Sue pulls out her phone and dials Bill. "We have a little problem. Carter doesn't have a dress, and it's going to take too long to drive and get one." She listens for a few seconds. "Thanks Bill, and tell the General thank you for me."

Carter, putting back on her jeans and shirt, looks at Sue. "What did he say I should wear?"

Sue smiles wide and grabs Carter's arm, walking her towards the door. "The General said we can do this one time, and not to get caught."

"One time what?"

"We can take the pod to go shopping."

Carter stops and lightly punches Sue on the arm. "Shut up! He did not."

"Yup, we can be back in half an hour. The General's going to the dinner too, so he wants you looking your best."

Carter glows with excitement. She has been such a social hermit for most of her life, and this is the first time since high school that she has gone shopping with a girlfriend. "Where are we going to get a dress?"

"Vegas is the closest town that has 24/7 formal dress shops."

"VEGAS!"

"Relax, we're getting the dress and coming straight back."

"What about my hair? And my make up? I've had the same makeup kit for eight years."

"Fine, we can go to the salon if there's no wait. I could actually go for a bit of that, myself."

Carter jumps up and down with excitement, using Sue's shoulders as a launch pad. They head to the TTRC and board the pod. Sue sits in Bills command chair and uses the computers map to find a dress shop in Las Vegas that also has a good place nearby to phase in. She brings the cloaked pod into the parking lot of a strip mall.

"There, a small thicket of trees where we can open the pod door. No one should see us." Sue points to a small wooded area.

After she parks the pod, they walk across the lot towards the shop.

"I've never been to Vegas before, this is so amazing." Carter looks up at all the casinos and not where she is walking.

"Focus sweetie, we only have two hours."

"Why can't we just get the dress and then spend a night on the town partying? Then we can time travel to right before the dinner."

"That's a good way to get us all fired. Not to mention me court marshaled. Besides, the pod is programmed to go back to the base only by using the return command. So whatever time passes here also passes there."

"No fun."

**

"Here's a nice formal one." Sue holds up a black dress with gold trim.

Carter crinkles her nose and shakes her head, holding a blue dress. "*This* is what they want to see me in."

"Holy cow, you'll give them all heart failure, they're so conservative down there."

Carter buys the blue dress anyway, and they walk a couple blocks to get their hair and makeup done. By the time they return the pod back to the hangar bay and drive across the base to the entrance of Agartha, it's 7:05 p.m. The dinner starts in half an hour, and Bill and the General have already taken a transit tube down to the Agarthan palace.

Like Bill and the General, Sue has never been to Agartha and is excited but nervous about the high-speed trip to the center of the Earth.

Sue and Carter lock themselves into the tube car.

"How long does it take to get there?" Sue asks.

"Oh, only ten or fifteen minutes."

The airman working the transit tube leans into the car before he shuts the door. "There's an Agarthan waiting for you when you arrive. She'll escort you to the palace."

"Thank you, Airman," Sue replies.

He closes the door and they begin their descent. Sue nervously chitchats as they pass at high speed through the Earth's crust. When they enter the crystal cavern portion, Sue stops mid-sentence, overwhelmed by the crystal structures. She had seen them before when the Earth was much younger and smaller, but the size took her by surprise. The only word coming out of her mouth is *crap*.

They arrive at the Agarthan transfer hub, where a tall woman greets them. She is very beautiful, in her mid-twenties or early thirties, a little over six feet, with long blonde hair and blue eyes like all the Agarthans Sue and Carter have seen.

She offers Carter her hand. "Welcome, I am Rosal, your escort."

Carter takes her hand and smiles.

Rosal nearly forgets that Sue is in the car and turns to offer her assistance, only to find Sue is already standing on the platform.

"Thanks, I got it," Sue snidely says.

"Sorry, I am nervous," Rosal says.

"Why?"

"It is just that I know who you are, and it is an honor to receive both of you in our city."

Sue and Carter look at each other and laugh. They're both celebrities now, but Carter is the one being stared at. Everyone they pass on the way out of the building gawks at her. Last time she was here the Agarthans were far less obvious, but this time her evening gown has provided just the right amount of jiggle and bounce.

"Carter you better not have a wardrobe malfunction in front of the king."

"I have dress tape on to prevent an international incident."

"You knew what you were doing when you picked it out, didn't you?"

"Of course, but this isn't for the Agarthans, it's for Bill. Other than dinners on base, this is our first real date. I want him to remember it."

"I don't think he or anyone else will ever forget it."

Rosal drives them to the palace, which is a short distance away. As they fly over the city, Carter recalls her visit a month ago and points out the places she learned about to Sue.

They approach the palace complex and something familiar strikes both of them.

"Sue, does that look like the same buildings when we stole the crown?"

"Speaking of which, we still need to return it."

"Yeah, almost forgot about that."

"It looks exactly like it, but a little bit cleaner, maybe."

Rosal hears the conversation and politely interrupts. "The palace complex is the only part of the old world we brought through during the exodus."

Carter leans in. "So it moves?"

"Yes, Atlantia is capable of moving wherever the king or queen desires."

"Atlantia? Is that the same as Atlantis?" Sue asks.

"Yes, in the past the palace has gone under different names."

"Interesting, we went here before."

Rosal smiles and nods.

They arrive in the courtyard at the center of the complex. A few levels above is where Carter and Bill had entered the tower last time, landing on the roof. It was too dark to realize the tower had been atop the palace.

Carter and Sue are greeted at the palace gate by guards dressed in heavy ornate robes. They stand at attention and hold long ceremonial spears at their sides.

Rosal walks them through the open thirty-foot tall palace doors. As they navigate the long corridor, music and voices echo from down the hall. The hall, adorned with statues and fine art, is lit with torches that have simulated fire. The floors, walls and columns are constructed from exquisite granite and marble.

As they reach the end of the hall, Rosal walks ahead to speak to a man writing in a large book with a quill. He stands at a large stone podium.

"Whom are you bringing to the palace dinner?" The man asks Rosal.

"Lieutenant Susan Philips of the TTRC, and the Prophet Evelyn Carter."

"Just Carter, please don't call me 'The Prophet'."

The man bows his head. "Yes, of course."

Rosal gestures for Sue and Carter to follow the man in to the ballroom.

"Rosal, I've noticed that everyone is speaking English. I thought English wasn't your first language?" Carter asks.

"The King has requested we speak it out of respect to you."

Rosal turns and walks away as the man from the podium steps down to escort them into the banquet hall. He leads them in through the arched entry, where they stand at the top of an elaborate staircase, looking down at hundreds of people who mingle with drinks in their hands. The man stands at the top of the stairs next to Sue and Carter with a small object that looks like a miniature trumpet.

He blows a quick two notes. As the people below turn towards the sound, he announces Sue and Carter. "Prophet Evelyn Carter and Lieutenant Philips."

He turns away and walks back to the podium. Carter and Sue, who now have the attention of all eyes in the room, walk down the steps to the banquet floor. The entire room erupts in applause.

"I'm not sure if they're clapping for everyone who enters, but I have a feeling the prophet announcement is the reason," Sue remarks.

When they reach the bottom, the crowd's eyes are glued on Carter. They stand next to each other at the foot of the stair case, shaking hands with the Agarthans, the majority of whom flock towards Carter.

"Sue's a prophet too!" Carter points to Sue.

"I appreciate your sense of fairness, but this is all about you tonight, sweetie."

After a few moments, the crowd spreads out to make way for King Solla. He approaches, followed by the General and Bill.

"Welcome Miss Carter, welcome Miss Philips. We were worried you would not attend. I am so pleased to receive you in the Palace," King Solla says graciously as he gently holds both of Carter's hands.

The King cordially invites Sue and Carter to follow him to his table at the head of the ballroom. As the King leads the way, Bill extends his arm to escort Carter.

"Carter you look amazing, and incredibly elegant."

Carter blushes. "Thanks. Sue helped me pick it out. I was going for sexy. Do you think it shows too much?"

"I think you made the Agarthan's evening, that's for sure. I'm kind of feeling a little jealous right now. If I didn't have to keep my uniform in a certain way, I'd offer you my coat."

"Good, that's the reaction I was going for. After all, this is our first date off base, and you did promise to bring me back here for dinner."

"That's right, this is the same island. Sorry it took four hundred thousand years to keep that promise."

They arrive at the king's table, where King Solla offers Carter the chair on his left. Bill sits in the chair on the right. After they take their seats, an Agarthan woman sits beside Carter.

"Hello Miss Carter, I am the Kings historical advisor. My name is Lumira."

Carter shakes Lumira's hand. "Nice to meet you."

"I hope this is not inappropriate, but I have been eager to speak with you for most of my life. I never imagined the prophecy would be fulfilled in my life time."

"Right. I guess I was as unprepared as you were." Carter reaches for a wine glass.

"May I ask, if it is OK, how did you know during your mission to the tower to reveal the truth to the queen about the coming solar activity?"

Carter sips the wine, surprised that it tastes awful. She doesn't show her displeasure, though. "Well, the main reason I knew was because there was no way your people could've known the solar flares were coming. Without satellites in space to monitor the sun, I figured someone had to have given you warning that was not from your world. It was a guess, really."

Lumira smiles, but is clearly disappointed that the story was not as magical as it reads in the history books. "I guess the truth of history is not always as it was written."

"Lumira, I forgot when I was choosing a dress today how cool it was in Agartha. Is there any way to make it a little warmer?"

"I'm sorry, no. We have a constant temperature of sixty-five degrees."

Carter grabs the wine and finishes it off, thinking it might help warm her up. "Is that because the night shade is on the sun right now?"

Lumira looks confused at the question. "The sun does not affect the temperature in Agartha, our temperature is regulated by geothermal vents."

"Oh, okay. No problem, it's fine, I've spent many nights in the cold."

Lumira stands and reaches to shake Carter's hand. "Thank you for speaking with me. Here is my card, perhaps when you have time, we can speak again?"

"Sure, I'd like that. Are you on Facebook?"

"I'm not sure what that is."

"Never mind, I wasn't thinking."

When Lumira leaves, Bill sees the empty chair and quickly occupies it. "Carter, see that kid over there? He's the king's son."

"Okay?"

"I'm in no way trying to pimp you out, so please don't beat on me or drop me off in the dark ages."

"And?"

"The King asked General Wilson if his son could dance with you after dinner."

"How old is he?"

"I don't know, maybe sixteen, seventeen?"

"I guess I can give him a dance. One dance, that's all!"

"Thanks, this seems to be important to the General, and he was really scared to ask you himself."

Carter leans over to look at Wilson, who sits with the king's son, staring at Carter. She mouths the word 'OK'.

After supper and desert is cleared from the table, a server delivers drinks. Once the king has his glass filled, he stands and the room falls silent.

"People of Agartha, please join me in thanking our visiting TTRC guests for joining us on this momentous occasion. Raise your cups and toast in celebration to the return of our prophet, Miss Evelyn Carter, after four hundred millennia. I have been told she prefers not to be called the prophet, so this will be the last time anyone does so. She prefers to be called Carter, so it will be so, and respectfully by all Agarthans."

Bill leans in to Carter. "I was the one who told him."

The King continues. "To Carter!"

The entire room of people in unison. "To Carter!"

"Now, the first dance. My son, Elon, has requested a dance with Carter."

Prince Elon suddenly appears over her left shoulder. "May I have the honor?"

Carter smiles at the young prince. "Of course you may." She takes his hand and they walk to the center of the ballroom floor.

As they walk past the King, she leans down and whispers to King Solla, "This isn't a marriage ceremony or anything like that right? It's just a dance?"

Solla laughs loudly. "Fear not, Miss Carter, it is but a dance. However, I cannot control it if my son expresses a desire for your affections."

Carter tries to smile but it's mixed with a tiny bit of fear. "Oh joy!"

Elon is shorter than Carter. At five-foot-seven, he's nearly eye to eye with her. They stand in the center of the empty dance floor, waiting for the music to start.

"I'm not familiar with Agarthan dances, so maybe you can show me?"

"It's easy, you put your palms on my shoulders, and I put mine on your hips. It's four steps, I will show you."

The music begins, and after only three measures of the waltz, she has it figured out.

"Miss Carter, are you married?"

"Wow, you move quicker than I expected."

"Oh no, I am not asking you, I was just curious."

"Elon, your way of speaking is quite different from everyone else. If it weren't for your Agarthan features, I'd think you were from the surface."

Elon leans in, "Please don't say anything, but I have access to surface communications. I can surf the web, and I downloaded lots of TV shows and movies. My favorite is Big Bang."

"Ironic, isn't it?"

"Ah yes, I never really thought about that until now. I guess it's no longer a theory any longer. You are proof of it."

"I guess. Wow, this is turning out to be pretty big. I wonder if I invented the wheel also."

Elon laughs. "Miss Carter."

"Just Carter is fine."

"Carter, would you ever want to, I don't know...go out with me?"

"What do you mean by *go out*? Like a date?"

"Oh, I mean maybe watch a movie with me here, or maybe I can come to the surface and we can do something together."

"Well, maybe. I'm a bit older than you though, and I have a boyfriend."

"Oh, I'm sorry, I didn't know. Wow, you smell really good. I have never smelled that before, what is it?"

"Oh, the berry spray."

"So that's what berries smell like. We can't grow all that many things here. I'll have to get my smuggler to bring me some, they smell great."

"So, Elon you don't have a girlfriend in Agartha?"

"No, not yet, our customs are really stupid with matching and courting. I really don't even like anyone around here. I talk to some surface people online, but you are the first surface person I have met other than the delegates. I mean, you are the first woman."

"Well, you seem like a very nice young man, and you'll find someone. Who knows, once the leaders on the surface tell everyone, which should be soon, you might go up and be really popular, being a prince and everything."

"You think so? Do you think I can meet a woman who looks like you?"

"There are lots of women up there like me."

Carter and Elon Dance for another song, then he escorts her through the palace and shows her around. The Agarthan customs are antiquated and uncomfortable for almost all the four of crew. The General, however, seemed to like the fish and wine.

***

When Carter and Bill get back to the apartment, it only takes a few seconds for Bill to finally release the lust he had been feeling all evening while watching her interact with the royals in her dress. After pressing her against the refrigerator in her kitchen and removing her dress, he swoops her up and carries her into the bedroom.

She's thrown on the bed and looks up at Bill, who unbuttons his uniform coat.

"Oh, my." She uses one finger to touch her bottom lip.

"Please don't say 'Oh my."

They both laugh at the uncomfortable reference to *Fifty Shades of Grey*, a book they're both embarrassed to have read.

***

The following morning in the hangar bay, Bill and Carter arrive to find Sue already there.

"Either of you feel sick this morning?" Sue asks as they walk up to the coffee machine in the ready room.

Carter and Bill both look at each other then shake their heads.

"Must be something I ate last night. That fish was nasty."

Bill stirs his coffee. "That was fish? I thought it was chicken."

"No it was definitely fish," Carter says.

"Sue, did you hear back from the engineering team on the status of the generator assembly?"

"Yes, sir, it's already stored in the matter collector on board. So we can deploy it when we are ready to go."

"Well, let's get on with it, troops." Bill phases the pod into orbit, where the plumestone sphere floats in space. "Sue, deploy the array."

"Deploying now, sir."

Sue materializes the generator array around the plumestone sphere. It's a lattice of stainless steel square tubing, forming a geometric shape surrounding the giant sphere. After the deployment, Sue goes through the generator start-up procedure and the plumestone starts to glow in a swirling blue and purple energy bubble. She starts the program which manipulates the phase shield into the shape required to wrap around the Earth and moon. As the shield takes shape, the pod is buffeted by the competing energy of the larger phase shield. The pod gets pushed back as the shield expands to its final shape.

"Activation complete, sir, the shield is operational and functioning well within normal parameters."

Carter claps her hands as she sees the final stage in saving the planet finally come into place. She gets up and gives Bill a hug, then another to Sue.

"TTRC Command, this is Colonel Adams."

"Go ahead, Colonel," General Wilson replies over the pod's radio.

"Sir, the Earth shield is deployed. Mission complete."

Back at the TTRC control room, dozens of engineers and scientists join the General waiting for the report of the completed shield. When they hear Bill's radio broadcast, they cheer loudly and exchange handshakes and pats on the back.

On the pod, the three of them watch as the new phase shield invisibly functions as designed. Sue runs through multiple start-up and shutdowns remotely to verify smooth operation.

"So, now we go forward and make sure it deflects the solar eruption?" Carter asks Bill.

"Yes, let's do that now. You know what I just realized? In the last month you haven't done the job you're paid to do."

Carter looks at Bill with a bit of confusion. "You mean filming?"

"Why don't you go down to the crew deck and get the camera out of the equipment locker? Let's document the shield doing its job."

Carter smiles and runs down to get her camera. She brings it back up and connects it to the rolling mount on the chrome rails above the command deck windows.

"Ready?"

Carter pulls out an elastic and ties her hair up in a ponytail "Ready!" She turns on the camera and presses her eye against the viewfinder.

Bill phases the pod ahead eighty years to watch the solar storm, parking far enough back so Carter can get the Earth and the moon in the shot. The angle at which she sees the Earth and moon has the sun directly behind them. She watches the coronal mass ejection begin its hours-long trip from the sun's surface to Earth.

"OK, speed up time a bit and orbit the pod slowly to the right," she calls.

"Got it."

Bill advances time slowly as requested and moves the pod to give her a panoramic shot. The solar ejecta moves closer and closer to Earth until its red plasma impacts the phase shield.

"Normal time speed now!" Carter commands.

Bill releases the spring-loaded time knob, and time resumes at normal speed. The plasma continues hitting the Earth and moon for a fifteen minutes and surrounds the planet, creating a red sphere of glowing fire. The blast wave reflecting off the shield causes the plasma to deflect from the planet and moon in all directions until the color starts to dissipate.

Carter zooms in on the fading plasma as it creates worldwide auroras that swirl into space. She adjusts her focus and zooms closer into Earth, looking down at North America.

She stares for a moment, then pulls her eye away from the viewfinder. "Bill? What month is it on your screen?"

Bill looks down at his monitor. "April, why?"

"Come here and look at this."

Bill walks over to her camera, putting his eye against the viewfinder. "That can't be right." He tilts the camera and looks down at the equator around South America. "It's all covered in snow."

"Look at the ocean."

"It looks frozen on top. Like the whole planet froze over."

Bill jumps down to his chair and maneuvers the pod closer to the planet. "Sue, send the code to deactivate the Earth shield, I want to go down there."

Sue deactivates the shield, which has been running for eighty years. Bill brings the pod down to one thousand feet above the ground. As they fly over the area that should be the desert of Nevada, they see the ground is covered with a thick layer of snow and ice. Bill brings the pod south of the base and heads towards Las Vegas. As they sink lower, down above the famous Las Vegas hotel strip, most of the taller buildings have collapsed and are covered in ice and snow.

"Sue what's the temperature out there?"

"Sir."

"What is it?"

"It's minus two hundred and sixty degrees. That's close to zero Kelvin. At that temperature, the molecular bonds start to break down and matter becomes subatomic."

"Wait, what does that mean?" Carter asks.

"It means matter, all matter can't exist lower than minus two hundred and seventy-three Celsius. It's so cold that atoms can't hold their bonds and simply fall apart."

"What! How can this even be possible?"

Bill stops the pod, aiming it at the Bellagio. "Are you still recording?"

"Yes."

"I'm going to reverse time until whatever caused this to happen becomes apparent."

Carter watches the demolished hotel through her viewfinder. The twisted frozen structure collapsed onto the famous water fountain at the front of the building. Bill grabs the time knob and turns it backwards, slowly at first, then speeding it up to a month per second. For the next sixteen minutes, Bill holds the time reversal steady, and in the last few seconds before arriving at nearly one month into their own future, the building reverses the collapse.

Bill lets go of the dial and brings the pod into normal time speed. "Sue, what's the temperature now?"

"Fifteen degrees."

Outside, on the normally busy streets of Las Vegas, not a single car drives, not a single person walks. Bill brings the pod above the city and rotates the pod to get a full view of the area. Snow is everywhere, and there are no signs of life.

Bill stops the pod and leans back in his chair, breathing heavy, and slaps his hands on top of his head. "Fuck! *Now* what did we do?"

Carter stops the camera, remembering something important. "The Agarthans don't get their heat from the artificial sun, they get it from the geothermal heat of the Earth!"

Sue smacks her hand on the console. "Of course!"

"Carter what are you talking about?" Bill asks in complete frustration.

Carter sits down and swivels the chair towards Bill. "When I first went to Agartha, I noticed that even though the artificial sun was only a few thousand miles away, the temperature on the ground was chilly. I had that red leather jacket on. Then last night I was freezing at dinner, and the woman I was talking to mentioned they get their heat for the entire place from geothermal vents. They pull the natural heat generated by the giant crystals in inner Earth."

Sue stands up. "The artificial sun only provides for photosynthesis of plant life. Its heat and radiation is blocked by the phase shield that contains it."

"So, when we were trying to shield Earth from that solar flare, we blocked all radiation from the sun to keep Earth warm," Carter concludes.

Bill sits and thinks for a few seconds. "So all we have to do is only turn it on when a solar flare comes."

Sue enters an equation on her screen. "Bill, the maximum time the shield can be on for before the temperature drops too low is twelve days straight."

"Well that's perfect, the solar flare only lasted a few hours."

"What about future solar activity? What if there's another flare that lasts longer than twelve days?"

"Well, let's find out if there is one. The furthest forward we've gone is eighty years. Let's go further."

Bill brings the pod back up to space, jumping to the point right after the first solar flare was deflected, moving time forward at ten years per second. After just a few moments, they see a flash of red light. Bill reverses time to the point of the flash and sees another solar ejection hit Earth only thirty years after the first. He advances time to see how long the plasma engulfs the Earth.

"God damn it!" He gets up from his chair and walks to the back of the pod, down the stairs to the crew deck.

Sue looks at Bill's screen, then up at Carter. "Four months."

Carter throws her hands up in exasperation and follows Bill down to the crew deck. Bill lays down in one of the bunks, his hands behind his head under the pillow.

"Carter, you know where I'd like to live? The 1950s. What a great time period. Maybe even the 1920s. I could be a gangster or something."

Carter walks up to the center table and sits in one of the chairs near the bunk. "So what, you are just going to give up now?"

"What's the point? Everything we do, everything we try always ends up with something else that goes wrong. Maybe it's just our time to go extinct."

Carter stares out the window at the snowball Earth below. "So you'd just go back in time and live the rest of your life knowing humanity is going to die?"

"No, I guess not."

"Then you need to figure out a solution to this!"

CHAPTER 20: EXODUS

After the team shuts down the Earth shield, they return to the hangar bay and find General Wilson waiting for them as they exit the pod.

"Colonel, how well did the shield work?"

Bill walks down the pod stairs, giving Wilson a look of disappointment as he shakes his head. "General, the shield deflected the solar eruption, however, just like the Agarthan shield prevents the heat from their artificial sun from warming their cities, our shield did the same thing."

"Colonel, I don't understand what the problem is."

Sue and Carter walk off the pod and stand behind Bill.

"General, the solar activity in eighty years only lasts a few hours, and everything works perfectly, but thirty years later, there are a series of eruptions that bombard Earth for four straight months. The problem is the shield can only be on for a few days straight before the temperature on the planet drops below freezing. In four months, we witnessed the Earth's temperature drop to minus two hundred and sixty degrees."

Wilson takes the news with a certain amount of ambivalence. "Colonel, thank you for all your efforts. I think you know what we're left with now. I have to inform the President that we've failed." Wilson walks out.

Sue moves past Bill to the ready room, where she flops into a chair. Carter faces Bill, looking at his face, which is that of a broken man. "What did the General mean? What is he about to do?"

Bill ignores Carter, who chases after him.

"Bill? Bill?"

He walks up to the coffee pot and pours a cup for himself, as well as Sue and Carter. As he passes them out, he points to the chair next to where Sue already sits.

Bill stands in front of Sue and Carter, working out what he is about to say.

"Tell her, Bill."

"Carter, before you got here, before any of us got here, we already sort of knew that the sun was a problem. You may find this difficult to accept, but we were warned about the solar activity in the 1950s by people who visited our planet."

Carters face shifts to a look of disbelief as she squints and presses her lips together. "Really? Aliens. Come on Bill." But she already knew about it from Aros's slip up.

Bill kneels to one knee. "It's true. Back in the late 40's they arrived and we began to talk with them secretly. Shortly after, they arranged an information exchange. Technology, culture and weapons.

They knew somehow with their own measurements of our sun that we didn't have much time left before the solar eruptions would intensify. They offered us sanctuary on their planet. However, in return, they wanted something we were not willing to sacrifice.

We made some unethical agreements with them while they were here. They wanted to learn about human physiology and our brains so they could try to create a sort of evolutionary jump back in their own species. They have the ability to pass down their memories to their offspring, so the next generation already has the knowledge of those who came before them. However, after centuries of genetic modification, their bodies began living shorter and shorter life spans. So, they went out searching for other species to mate with or who might possess the potential to mix into their genetics and create a longer living hybrid. "

Carter stands up and walks to the podium at the front of the room. "What do they want in exchange?"

"In exchange for their advanced technology, we allowed them to do very limited experiments on humans. After a number of years, they started violating the agreement and began abducting people all over the world. We tried to reason with them, but it ended in a fight. They left and told us no more technology would be shared unless we gave them access to more people. Their offer was they would use their giant spacecraft to transport the entire population to their planet, only under the conditions they could have access to us for experimentation."

"Fuck that shit!"

"Carter, we don't have a choice now. The President is going to authorize the operation. It's the failsafe option. Our mission is over."

Carter stands silently, staring at Bill and Sue, growing more and more frustrated as she thinks about all the things they've done over the last month to try and save the planet. "So how are they going to convince the people of the world to go to this concentration camp planet? I mean, when people are given the choice they'll resist!"

"They're not going to be given a choice. The procedure is we take the pod to the alien planet and inform them we agree with the terms. A year or so later, they send ships and they collect the people. The ships are massive, and can transport everyone in a sort of suspended state. The trip for their ship to get here is about a year, so everyone is asleep during the journey. When the people wake up, they'll already be on the planet. The government's plan is to claim ignorance and deny any collusion with the aliens."

"I can't believe you're even *considering* going along with this! I thought we were trying to *save* people, not put them into slavery."

Bill walks over to Carter, who is exhausted mentally and physically. He breaks his own rule and hugs her right at the podium. Sue gets up, walks behind Carter, and embraces her as well. General Wilson strides into the ready room holding an old leather briefcase.

He stands and watches as the team silently are holding each other. "Colonel."

Bill looks up at Wilson. They all release each other and retreat to different areas of the room. None have dry eyes. Bill approaches Wilson, who hands over the briefcase.

"Colonel, the plan is in here. I never thought I'd see this thing again."

Carter walks up to them as Bill looks inside the soft leather top opening of the case.

"General, what alternatives do we have? Can't we just wait and see if we can come up with something better?"

"Miss Carter, I understand this is a shock to you, but we've been preparing for and fearing this moment for over sixty years. The aliens from Serpo are our only hope of survival. Either way, we'll sacrifice."

"General, when the people wake up on an alien planet and are herded like cattle they won't stand for it. They'll fight back!"

"Miss Carter, we've been searching for a habitable planet for a while. Theirs is the only one we know of, and it already has the resources humanity will need to survive. Over time, the people will adapt. Their planet is big enough to accommodate the entire human race, and they have the infrastructure to handle it. The people will have food and water, as well as shelter. It may not be ideal, and we may have to sacrifice our freedom, but at least we'll live."

"But General..."

"The decision has been made Carter, and as much as we all appreciate everything you and the rest of your team has done over the last few weeks, please understand my hands are tied. I cannot disobey direct orders from the President." General Wilson leaves the room.

Bill puts his arm around Carter and squeezes her tight. "It's time to go."

The team boards the pod, and Bill pulls out the documents from inside the briefcase, spreading them out on the command deck conference table. Among the documents are a contract signed by former President Dwight Eisenhower, agreeing to the original human alien exchange program from the 50's. There was a folder titled 'Project Serpo' as well as a new contract that had been printed from a fax machine with the current President's signature. The terms of the new contract spell out that the aliens had the authority to experiment on 1% of the Earth's population per year as long as the population didn't shrink by more than 1%. In return, the human population would be given exclusive use of 30% of planet Serpo.

Carter reads the contract with tears streaming down her face. "What about everything we've built? All of our achievements throughout history?"

"We'll transport as much as we can fit on our own ships. There are plans in place to try and protect as much culture as we can. We can set up a new government and bring weapons for defense. We can also bring different species of plants and animals, but the planet isn't suitable for many life forms, and we'll need to adapt our diets to what they have."

He pulls out a laminated index card from the pile of documents that has the coordinates of Serpo. He stares at it for a few seconds, then begins typing the coordinates into the navigation screen. A red flashing message appears. 'Access Restricted.'

"Pod One, request permission to depart for project Serpo, authorization code requested," Bill calls to the hangar bay control room.

"Pod One you are clear for departure, transmitting access code now."

General Wilson stands in the control room, watching through the window. He pulls his identification off his uniform and swipes it through the card reader on the control room console.

The Access Restricted message disappears, replaced with a button which reads 'Phase now?'

Bill looks at the button, then back at Carter, who still slumps at the conference table. She nods, and Bill turns back to the console, pressing the phase button. As the ship phases out and the light flashes, Carter is suddenly overwhelmed by the emotions she has been trying so hard to suppress. She cries out as if she had just been punched in the gut.

The pod arrives in orbit above planet Serpo, which orbits around a star in the constellation of Aquarius. The star is almost identical to the sun, but is much younger and more stable.

Carter gets up to look down at her future home. As she approaches the window, she sees the giant dry-looking planet. There are no visible oceans or polar ice caps. The few clouds in the sky look weak and wispy. She stares in utter disgust at this ugly planet, and her anger grows. Sue is visibly disturbed as well, but keeps her head down and stares at her screen.

Bill places his hands on the flight sticks and begins flying around the planet so they can see the entire surface. As they fly around the equator, some small seas and lakes become visible on the other side.

"Where are we going to live, Bill?" Carter asks.

"I don't know, I just hope it's near the water on this side of the planet."

"Yeah, but what are the odds of that?"

Bill just shakes his head as he finishes a full orbit.

Carter points. "Look at that!"

"That's a gas nebula. Wow, it's really beautiful, isn't it?"

"Yeah, it's about the only beautiful thing here. It's almost heart shaped and has so many colors." Carter becomes more and more disappointed by the way this is going.

"This is the only planet orbiting this star, but it's just at the inside edge of the habitable zone. Had it been a few million miles further out, it might not have been like this. It's on average 105 degrees Fahrenheit year-round. The ultra violet index is about 20% higher than on Earth, so we'll need to build lots of indoor temperature controlled cities," Sue says.

Bill begins descending towards the surface. Ahead, there are signs of civilization. A large city made from tan stone is visible below. They start heading towards the capitol of the city, a large complex laid out like an eight-sided building with a courtyard in the center, very similar to the Pentagon.

The pod lands on the sand-dusted rocky surface in the center of the courtyard. Bill phases the ship in, and the aliens standing nearby suddenly turn to look at the pod as it emerges from its cloak.

Carter, suddenly overcome with fear, realizes the aliens are exactly what she thought they would look like, standing three to four feet tall, and bluish grey color. They have large heads similar to the way an ants head looks, with big black oval eyes.

None of them wear clothes or carry weapons and seem almost robotic in the way they move. Bill stands up and walks over to the conference table to gather up the contracts. He places them back into the leather case and stands near the edge of the table.

Carter and Sue make to stand, but Bill raises his hand. "Stay here. I'll be back in a few minutes after I deliver the contract." Bill walks down the stairs to the crew deck.

Carter walks after him, but Sue grabs her arm . "No, this one he has to do himself. He holds himself responsible."

Carter wipes a tear from her cheek as she watches Bill's head disappear down the stairs. She sits back down and stares out the window. She puts on her headphones and presses play. The song 'Resistance' from Muse, ironically, is next on her playlist.

Below deck, Bill stands at the pod door, dreading pressing the button, but he does anyway. A blast of heat rushes into the pod, causing him to raise his arms to protect his face from the heat and bright light. The heat rushes up to the command deck where Sue and Carter sit. Their backs burn as if the devil had just breathed down their necks.

Bill steps down to the hot surface. He's not the first human to walk on this planet. Back in the 1960s there had been a short-lived alien/human exchange program. All those humans left and returned home after two years on Serpo. When they returned, they reported the horrible living conditions.

Bill walks around to the front of the pod, heading toward the building. The walk is a long one, over two thousand feet.

Inside the pod, Carter and Sue sit and wait. The environmental system kicks on to adjust the cabin temperature back down to a decent level. As the cold air hits their hair, it flutters about both of their faces, which have begun to perspire. Carter watches Bill trek across the arid alien surface carrying the enslavement of the human race in his right hand.

She sits and thinks of something she had just heard. In her head, something turns, and she's suddenly overcome with a sense of urgency. Carter panics as she taps her palms on the armrests of her chair. She has something—she doesn't know what it is, but something important is coming to mind.

"We have to stop Bill!"

"What? Why?"

"We missed something important. Don't let them sign the contract."

"Are you sure?"

"Yes, stop him, get him back here, now!"

Sue reaches for the microphone. "Colonel, Come in."

Bill is still in view, but he forgot his radio in the pod. "Colonel?"

Sue jumps out of her chair and runs around Carter to Bill's chair. She grabs the control sticks and lifts the pod up in the air, flying towards Bill, who draws close to the building ahead of him. Carter gallops down to the deck and opens the pod door just as Sue lands the pod hard in front of Bill.

The pod slides on its landing skids, kicking up dust and sand which makes a cloud of debris blast against the building. As the pod comes to a stop, Bill sees Carter standing in the doorway. She holds out her hand.

"Bill! There's another way, there's *always* another way."

Bill stops twenty feet from the pod door. Their eyes meet, and he can instantly tell she does indeed have another way. After weeks of seeing her use little tiny bits of information to complete a bigger story, he trusts her judgment more than anyone he has ever known. He jogs towards the pod door. The sweat on his face is covered with dust. He grabs Carter's hand as he climbs up the pod steps. As soon as he's aboard, Carter calls out to Sue.

"Get us the hell out of here."

Sue lifts the pod up into the air as Carter closes the door. Carter throws her arms around Bill and kisses him, looking him in the eyes.

"Do you trust me?"

"With my life."

The pod flies up and out of the planet's atmosphere. Sue places the pod in a cloaked orbit about a million miles from the planet. After Bill washes his face, he, Carter, and Sue discuss the new plan Carter came up with. After about an hour of working out the details and Sue running the calculations, Bill brings the pod back to Earth.

He reaches for the microphone and calls down to General Wilson. "TTRC command, Pod One. Over."

A few seconds later General Wilson answers. "Go ahead, Colonel."

"General, we have a new plan."

"Colonel, did you deliver the contracts to Serpo?"

"Negative, General, we found a new solution. Correction, Miss Carter found a new Solution."

"Colonel, I cannot authorize a new mission until the President rescinds this order."

"Understood. Could you get him on speakerphone for us? We only have a few seconds before power cells are charged to maximum."

General Wilson picks up the phone and dials the Presidents emergency line. "Colonel, I have the President on the phone now."

"Thank you, General. Mister President, do you read me?"

"Yes, Colonel Adams, I'm assuming you're not following my direct orders?"

"That is affirmative, Mister President. Carter has come up with a new plan, sir."

"Miss Carter has, huh? And what exactly is this new plan, if I might be allowed to approve it?"

Sue calls out, "Power at 100% Colonel, we have to execute now!"

"Mister President, are you near a window?"

"Yes, I'm in the Oval Office."

"Sir, you might want to look outside."

The President swivels his chair around and looks out the window. It's nighttime, and he can see the stars through the cloudless sky.

Bill looks at Carter and smiles. "Press it."

Carter leans over to Bill's screen. She puts out her finger and presses the 'Phase now?' button on his console.

The phase shield shuts off, and a hissing can be heard as air escapes through the closed doors. The pod shield off, they're now exposed to the vacuum of space. An electrical hum builds as the power cell activates.

Suddenly, there is a flash of light.

The President looks out his window and the blue flash fills the entire night sky. All over the world, people see the sky flash an electric blue that disappears as quickly as it appeared.

On the pod, the phase shield suddenly turns back on, and the leaking door stops hissing.

"Phase complete, Colonel," Sue calls.

"Shut down the Earth phase shield."

"Shield deactivated."

Bill reaches over to the screen and presses the return button. The pod returns to Hangar Bay One, where General Wilson and other TTRC personnel are waiting. The pod doors open and Bill, Carter and Sue get out.

"Colonel, what the hell just happened?"

Bill walks up to the General and shakes his hand. "General, we just saved the Earth. I think we all need to go to a sun tower and take a look."

"Colonel, what did you do?"

The four head over to the sun tower. When they arrive at the top, the General looks up at the sky. He scans the stars and the moon, then looks back at Bill.

"Colonel what exactly am I looking at?"

Carter takes Wilson's hand and turns him around to look the other way. Wilson stands and stares at a large heart-shaped multi colored nebula.

"Miss Carter, what exactly did you do?"

"General, we found another way. Since the choice was between burning under our sun or enslavement under a different sun, we decided to go with door number three, and find a new sun. We used the Earth's phase shield to transport us to a new star. We transmitted coordinates to the Earth's shield to transport the Earth and the moon to perfect orbit around the Serpo sun."

Wilson's jaw drops as reality catches up with him. Sue steps next to the General, who stares up at the new star field above him.

"Carter came up with the plan, sir. When we went to Serpo, we realized the planet was at the inside habitable zone. It's like where Venus is on our own star, just a little further away, so it's hot, but not too hot for life. The prime area of the habitable zone was empty. There were no planets other than Serpo, so we calculated the perfect orbit to the star, and other things like orbital speed as well as angle. Then it was just a matter of sending the frequency signal to the Earth's phase shield at a high enough level of transmission power. We shut off our own phase shield momentarily so the shield would react, and not our pod. Then when the phase completed, we turned our phase shield back on and turned off the Earth shield. It was actually easy. I'm surprised I didn't think of it."

Bill puts his arm around Carter as they look at the nebula. "I don't think you could've picked a better view."

"It's a great Valentine's Day present."

Bill looks at his watch and sees it's February 14, 2018. Before he can say anything, Carter decides to throw Bill's 'no romance out of the apartment' rule to the wind. She reaches up and throws her arms around him. They stare into each other's eyes and kiss.

Wilson looks back and smiles. "It's about time you two stopped trying to hide it."

Bill and Carter look at Wilson, who smiles and winks.

"My lips are sealed, Miss Carter," Wilson says as he and Sue walk towards the elevator. "I have to go inform the

President that his disclosure speech has been pushed up a bit."

"So Bill, do we go back to our normal mission of documenting history again?"

"I think our mission just got a bit more interesting."

"Let's see, tomorrow morning the world will find out that there's an entire civilization living in the center of the Earth. The Earth and moon were just teleported and are now orbiting a different star, hundreds of light years away. That red dot up there next to the nebula is a planet that has aliens who are hell-bent on experimenting and enslaving us. Yeah, I'd say it'll be very interesting to see what happens next."

Bill reaches down to the ground and pulls a flower from the garden. He slides the stem of the flower into her hair.

Author's Note

Thank you,
Elle Turner my editor.
Harald Johnson for helping with the cover
layout
The many people who beta read.
My friends and family for encouragement.

Keep an eye out for the sequel to this story.
Follow me on Facebook,
https://www.facebook.com/timetravelerchroniclesnovel/

www.ingramcontent.com/pod-product-compliance
Lightning Source LLC
Chambersburg PA
CBHW032258260626
47157CB00022B/397